Nathaniel Hillyer Egleston

The home and its surroundings

Nathaniel Hillyer Egleston

The home and its surroundings

ISBN/EAN: 9783337185138

Printed in Europe, USA, Canada, Australia, Japan

Cover: Foto ©Andreas Hilbeck / pixelio.de

More available books at **www.hansebooks.com**

THE

HOME AND ITS SURROUNDINGS

OR

VILLAGES AND VILLAGE LIFE

WITH HINTS FOR THEIR IMPROVEMENT

BY

NATHANIEL H. EGLESTON

NEW AND REVISED EDITION

NEW YORK

HARPER & BROTHERS, FRANKLIN SQUARE

1884

TO THE MEMORY OF

THE LATE

ANDREW JACKSON DOWNING,

WHOSE WRITINGS HAVE DONE SO MUCH FOR THE IMPROVEMENT OF OUR
COUNTRY LIFE, AND TO INSPIRE OUR PEOPLE WITH
A TASTE FOR RURAL ENJOYMENTS,

THESE ESSAYS ARE GRATEFULLY

𝕵𝖓𝖘𝖈𝖗𝖎𝖇𝖊𝖉.

PREFACE.

In answering the call for a new edition of his work, which its favorable reception by the public has made, the author has taken occasion to modify its title somewhat, in order to indicate more clearly and definitely the purpose and character of the book. He has also improved the opportunity of a new issue to make its statements conform to the most recent facts in relation to certain subjects, in respect to which even a year may effect important changes.

The book was written with the hope of doing something to improve our country-houses and the grounds around them in respect to tastefulness and comfort, and so to make them more truly *homes*, to which their inmates would be bound by life-long ties of endearment and remembrance. The many letters which the author has received from time to time from unknown readers in various parts of the country, and the pleasant acquaintances thus made, are the ample assurance that his expectation in writing has not been disappointed.

The work might also be called a treatise on Village

Improvement. But, while it deals with what is commonly understood by that phrase, it takes a wider range and embraces still more general interests, such as some of the sanitary problems of the day, and the subject now rapidly—but none too rapidly—gaining attention, the preservation of our woodlands, a matter of the first importance in its economical and other aspects. In sending forth his work afresh and for a wider reading, from a place also to which he has been called for the purpose of promoting the interests of forestry in our country at large, the author would especially commend to his readers what he has to offer upon this subject.

N. H. EGLESTON.

DEPARTMENT OF AGRICULTURE, FORESTRY DIVISION,
WASHINGTON, D.C., *September*, 1883.

CONTENTS.

INTRODUCTION.

CHAPTER I.

VILLAGE LIFE AS IT IS AND AS IT SHOULD BE.

CHAPTER II.

TOWN AND COUNTRY.

CHAPTER III.

A DOUBLE INJURY.

CHAPTER IV.

CAUSES OF OVER-POPULATING OF TOWNS.

CHAPTER V.

DULNESS OF THE COUNTRY.

CHAPTER VI.

MEANS AND OCCASIONS OF SOCIAL INTERCOURSE.

CHAPTER VII.

VILLAGE-IMPROVEMENT SOCIETIES.

CHAPTER VIII.

THE LAUREL HILL ASSOCIATION.

CHAPTER IX.

TREES AND TREE-PLANTING.

CHAPTER X.

VINES AND CLIMBING PLANTS.

1*

CHAPTER XI.

FRUITS AND FLOWERS.

CHAPTER XII.

THE COUNTRY DWELLING-HOUSE.

CHAPTER XIII.

FENCES AND HEDGES.

CHAPTER XIV.

LAWNS.

CHAPTER XV.

WATER.

CHAPTER XVI.

SANITARY ASPECTS OF COUNTRY LIFE.—DRAINAGE.

CHAPTER XVII.

SANITARY ASPECTS OF COUNTRY LIFE (*continued*).—
VENTILATION.

CHAPTER XVIII.

SANITARY ASPECTS OF COUNTRY LIFE (*continued*).—
CARE OF THE SICK.

CHAPTER XIX.

CEMETERIES.

CHAPTER XX.

ROADS AND BRIDGES.

CHAPTER XXI.

PRESERVATION OF WOODLANDS.

CHAPTER XXII.

SCHOOLS AND SCHOOL-HOUSES.

CHAPTER XXIII.

THE VILLAGE CHURCH.

CHAPTER XXIV.

THE VILLAGE LIBRARY.

CHAPTER XXV.

WORK AND PLAY.

CHAPTER XXVI.

OUR VILLAGE FESTIVAL.

" Would I a house for happiness erect,
    Nature alone should be the architect,
    She'd build it more convenient than great,
    And, doubtless, in the country choose her seat."

COWLEY.

"In those vernal seasons of the year, when the air is calm and pleasant, it were an injury and sullenness against Nature not to go out and see her riches, and partake in her rejoicing with heaven and earth."

MILTON: *Tractate of Education.*

INTRODUCTION.

"I never had any other desire so strong and so like to covetousness as that one which I have had always—that I might be master at last of a small house and large garden, with very moderate conveniences joined to them, and there dedicate the remainder of my life only to the culture of them, and study of nature;

And there (with no design beyond my wall) whole and intire to lie,
In no unactive ease, and no unglorious poverty."—COWLEY.

THE love of the open country, the fields, the woods, the streams, seems to be a peculiarly Anglo-Saxon trait, and to have come down to us even from our Teutonic ancestors. The historian Tacitus, in his *Germania*, has noticed the difference in this respect between the people of that country and the Romans, and says of the former, "They live apart, each by himself, as woodside, plain, or fresh spring attracts him." But it is in England that this love of the country has reached the highest development. The Englishman lives in the town or city only under protest, and is all the while claiming the country as his true home. Our people, so far as they are of English descent, have the same inherited trait. The child is hardly out of leading-strings before he fairly revels in the scenes of rural life, if he has the opportunity; and, though this delight of early days may be seemingly supplanted by the occupations or pleasures of maturer years, it is yet very sure to assert itself from time to time, and usually with a strength that increases with our years. To many a one chafed by the cares and anxieties of busy life in the city or town, the one hope that has buoyed him up and enabled him to keep a cheerful spirit amid his struggles has been that of a home to be secured by-and-by, on the old ancestral farm, perhaps, where the memory of boyish days and boyish pleasures exhales a perpetual aroma; or, on some other favored spot, where he may look out upon trees and rocks and sky and clouds, cultivate his acres at his own will, and, after the gentle and unexciting toils of the day, be lulled to rest by the

"Liquid lapse of murmuring streams."

And is it not the token of man's essential kinship with nature, and of his true dignity, that he has such longings for the aspects of natural scenery; that more and more he cleaves to the earth, loves to press the sod with his feet in daily tread, and to engage, though it may be with feeble hand, in the occupations of country life? Is there not the manifestation of one of the best feelings of his nature in this longing in his advancing years—his second childhood, as we call it—to throw himself again upon the bosom of "Mother Earth?" That second childhood is the time of man's return, so commonly, to the purity and healthfulness of feeling which are the special mark and the true glory of our opening days. And so, though it may sometimes be accompanied by bodily feebleness, it is really the ripened glory of life, as it stands calm and serene, after the manifold discipline of earlier and more active years, the successes and disappointments which have attended our various occupations; when we have learned by experience what is essential to our happiness and what is only adventitious; and when we turn from the personal and selfish conflicts of the world around us, and find pleasure in the kindred openness and unselfishness of little children, and in communion with nature, and through it with Him who framed its diverse forms.

It must be confessed, however, that in many cases we live amid the beauties and glories of the natural world, but, "having eyes, see not," or only half see at the best. "Ask the connoisseur," says Ruskin, "who has scampered over all Europe, the shape of the leaf of an elm, and the chances are ninety to one that he cannot tell you; and yet he will be voluble of criticism on every painted landscape from Dresden to Madrid, and pretend to tell you whether they are like nature or not." So we have known a whole roomful of farmers, and farmers' wives and daughters, to puzzle themselves over a bunch of common corn-tassels on a mantel, utterly unable to tell what they were, though familiar with them all their lives. It was simply because they had never looked at them except in the hazy, indefinite way in which so many look at most things, and so were unable to rec-

ognize these well-known objects when removed from
the cornfield to the drawing-room. These are only a
few illustrations of a very common defect—a neglect
to use faculties aright—as a consequence of which we
fail to find in natural objects many delights which they
were designed to afford and which they are ready to
give us.

Everything, therefore, which helps us to see nature
with appreciative eyes is to be welcomed. Much has
been accomplished in recent years in this direction by
the wide diffusion, through the press, of what our most
tasteful and discriminating writers have had it in their
hearts to say. We have followed our poets and essayists into the fields and woods and along the sounding
shore. The greatly increased facilities of travel, also,
have brought multitudes into the presence of some of
the most impressive natural scenes, and wrought upon
them, thereby, a lasting and precious influence. The
pleasant aspects of rural life have thus been presented
to view, and an interest in rural scenes has been awak-
ened which gives promise of most beneficial results.

If the following essays shall help any to a better appreciation of country life, or aid in making that life
more nearly what its ideal should be, the object of the
writer will be gained.

WILLIAMSTOWN, MASS., *June*, 1878.

THE
HOME AND ITS SURROUNDINGS;
OR,
VILLAGES AND VILLAGE LIFE.

CHAPTER I.

VILLAGE LIFE AS IT IS AND AS IT SHOULD BE.

"For it is not in great cities nor in the confined shops of trade, but principally in agriculture, that the best stock or staple of men is grown. It is in the open air—in communion with the sky, the earth, and all living things—that the largest inspiration is drunk in, and the vital energies of a real man constructed. The modern improvements in machinery have facilitated production to such a degree that when they become diffused through the world, only a few hands, comparatively, will be requisite in the mechanic arts; and those engaged in agriculture, being proportionally more numerous, will be more in a condition of ease. Here opens a new and sublime hope. If a state can maintain the practice of a pure morality, and can unite with agriculture a taste for learning and science and the generous exercises I have named, a race of men will ultimately be raised up having a physical volume, a native majesty and force of mind, such as no age has yet produced."—BUSHNELL.

HARDLY any one can pass through the villages of the older portions of our country, particularly those of New England—in the warmer seasons of the year especially, when the vegetation is in its freshness and luxuriance—without being impressed by their general beauty, and feeling that many of them are choice places for family homes. The happy combination of hill and valley, mountain and plain; the dense masses of woods crowning so many of the more elevated portions; the wide stretches of meadow with their emerald beauty; and the great abundance of streams of water, from the broad rivers to the almost threadlike springs which gush out of the ground at such brief intervals, these, together with a reasonable fertility of soil — a fertility which sufficiently rewards honest industry while it does not invite speculation nor encourage idleness—and a climate which, though somewhat rigorous, is probably as healthful as any, combine to make New England one of the choicest dwelling-places of man. If to these we add the tokens of peculiar civilization and culture which characterize New England — the influences of the schoolhouse and the church, which have been felt here from the beginning, and which every traveller sees and feels, however hurriedly he may pass along—we shall not be wrong in thinking that few places on the globe are better fitted to furnish homes of the highest type. The fertile plains of the West may offer the prospect of a more rapid accumulation of wealth. The warmer latitudes of our Southern States may appeal to the senses and tempt with their languid charms, but

> " Man is the nobler growth our realms supply,
> And souls are ripened in our northern sky."

It was something besides accident that swept the *Mayflower* from her destined port in more southern waters and landed her precious freight of souls on the coast of New England, there to plant the seeds of a civilization that was to overspread a continent. Man comes to his best only through a struggle; and to wrestle with storms and rocks seems to be about the best gymnastic for the development of the sturdiest and most effective character. The man who has his home in New England certainly need not envy the dwellers in other places. They may have more of ease in their lot. Their fields may yield a larger harvest and with less demand of labor; but it is likely to be at the expense of temptations or deprivations which more than counterbalance such advantages. "A man's life consisteth not in the abundance of the things which he possesseth." It is the quality, not the quantity, which decides the case.

"He most lives,
Who thinks most, feels the noblest, acts the best."

Whatever inspires the best thought and feeling is to be desired rather than mere fertility of soil or balminess of air. And New England has, in her character and scenery, as well as in her institutions, a perpetual stimulation of what is best.

But, after all, our village life, whether in New England or elsewhere, is not yet what it ought to be. Much of it is crude and low and gross. We have not improved our advantages as we might and should have done. Culture, as yet, has made comparatively little advancement. The school, which is the boast of our country, has not yet done for us what it should have done. It has done much; but how much more remains to be accomplished before we can claim to be a truly educated people! Then, the lessons to be learned in the school of nature have been learned only in small part. How few have their eyes open to see the forms and read the language of the world they daily live in! How little impression do the objects of nature make upon the mass of people! The higher faculties of the soul too often lie in a dormant state. We wait for a better time. In too many of our village homes the life is of a low and animal type; the energies are too much on a level with those of the cattle. It is too often a digging drudgery for the sake of food or for the accumulation of money, unrelieved by any higher object or the cultivation of the refining tastes. The body is cared for, while the mind and heart are neglected. Books are few and too commonly of the trashy sort. Or if there is any waking-up of the mind, it is in being sharp at a bargain. We are often far more ready to overreach than we are to help a fellow-man; and many a father will be found to give indubitable signs of pleasure at seeing his child get the better of another by some trick of shrewdness or audacity. It argues a capacity in the child to get on in the world, and that, in the estimation of many, is the chief end of man. Meantime the softer, gentler feelings are hardly thought worthy of cultivation; the finer tastes are not developed; and the child grows up too often a dull, hard, selfish man; his whole life "of the earth, earthy," when it might be all the while so much higher, better, and happier.

And so, in the cases where our village life has reached a superior development, how charming is the sight! Some simple little cottage, lacking even paint, it may be, but wearing the look of neatness all about it, needs no opening of the door to tell that all is neatness within. A few flowers under the window, an unmistakable look of thoughtfulness and tender feeling stamped upon everything, even upon the grass in the door-yard—how much more delightful is the sight of such a place than that of so many of our ambitious houses, set up in their stilted fashion, unmeaning masses of brickwork and carpentry, the bold advertisements of newly acquired riches, as vulgar as they are expensive! And then, when one goes within such an unpretending cottage, and finds it at once the home of mind and heart—everything plain and simple, perhaps, but taste making all beautiful, and, with more than the power of Midas, converting everything it touches into something better than gold; when he finds only a few books, it may be, but these of solid character, and evidently for use rather than show, and the talk not vulgar gossip or neighborhood scandal, but of a character thoughtful and elevating, pure and good—one feels how precious to the country and the world are such homes.

If our village homes were generally of this character, what a renovated country would ours be! If even a majority of the houses in any of our country villages

2

were really homes such as we have just sketched, how changed and heightened in character would the life of such a village become! The many petty jealousies and causes of dispute which now so commonly exist, followed, as they so frequently are, by open animosities and disgraceful quarrels, would be prevented by the prevalence of a general kindliness of feeling, and a mutual regard for each other's interests in place of the selfishness which now so often reigns. The village households would become, so to speak, members of a larger family —the village family—and a common interest and common feeling would characterize the place and regulate the style and tone of life, while yet leaving the freest play for individual tastes and feelings. In such a community a thousand good influences would surround the young from the beginning, and give them such helps towards a noble spirit of life that their advancement in character would be sure and rapid. Many sources of entertainment and improvement would be found in such a community which in others are almost unknown, and life would become a nobler, sweeter, happier thing than it is or can be in most communities as they now are.

And so, perhaps, we shall be thought to be wasting time upon an ideal which is never, or at best only in the far-away distance, to become real. But if that ideal is only to be realized, if at all, at some distant time, this should not prevent us from doing something to secure the fruits which lie in that direction. Here is a man, for instance, who has the reputation of being a good farmer. He has been diligent and industrious. He prides himself on raising as good crops as any of his neighbors, and his fields are kept in good condition. He is not ashamed to have them looked at. And as the result of his labor he has a handsome sum laid away in the bank, or where it is equally safe. But perhaps in his busy industry upon the farm, the surroundings of his house have been somewhat forgotten. Perhaps the sight which meets his eyes, and the eyes of his family, most frequently is that of a door-yard filled with the waste material of farm and house, with carts and ploughs, some serviceable, and some for many years past use; with unsightly heaps of wood and chips lying about in disorderly confusion. There are, it may be, no convenient walks by which one can get to the well with comfort, or to the road when the rain has been falling or the dew is heavy on the sward. Perhaps the ground about the house shows a growth of weeds rather than grass. The fences, it may be, are not kept in as good repair just around the dwelling as they are out upon the farm, where the protection of the crops seems more to demand them. The gates, seldom closed, have fallen down. In short, there is about the house of this well-to-do and successful farmer an air of neglect and carelessness. Things look untidy. The poultry, and possibly the pigs, have free range of the door-yard, and there is no place where the wife and daughters can go and sit down comfortably out-of-doors in pleasant weather when the household work is done. They are fairly imprisoned at home.

Can there not be an improvement here? A few days' work in the autumn season, after the harvest toil is over, or in early springtime, before other work presses, would change many such places for the better. Let there be a determination that the home of the family shall at least look as well as the home for the cattle. Let the unsightly bushes and weeds in the fence corners be cut away and rooted up, so that they shall not appear again another year. Let the pigs and the poultry go to their own place. Let the ruins of old carts and wagons, ploughs and scrapers, be broken up and conveyed to the wood-pile and the receptacle for old iron. Let the wood and chips be gathered and properly housed. Let the rubbish of any and every sort be removed to its appropriate place. Let trees and shrubs be planted, and the green grass be invited to grow, where now perhaps only dock and plantain thrive. Let a few roses and vines be set within easy reach of doors and windows. How soon will such touches of taste and care change the whole aspect of the place, and change perhaps the character of the occupants as well! for the cultivation of our grounds is often a cultivation of ourselves.

It is an easy step, also, from the improvement of one's immediate surroundings to the endeavor to do something for the entire village where one lives. But in regard to what is desirable, both for the individual and for the community as a whole, we shall speak more at large in subsequent chapters.

CHAPTER II.

TOWN AND COUNTRY.

"God the first garden made, and the first city Cain."—COWLEY.

THE pointed contrast between life in the open country and life in the city, set forth in the above quotation
from one of our elder poets and essayists, has been made
by many another writer. Indeed, it is one of the com-
monplaces of literature. We may trace it all the way
from Cowper's

"God made the country, and man made the town;"

and Lord Bacon's opening of his "Essay on Gardens"
with the words "God Almighty first planted a garden,"
up to old Varro, who, in his *De Re Rustica*, says, "*Di-
vina natura dedit agros, ars humana œdificavit urbes.*"
Essayists, poets, travellers, and philosophers alike have
been wont to pay tribute to the charms and attractions
of the country as compared with the scenes of city life.
Every schoolboy who has gained admission to college is
familiar with the "*Beatus ille qui procul negotiis*" of
Horace; and it is almost the singularity of the many-
sided Macaulay that he seems to have cared little for the
aspects of external nature, content if he could be allowed

to live in London, and walk from day to day the old his-
toric streets and courts of the " City," or busy himself
amid the books and manuscripts of the British Museum.
A poet himself has said that " Poetry was born among
the shepherds," and that " one might as well undertake
to dance in a crowd as to make good verses in the midst
of noise and tumult."

And yet, with all literature and philosophy against it,
there is a large and ever-increasing practical vote in favor of the town as a place of living. Very good people, also, some of the best and most intelligent, seem to
prefer the man-made town to the God-made country.
There is, moreover, a manifest and increasing tendency
of population to concentrate in towns and cities. One
third of the people of our new and essentially agricultural country are already thus gathered. The growth of
towns and cities is disproportionately rapid as compared
with that of the villages and hamlets of the open country.
And this is the fact not only with us, but with many
older nations. London and Berlin never before were
growing so rapidly as now. The same is true of other
European cities — cities which have no such ample
spaces around them as ours have, no such spaces from
which to draw their population, and in supplying the
wants of whose people they may find a sustaining
market for the commodities of their mercantile and
manufacturing industries.

Nor is it, with us, the new towns and cities of the
West merely that are making disproportionate growth

in population, but the oldest cities of the East are showing a like rapid increase. New York, Boston, and Philadelphia are populating themselves more rapidly than
the country around them, as truly as Chicago and San
Francisco. Indeed, so strong is the flow from the country to the cities and manufacturing towns, especially in
New England, that in many of the country districts
there is not only a comparatively slow growth of population, but an actual decline. The sight is only too common, and painful as it is common, among our Eastern
villages, of houses going to decay or actually fallen down,
with none to take their place. The people who once
dwelt in them have left them, and no children of theirs
have come in their stead. The farms, once teeming
with grain and cattle, are now, in many cases, overgrown with bushes or young forests, or only partly kept
under cultivation by some immigrant from Ireland, Germany, or Canada, who has bought them because they
were cheap, and too undesirable to find any other pur-
chaser.

The last census has made some surprising revelations
in this respect. The population of our hill-towns especially seems to have slidden down, in large measure,
into the valleys, along whose streams have grown up important centres of manufacture. As a consequence, not
only have many of the older villages not held their own
in population, but they have lost in character as well as
in people. The more enterprising having gone away,
all the movements of society become less vigorous in

consequence. There is less wealth, therefore less expenditure upon roads, upon houses and buildings of
every kind, upon schools and churches, upon books and
papers, and in travel and intercourse with other places,
which is such a fruitful source of intelligence. All
these educating and civilizing forces are lessened in
quantity, if not entirely lost. So, there will no longer
be found rising up in such a place from time to time, as
formerly, one and another fit to stand as leaders in society, and to have an influence reaching perhaps far beyond the local limits of the place. There will be no
skilful lawyer or wise magistrate, no highly cultivated
clergyman, fit to be looked up to as an authority in all
matters of general knowledge as well as in his special
professional studies. The place can no longer, by its
character, or the compensation which it offers, attract the
presence or command the services of such. The great
law of supply and demand rules here as elsewhere, and
forbids it. And this decay once begun, the tendency of
things becomes strong in this direction. For a time the
influence of certain families of culture and of wealth
may successfully resist the downward course of things,
and hold up the life and spirit of the village. But it is
only for a few years. The next generation will very
likely feel the downward drag of the community around
them too severe to be longer endured, and sons and
daughters, though loath to leave the consecrated home
scenes, will take their departure to more congenial
places.

And now there will be less to hold any to the place. The depopulation will go on with accelerated speed. Family after family will disappear. Their places, if filled at all, will probably be filled with aliens, with people of a lower grade of culture, and such as have no ties of relationship or of historical connection with the place which might form a bond of union with the existing society. Thus the attractions of social interest are lessened all the while. Social life stagnates. The place is no longer a *community* as it once was, but a loose aggregation of individual atoms, as it were, each living by, and for, and in himself. There is no longer any *esprit de corps*, such as there should be in any community, making it an occasion of pride to every resident there that he can say that it is his home. In fact, it will sometimes be found that the process of decline has gone so far, and the change become so great, in some of our once honored villages, that the present inhabitants seem at the best but dwarfs and pigmies under the great name of the place where they live, and where great men and noble women once dwelt.

Such is the tendency to check the growth of many of our villages; and as this is checked by emigration, the growth of the larger towns and cities is proportionally increased. They are the receptacles not only of the enterprising, but of the discontented and dissatisfied. So, in addition to those who may be said to be needed for the proper life and work of the city, or the trading and manufacturing town, there is a large inflow upon them

2*

of those who are not needed, who crowd every avenue
of industry, make life a hot competition for gain, and
even a struggle for very existence, and many of whom,
in the end, become a burden upon society, if not an absolute danger to it.

Life burns fast in the crowded city and the busy mart.
These places must be recruited from the open country.
But more recruits offer than are wanted. More recruits
offer than will fill the ranks. There is a large mass
gathered in every such place, who can only be mere
camp-followers, a poor, or rough and lawless set, who
live upon the waste or the plunder of the great moving
and effective army.

.

CHAPTER III.

A DOUBLE INJURY.

"In town one can find the swimming-school, the gymnasium, the danc-
ing-master, the shooting-gallery, opera, theatre, and panorama; the chemist's shop, the museum of natural history, the gallery of fine arts ; the
national orators, in their turn; foreign travellers, the libraries, and his
club. In the country he can find solitude and reading, manly labor, cheap
living, and his old shoes; moors for game, hills for geology, and groves
for devotion."—EMERSON.

IT is easy to see that the tendency of which we
have been speaking in the previous chapter works a
double harm. The country is depopulated ; the city
and town are overcrowded. The proper balance of
population, and so the proper adjustment of life, of
business, and of society, is lost. Life is not so desirable either in city or country as it otherwise would
be. In the city, and largely because of the overcrowding, it is feverish and frivolous, and, sometimes, fero-
cious. The extremes of good and evil there meet.
In the country, on the other hand, life is often dull
and enfeebled and greatly deficient in the social element. The great expanses of the country want more
people, or more contact of the people with each other.
The city, also, wants the country. It is dependent
upon it for its very existence. In its rapid consump-

tion of life, it must draw from the country a supply of fresh mind and muscle which it cannot produce from itself; and it must have the products of open field and forest, and of the mineral deposits of the wide country, to furnish the staple of its trade and manufacture. The country, also, needs the city. It needs it as the ultimate market for its surplus products, as the place of exchange by means of which the productions of one clime or one continent are made the possible possession of every other, and by which the cottager of Vermont or of Oregon may make the whole world tributary to his daily comfort. The country needs the city also for the stimulating power of its concentrated enterprise, its quick and intelligent action, its speedy reception and utilization of every new thought and every wise plan. Great national undertakings are dependent very much upon great cities and towns. The country villages of New York would never have built the Erie Canal, though all felt its desirableness as a means of getting the products of their fields and forests to market. Our villages would never have given us the Pacific Railroad or the Atlantic Telegraph. They would never have given us the daily newspaper, or the daily meteorological reports of the Signal Service Bureau, for which he who ploughs the open sea, and he who ploughs the open field, look daily with expectant interest. They would never have originated, certainly never have carried on with efficiency, our great missionary and philanthropic enterprises. The American Board of Foreign Missions, or any of our Home Missionary Societies, would die, or dwindle to a feebleness next to death, if they were dependent for success upon their village supporters alone. The mainspring of these, and of all great enterprises, is in the populous, busy town or city. It is our merchant princes by whom these are originated or pushed forward. It is they who send our commerce to the ends of the world, who cover continents with iron highways, and with their telegraphic wires fulfil the promise of Puck—

> "I'll put a girdle round about the earth
> In forty minutes."

It is they, largely, who endow our colleges and schools of highest grade, who push geographical research, if possible, even to the poles, and who are ready to send the Gospel of Christ wherever the most adventurous explorer shall find a fellow-man.

Let us not forget, then, in our love of the country, or when we hear its praises spoken, how much all owe to the city and the busy town. Let us not forget what treasures of power, of wealth, of civilization, of enterprise, of art, of science, of philanthropy, and of religion are garnered up in such a metropolis as New York or London. Why, they are worlds in themselves. The whole earth is there in miniature. It is easy to talk of cities as being "great sores" and the like; to say they are slums of foulness, haunts of vice and crime;

to point to their thousands of paupers, and their thousands more ready for any violence and to prey like
tigers upon the peace and order of society. It is easy,
also, and too common, to talk of the purity and innocence of those who dwell in the open country, when it
may be questioned whether, if the same number of
people in the country as compose the city's population
were to be suddenly confined to the city's space, and
their character and conduct as closely scrutinized, there
would not be found as much of evil as among the habitual residents of the city, though not, perhaps, in the
same forms. Says the author of " Recreations of a
Country Parson," "I have long since found that the
country, in this nineteenth century, is by no means a
scene of Arcadian innocence; that its apparent simplicity is sometimes dogged stupidity; that men lie
and cheat in the country just as much as in the town;
and that the country has even more of mischievous tit-
tle-tattle; that sorrow and care and anxiety may quite
well live in Elizabethan cottages grown over with
honeysuckle and jasmine, and that very sad eyes may
look forth from windows round which roses twine.
People may pace up and down a country lane, between fragrant hedges of blossoming hawthorn, and
tear their neighbors' characters to very shreds." Certainly we could not do without our cities except at the
peril of almost all that distinguishes our present life
from that of the Dark Ages. Our civilization, with
all that we include in that term, what is it, as the very

word tells us, but the character which properly belongs to the *civis*—the one who lives in the city?

While, therefore, we deplore the tendency to leave the country for the city, so far as it results in the depletion of the country and the overcrowding of cities and towns, and the disturbance of the proper balance between them, and while the object of our writing is to do something, if possible, to counteract this, it will not be, we trust, out of any lack of appreciation of the importance of the city, or the peculiar and unequalled privileges which it holds in possession.

CHAPTER IV.

CAUSES OF OVER-POPULATING OF TOWNS.

"Man in society is like a flower
  Blown in its native bed; 'tis there alone
  His faculties, expanded in full bloom,
  Shine out; there only reach their proper use."
                                        COWPER.

"Plain living and high thinking are no more."
                                        WORDSWORTH.

IN looking for the causes which occasion the strong
tendency of population towards the city or town, and
the readiness to forsake the country for them, it is evident that business considerations alone are not sufficient to account for it. The demands, or the possibil-
ities even, of trade would not draw the masses so
strongly to the city, nor would the prospect of increased gain lead them in such crowds to the manufacturing town. Of course, cities and trading and
manufacturing towns are naturally built up as the
country around them grows. They are places for the
exchange or manufacture of the products of the soil.
They can exist only as these first exist. This is their
foundation, and they should grow as the country grows
in population and productiveness. But, as we have

seen, and as is only too apparent to every one, cities and towns are growing far more rapidly than the country, and at the expense of the villages, as well as to the detriment of the cities and towns themselves. The reasons of this lie deeper than the simple inducements of trade.

If those who come from their city homes as temporary visitors to the country, or even a majority of those whose habitual residence is in the country, were asked to characterize country life by a single word, they would pronounce it *dull*. The occasional visitor from the city finds the change so great that life in the country has for a time the zest of novelty and striking contrast. All scenes and habits are new. There is a piquancy and flavor in everything that for a while delights. The commonest things provoke attention because new. But this soon passes away, and he begins to weary of the new scenes and objects. Our city guests of the summer, for the most part, are so ready to bid good-bye to the country that they willingly lose the most charming portion of the country year, the ripening days of autumn, when the heats are lessened and the fruits are offering their luscious juices and delicate aromas, and the trees are ready to march out, like a bannered army, in all their gorgeous array of color. And how often does the man who goes to build his villa in the country tire of it in a year or two, and go back to his city home! As he returns he finds himself moving also with the tide, whereas before he had been struggling against it. There is a general pressing from country to city. The young men are eagerly looking for any employment that will take them from the farm. They jump at the chance of leaving a good home, where friends and food and clothing are abundant, for the store, where they may sell dry-goods or groceries at a salary which will not enable them to live with comfort, if with decency. Young women will stitch all day, and evening too, in a milliner's shop, and sleep in a garret, rather than give themselves to the wholesome work of housekeeping in the country. Not the smallest or poorest-paid situation in town or city offers but a hundred are ready to take it, while it is a matter of the greatest difficulty to procure competent farm-laborers or tolerable domestic service for the country household. If you ask these people why they are so eager for the town, and so ready to leave the country, their answer, when you fairly get it, is, *the country is dull.* And by country they mean life in the country, not the visible, material world. The country, as a physical thing, is not dull or uninteresting. In contrast with the uniform streets and blocks of the city or large town, the country is infinitely varied and picturesque, and full of the charm of new and beautiful objects.

> " There are flowers in the meadow,
> There are clouds in the sky,
> Songs pour from the woodland,
> The waters glide by ;

Too many, too many
For eye or for ear,
The sights that we see,
And the sounds that we hear."

It is not the country, physically considered, that is dull, but country life—the life of the people who live in the country. Their life is not in keeping with the material world around them. It is not, in a large majority of instances, what life in such a situation ought to be. We throw out of account, of course, the life of the pioneer, the man who is just hewing himself a lodging-place in the forest˙or breaking up the soil of the prairie now for the first time. The attractions of place or of society are little to be considered in such circumstances. We speak of established communities. And it cannot be denied that in many, if not in most, of our country villages the spirit and usages of society are dull. There is a heavy weight upon the general life, which presses fearfully upon the spirits of the young especially. The movement of things in the country is like that of the cattle, sluggish. It may be sure ; it may tend, on the whole, in the right direction. So does that of the cattle. But this is the day of roads and of the locomotive, and the sound of these is in the air and echoing among the hills and valleys, even when they are not in sight. The young hear it, if the old do not, and it stimulates a quickened movement in them, or the desire to be where a quickened movement will be possible to them.

Life in the country may be in general on the side of good order, thrift, and virtue, but it is slow and heavy. It drags. It does not readily take the stimulus of new ideas. It does not believe much in improvement. It is content with old methods, and not much disposed to consider whether there can be any better ones. The general life in the country is unquestionably sluggish. It is withal a life, too much, of dull, hard drudgery. The yoke also comes on the shoulders at an early age with excessive severity; and the boys, like too many of the colts, are broken down before they reach the years of mature strength and endurance. The late war showed that the town and city boys could endure a strain under which those from the country frequently failed. To this drudgery of country life there is little relief, whether to the man in the field or the woman in the house. Day in and day out, year in and year out, it is very much the same hard, heavy strain. There is little change except from work to idleness or sleep, or perhaps the dull gossip of the neighboring kitchen, or the duller and worse gossip of the store or tavern. The talk is, in large part, the dripping of scandal or story-telling of a low cast. There is little of earnest or high-toned thinking, little grappling with things which are not material. There is little alertness of mind, little of the spirit of inquiry; as how could there be much, when body and mind are so dragged and spent with the heavy, incessant tug of such an unvarying round of life?

As for amusement and recreation, there is next to
none, at least that is worthy of the name.   It has been
said of the New England villagers particularly that their
only recreations are their funeral occasions.   There is
too much ground for the sarcasm.   The very general
attendance of country people at funerals is not altogether a token of sympathy and respect.   It is, in no
inconsiderable measure, the assertion by human nature
of its right to break away from dull drudgery of the
house and the soil, and, as a thinking, feeling being, to
become a participant in society.   And so you shall see
the people, assembled from distant parts of the town,
as they stand about the doors before and after the
solemn service, hearing and telling the news, shaking
hands with a new feeling of brotherhood, and so going
home in some sense refreshed, for anything is a refreshment and recreation which takes one out of the rut of a
dull, plodding life.   This getting together at a funeral,
as also the gathering in company at the church on the
Sabbath, is a very important matter, therefore, apart from
the religious solemnities of such occasions.   If what is
solemn leads to the joyful and the genial, through the
pleasant interchange of thoughts and feelings on the
doorstep or under the horse-sheds, all the better for the
people, and none the worse, perhaps, for the worship.
It is the easier and more frequent getting together for
various purposes and on various occasions, it is the
more palpable presence of society which town and city
afford, that give them the preference over the country.

It is the more manifest presence of the human, the more constant and intimate commingling of the human, that, beyond and above all the attractions of fashion or wealth, draws people to the city. Bridget will consent to be shut up in a basement kitchen during work-hours, because, when work-hours are ended, she can quickly have around her a company of like spirits, or can meet them as she goes on her errands to the corner grocery or to the baker, when she will utterly refuse to share with the farmer's wife an ample apartment whose windows open upon boundless views of beauty and admit none but healthful airs.

It is society, and varied society, which the soul craves, unless its cravings have been so long ungratified that it settles down into an ignorant or enforced contentment with itself and its habitual surroundings. All physical and material things will not make amends for the lack of society, for the commingling of soul with soul. Much as the human being may grasp after what is material, and material as his life may seem to be, he is, after all, a spiritual being, a creature of feelings and sympathies, and all riches cannot satisfy him. Money, land, food, drink, dress; these are not enough. There must be something more,.and something higher — communion with his kind, the interchange of thought and feeling with others. This he finds most, and most easily reached, where those of his kind are massed together in the town or city. Here, too, in the large community, society of the most congenial character is easy to be found.

Then, growing out of this consolidation or aggregation, come facilities for various social delights ; such as
books, plays, concerts, lectures, and shows of different
kinds, reaching in quality through a wide range, which
adapts them to all tastes and all grades of feeling and
culture.

Now, grant that there is an abnormal and unhealthy
craving for excitement which impels many to turn away
from country life and seek the city with its crowds and
varied sights and scenes. Grant, also, that low passions
tend thither, because of the easier gratification afforded.
Enough remains in the prevalent habit of life in the
country to account for the readiness to forsake it for
the town. It is not to be wondered at that our boys
and girls, not to speak of those older, who have any enterprise of spirit, should be willing to leave the paternal
acres. It is the defective social element of our country
life which is the most efficient cause of the depletion of
the country and the disproportionate gathering of population in the large towns and cities. Other causes do
their part to occasion this result, but this is the grand
and most constantly influential cause. The remedy for
the evil, therefore, if remedy there be, is to be applied
principally at this point.

CHAPTER V.

DULNESS OF THE COUNTRY.

"Accuse not Nature, she hath done her part."—MILTON.

"'To smell to a fresh turf is wholesome for the body."—THOMAS FULLER.

LIFE in the country ought not to be dull or unattractive. There is no necessity for it. In certain respects, as we have seen, the city may possess advantages not to be found in the open country. This must be so, else cities would never come into existence. And so to many persons the city or great town must be the most desirable place for residence. But the mass of people dwell, and ever will dwell, in the country. Cities can exist only as there is a country back of them to create and sustain them. They have no self-creative power. "The profit of the earth is for all: the king himself is served by the field." So says the Scripture. Agriculture, the tilling of the ground, is the bottom and foundation of all life, of all industries, of all enjoyments. This dependence of all upon what is produced in the open country is often forgotten, and multitudes who flock to the city, without any legitimate call of business, find that they have escaped discomforts and troubles which might have been removed, only to meet those far greater and more persistent in character.

We might conclude beforehand that the place designed by a good Creator for the larger part of mankind to live in would be as desirable, because as promotive of comfort, as any. Nay, it ought to be the most desirable. And so who does not know how the poets, who are the true seers and have the deepest insight of things, are always singing the charms of the country and taking us out with them through woods and fields, and under the open sky, and fixing our gaze upon a thousand delightful objects? The material world becomes a living thing to them. And thus our own Bryant, clinging to the country as he did, resting—and may we not say revelling—there after his daily business in the city was done, expresses a wide-spread feeling when, in the familiar words of his "Thanatopsis" he says—

> "To him who, in the love of Nature, holds
> Communion with her visible forms, she speaks
> A various language. For his gayer hours
> She has a voice of gladness, and a smile
> And eloquence of beauty; and she glides
> Into his darker musings with a mild
> And gentle sympathy, that steals away
> Their sharpness, ere he is aware."

So Wordsworth says—

> "The sounding cataract
> Haunted me like a passion; the tall rock,
> The mountain, and the deep and gloomy wood,
> Their colors and their forms, were then to me

3

> An appetite—a feeling and a love,
> That had no need of a remoter charm
> By thoughts supplied, nor any interest
> Unborrowed from the eye."

Cowper in like manner gives this expression to his feelings in respect to the country:

> "I never framed a wish, or formed a plan,
> That flattered me with hopes of earthly bliss,
> But there I laid the scene. There early strayed
> My fancy, ere yet liberty of choice
> Had found me, or the hope of being free;
> My very dreams were rural."

It were easy, by turning the leaves of our volumes of poetry, to bring the very woods and fields about us, odorous with their scents and vocal with their peculiar sounds. And if there were more of this poetic feeling or sensibility, the country would be more attractive than it is as a place of living. As it is, we often find those who are dwelling amid the most delightful scenery quite insensible to its charms. The most beautiful landscape is but "common earth" to many. "Having eyes, they see not, neither do they understand." And one of the problems involved in making country life properly attractive and giving it its true interest is that of giving people this power to see, the ability to behold what a world of life and beauty they are living in, and so to have all the powers of their souls brought into communion with it, and, through it, with all the creation and with the Creator himself. What is wanted is to lift our country life out of the dull,

mechanical, and monotonous condition in which it is
found to so great an extent, and to bring it into a condition of inspiration from all the life of nature and society.

The problem is seen to be twofold, therefore—to bring
those living in our country villages into closer and more
frequent contact with one another, and thus to develop
the social element which every soul so much needs;
and, secondly, to bring all into contact and communion
with nature, and thus give a higher tone and inspiration to the life of each and all.

The country is dull and irksome to many, and especially to the young, because there are so few occasions
of coming together and uniting in common pleasures,
and thereby gratifying the social instinct of our nature.
We are made for society. We may be absorbed for a
time in the busy cares and ambitions of middle life so
as to be temporarily oblivious of, or indifferent to, the
claims of society. But in our younger, and again in
our older years, we feel that life is a partnership affair,
that to be alone is not to live. We yearn for our kind.
We want to exchange thought and feeling with others.
We want to touch hands and to touch hearts. We want
to look at pleasant things with other eyes as well as our
own, to see and hear in company with others.

Now, the too common fact is, that our country vil-
lages furnish few opportunities for social intercourse.
Life drags on with an almost unvarying round of toil.
There is little to break up its monotony. There are

few sources of rational amusement open to all. And
amusement certainly has its place as one of the needs
of a truly healthy life, healthy in the largest and best
sense. As the cattle cannot profitably be kept in the
yoke all the while, no more can the man. The farmer
himself will accomplish the most in his farm-work if
now and then he gives himself up to some social enjoyment. He will be the fresher and more vigorous for it,
and he will find more of enjoyment in his life of toil.

The young feel a special craving for society. It is,
in fact, their life. And it is because this craving of
their nature is not adequately gratified, but is even often rudely rebuked, and the means of innocent pleasure
denied, that they are so frequently ready to leave home
and friends and try the chances of town or city. The
son and daughter not only feel the absence of occasions
of social enjoyment, but they see father and mother
leading a monotonous round of drudgery in the field
and in the house alike, with little variation, the joints
of the body stiffened prematurely by the steady drag of
unremitted work, and the joints of the mind stiffened
at the same time by the dull and narrow and unvarying
habit of thought. And who can blame them if they
shrink back at the prospect of leading such a life themselves? The wonder is rather that more do not flee
from the country.

But this may be changed, and should be. The boys
and girls at school, or just emerging from it, in the
fresh fervor of youth, feel that there is, or ought to be,

something better for them than such a dull, mechanical life as they see most of those around them are living. And they are right in this. Life in the country ought to be full of freshness from youth to oldest age. The life of a farmer ought to be a truly royal life. There is no life more independent or free from wearisome care than his may be. There is none that has more abundant natural resources for delight and for that which will interest and occupy all the faculties of the man. There is none which better affords place for the use of all knowledge, even that which is most scientific. There is none which can supply a larger variety of employments and thereby guard against monotony and dulness more effectually than a life on the broad acres of the open country. The husbandman is king, or may be. It is his own fault if he lives as a serf, or in a way only to dull and dwarf his higher and better nature.

CHAPTER VI.

MEANS AND OCCASIONS OF SOCIAL INTERCOURSE.

"How sweet, how passing sweet is solitude!
But grant me still a friend in my retreat,
Whom I may whisper, solitude is sweet."

COWPER.

RECOGNIZING the deficiency in the social element of
country life as that which principally renders it dull
and distasteful to so many, and the chief reason why
there is such a disposition to forsake the country and
crowd the towns and cities with a disproportionate population, it is manifest that the first thing to be done, if
we would remedy the evil, is to make some resolute endeavor to improve the social life of our country villages.
Something is needed to draw out in the inhabitants of
our villages the feeling that they are dwellers together
in a common home, and that they have a common interest in it and in each other. Something is needed to
stimulate into more active exercise the feeling of mutual interest and common enjoyment as well as a common
responsibility for the general ongoing of things around
them. There is need of something to draw the people
together, in one way and another, and in larger or
smaller numbers, from time to time, old and young, and

men and women alike, that they may look into each other's faces, and, for the time, engage in some common work or common pleasure, and thereby have the bonds of a common interest and fellow-feeling cemented and strengthened. Something is needed which shall localize their feeling and cause their thoughts to gather about the place in which they dwell with a special interest, to give them a certain pride in their own village, and make them feel that it is a good and desirable place in which to live; that if it has not something of celebrity and attractiveness, which other places may have, it has yet something which they have not, or has it in better form and degree.

This feeling needs to be cultivated, especially in the young, who naturally have as yet felt the fewest ties of attachment to any place or society, and who are readiest to move whithersoever the attractions and pleasures of society may be, or seem to be, strongest. Parents, and the older members of our village communities, have been greatly at fault in not cultivating in the young a feeling of interest in, and attachment to, the place in which their home has been fixed. They have been at fault in not having more of it themselves, and in not manifesting more what feeling of this sort they have had. "This is our village;" "This is our home." Too seldom has there been the feeling which stood ready to vent itself in such words. So far as it has existed, as doubtless it has to a considerable extent, it has been for the most part a dumb and voiceless feeling. As a consequence, the young have grown up commonly in great ignorance of the place where their very life originated, and, while they may have come to have a respectable knowledge of the geography and history of the world at large, have often been lamentably ignorant of the features and objects of interest in the village where they were born. Many a boy has been able to give a more intelligible account of Patagonia or Greenland than of the town and county of his own residence.

Now, what is wanted is something that shall develop the local interest of the dwellers in our villages in one another and in the place where they live; something to cultivate in old and young alike the feeling of attachment to their local home. Almost anything, therefore, is to be encouraged which will serve to bring the people together. A mountebank show is better than nothing. But other and better occasions may easily be had. The national anniversary and Decoration-day might easily be improved in every village, not only as the means of stimulating the feeling of patriotism, but the feeling of local attachment as well. The old "Mayday" of our English ancestors might be revived. So, also, farmers' clubs are to be encouraged, or something of the sort, under a different name. These should not only draw the whole village together once a year for a show of the annual products in cattle, grain, and fruits, but on more frequent occasions, though, perhaps, not in so large numbers. They may not always result in securing a larger immediate pecuniary return for the farmer's labor; though nothing is more certain to bring an increase of this sort than an increase of intelligence in the methods of labor which such gatherings are well calculated to promote. But, however this may be, they do result in a culture of the better feelings and sensibilities, which is of more importance than the best and most profitable culture of the soil. No company of men can come together as friends and neighbors to discuss corn or potatoes, or anything that concerns their common life, without going home the better for so doing. They feel anew the touch of a common humanity, and they are better men for what they have mutually given and received in the interchange of thought and by the secret magnetism of their personal presence. They have a new and deeper interest in one another and a kindlier feeling towards each other. The farmers' sons should, of course, be included in these gatherings, and be made to feel that they are for their sake as much as for that of their elders. Instead of being merely allowed to hang about upon the outskirts of such assemblings, as has been so commonly the usage, they should be made to feel that they are an essential part of them. It has been the bane of our agricultural life too commonly that the sons of our farmers have been made mere drudges and dependents, instead of being early recognized as having a partnership in the common work and the common rewards of the home husbandry, and thus too often have been fairly driven off from the place which had become more a place of ser-

3*

vitude than a home, and, therefore, had little to attach them to it.

If these meetings are also open to the farmers' wives and daughters, as they should be, the result will be all the better. The tone of the talk will be more refined—more of the soul and less of the soil—while the light of woman's eye shining upon the scene, even when her voice, perhaps, may not be heard, will serve to quicken all the better sensibilities of man's nature. And then there will be the little hand-shakings and interchanges of family and neighborhood news in the doorway and on the steps before and after the formal gatherings and discussions. Or there will be the free loosing of the tongue and the unbosoming of the heart, perhaps, at the social dinner or tea which is the accompaniment of the meeting, that will make the result all the better; for this dining or supping together is, after all, one of the great motive forces of a truly human society. A good dinner is recognized in political circles as an important instrument of diplomacy. We have it, also, on the authority of a very eminent and very intellectual clergyman that it is impossible to carry on a ministerial club successfully without having a good dinner or supper as one of its adjuncts. And ever since Jacob secured Esau's birthright by a mess of pottage, and conquered his will by an assault on his stomach, the importance of this organ has been recognized. Body and soul are strangely linked together. We are not all body, and we cannot be all soul if we would. The attempt thus to etherealize ourselves makes us ghosts or dyspeptics, and not men.

And so fairs and festivals of almost all sorts are to be encouraged on the same account. In a pecuniary view, the former are expensive. They commonly cost more than they come to, though many persons have an easy way of cheating themselves into the belief that they thus secure large returns upon a small investment. And, accompanied as they frequently have been by grab-bags and lotteries in one form or another, their moral influence has been bad. Their real value is social, not pecuniary; and as man is worth more than money, so these occasions for the development of the social part of our nature are worth more than all the most successful speculations of the Exchange. The heart at such times coins feelings which are more precious than any coinage of the mint. Let fairs and festivals, then, be encouraged and multiplied as often as fit occasions for them can be found. They may occupy time. But how can time be better employed? They may require the expenditure of some labor in preparing for them. But what labor is spent to better purpose? And when the work is over, how many pleasant companionships will have been formed or cemented anew, and how many pleasant memories will remain! The community will have been drawn together; hearts will have come into closer fellowship; the sense of a common humanity will have been deepened; and something besides dollars and cents, or digging and ditching, will have been thought of. And then, so far as digging and ditching are a necessary part of the villager's life, he will go back to it from these social and festive occasions with a freshened spirit and a more willing heart; he will go back to it feeling that he is not a mere dirt-digger, after all, but that there is another and better side to his life.

It is but a short step from these farmers' clubs and fairs and festivals to many other things which appeal to, and at the same time cultivate, the social feeling, and which tend to give attractiveness and interest to the place where they are found. Such are debating societies and lecture associations, either separately or combined. The former may easily be established in connection with every district school; and one can hardly be established without proving a source of interest and entertainment to the whole neighborhood. And every town may have an instructive course of lectures, as the leisure winter evenings come on, which will prove a happy occasion of reunion to the entire community. Nor is it necessary to send abroad, unless occasionally, perhaps, for the brilliant stars of the lecture firmament. Let there but be a readiness to give a modicum of honor to a prophet in his own country, to cherish and appreciate home talent; and then, when the schoolmaster has given his address on some theme which he has studied, and Farmer A—— comes with his experience on the cultivation of corn or on the improvements which have been made in the art of husbandry; or Blacksmith B——

gives his essay on iron, or the strength of materials, or some other subject with which he is familiar; or Carpenter C—— his discourse on house-building or the various qualities and uses of timber; and the doctor, the lawyer, and the minister contribute their quota from their various stores of knowledge and the contents of their libraries, the people who come to hear will listen to honest and instructive thought, if not always to the smoothest or most startling periods; and the home life and society of their own village will have new value in their esteem, and they will be more ready to think that the lines have fallen to them in pleasant places, and be more content than ever with their country home.

Then how easy to have, in almost every village, some organization for musical purposes — a glee club, perhaps, or a band of instrumental performers — which shall from time to time call the people together, in larger or smaller numbers, and in different neighborhoods, it may be, for a pleasant entertainment of music, combined with cheerful conversation and harmless games of various kinds.

It is easy to see, when we come to look at the subject thus, how readily means are afforded for developing the social spirit of our village life, and thus waking that life from the dulness and seeming torpor which too often characterize it, and giving it a new interest and attractiveness.

CHAPTER VII.

VILLAGE-IMPROVEMENT SOCIETIES.

"The real elements of beauty in a village are not fine houses, costly fences, paved roadways, geometrical lines, mathematical grading, nor any obviously costly improvements. They are, rather, cosiness, neatness, simplicity, and that homely air that grows from these and from the presence of a home-loving people."—GEORGE E. WARING, JR.

WE have spoken of fairs, festivals, farmers' clubs, and the like as deserving encouragement on account of their contributions to the social life of our villages and consequent tendency to make our village life more attractive. But when these means of social improvement have come into use to any considerable extent, there will grow up such an interest in the village home as will lead many to wish to do something to make it additionally attractive — to add something of method and system to the work of improvement. As a new spirit is developed in one and another; as the social feelings are quickened; as something of taste is felt stirring in here and there one, there will be more and more of desire, on the part of those so affected, to do something for the whole community of which they form a portion. Very naturally they will desire to see a better outward look on the village itself—the houses in which they live, the streets along which they have occasion so often to walk or ride. The desire is a laudable one; and yet it often fails of attaining its object, except very slowly and partially, for want of the aid of systematic and associated action, and because action in this direction and for this object is something unfamiliar in practice. There are some, if not many, in nearly every village, probably, who have, in a degree at least, the spirit of improvement; who desire their own advancement in culture and character, and who carry this feeling, to some extent, into the arrangement of their own houses and their surroundings; and who would gladly see an improvement in the aspect of the whole town or village where they live. But, alone, they are comparatively powerless to effect the desired object. It is true that what any one may do to improve his own residence, or to improve himself, has the force of example, and is likely to stimulate the feeling of improvement in others, and thus produce some good result. But this influence works slowly. The desired result may be much hastened by bringing together and combining the power of those who have like feeling and taste. And there is often a good deal of feeling and taste existing in a latent state, as it were, which any such organization calls out and makes manifest, which otherwise would never have made itself known.

Hence, among the most hopeful agencies for the improvement of our village life are those various organizations and associations which have been springing up within the last few years, known generally as Village-improvement Societies, though sometimes bearing other names. Such organizations deserve to be encouraged on very many accounts.

  They may begin, if need be, in a very humble way. They may begin in almost any neighborhood. It is not at all necessary to wait till the whole village or town can be set moving in this direction. If only those living on some one street or in some one neighborhood, or a considerable part of them, associate themselves for purposes of improvement, their aim will sooner or later extend so as to take in the entire town, and their organization will enlarge itself proportionally or be merged in another of wider scope. Sooner or later the thing will expand so as to meet to the fullest extent the result desired. What is most needed is a *beginning*. If there are but half a dozen neighbors, or half a dozen in the whole town, known to each other as having some desire to see a better state of society and a better look to the village where they live, let them get together some evening and resolve to do what they can, by their combined efforts, to bring about the desired result. But let the meeting and the earnest talk not end in talk; and that it may not so end, let not those assembled be afraid to organize themselves into a visible and formal society or association. Some organization is indispensable to success. They need not fear that such a course will look ambitious or presuming.

  And now, having sufficient courage and earnestness

of purpose to organize themselves into a visible body or corporation, they need not waste time in deciding by what particular name they will be known. This is, comparatively, unimportant. If they happen to have most prominently in mind at the start the desirableness of trees to cover the nakedness of some place from which the ruthless axe at some former time has swept away every green thing, let them call themselves the " Tree-planting Association " of such a town or village. If it is a neighborhood movement for the general betterment of things around them, they may designate themselves the "—— Neighborhood-improvement Society." Or, if it is a more wide-spread movement at the outset, they may style themselves the " Village-improvement Society of ——." The name is of little consequence. It is the action under it which is of importance. What is wanted is something to hold them together in a visible unity, so that they may act unitedly, systematically, and with their combined force and efficiency. Being thus organized, and having taken some name, it is very important that their few officers should be selected with reference to their earnestness and efficiency rather than their dignity or the personal position which they may have in the community. Our societies are not unfrequently so loaded down with dignity in their officers that their effectiveness is very small.

The constitution of the society may be as simple as its name. Nothing elaborate or long-drawn is necessary. Let the object or objects of the association be stated in as few and simple words as may be. Let there be a president, secretary, treasurer, and an executive committee of two or three—it may be a few more —and then the society is ready for work.

With what work it shall best begin will depend upon the peculiarities of the place and also upon the season of the year. Some places need improvement most in one direction; others, in a different one. With some it will be most needful in outward things, while in others it may be most demanded in respect to things within doors and those which more directly respect social feeling and habits. If the association comes into being and takes form in the cooler season of the year, then it will naturally turn its attention first to the promotion of social enjoyment by means of pleasant gatherings in one place and another—festivals, concerts, games, and the like; while it will also be discussing, from time to time, in its meetings, plans for operations when the right season comes, which will do something for the improvement of the outward appearance of the village. If the organization of the society takes place in springtime, its first efforts will naturally be put forth in the endeavor to secure some outward improvement or embellishment; and, perhaps, no better start is likely to be made than by planting trees along some naked street or upon some open ground which has been left at the confluence of two or three roads waiting to be fashioned, with little effort, into a lovely park. Or it may be the village church has been left, like a great rocky boulder, standing in some bleak place, exposed alike to the blaze of the sun and the blasts of the storm, forlorn and cheerless. It would be a thing welcomed by all if this could be changed, as it could be by only a day or two given, at the right season, to the planting of trees. If the parish minister should be a member of the Improvement Society — as he very likely would be — he might be willing to lend a voice in church on the Sabbath as well as a hand at the right time elsewhere, by doing as one clergyman we wot of did, who one day, calling to his aid the words of Isaiah, gave the following among his Sabbath notices: "All those who are willing to aid in making the surroundings of the house of God pleasant and comely are invited to go out into the woods with me to-morrow and 'bring the fir-tree, the pine-tree, and the box together to beautify the place of God's sanctuary, and make the place of his feet glorious.'" The result in that case was a pleasant, social day on the hill-sides spent in gathering the trees, and nearly a hundred of them, of various kinds, planted around the church, where they now stand, the adornment of the village and a monument to the memory of that minister to which the people point with pride and affection.

Perhaps the village cemetery has been neglected, and is an unsightly and disagreeable place. If so, here is a feasible point at which to begin the work of village improvement. No other work could be undertaken, either,

which would be likely to excite a more general interest
or elicit a more general co-operation, for all have a manifest concern in the good keeping of the place where lie
the remains of friends and kindred, and where all are
so soon to lie down. Let the work be undertaken of
surrounding the place of the dead with some barrier
which shall protect its sacred ground from the intrusion of wandering cattle. Let it be girt about with an
evergreen hedge, emblematical of our immortality, our
essential life thus asserting itself, as it were, in the very
citadel of death. Let the paths that lead through the
cemetery be cleared of their grass and weeds; the half-
fallen gravestones be set up again, and trees and shrubs
planted along the avenues, or in other places, under the
grateful shadow of which the visitor to the graves of
dear friends may sit down for rest and tranquil contemplation.

In the various ways now suggested, and in many others not named, the desired work may be begun and carried forward. It matters little, as we have said, where
the beginning is made. One thing will naturally lead
to another until the whole field is covered. One thing,
too, will commonly be enough for any one year, while
several years will be required to accomplish some of
the objects which a village-improvement society will
be likely to undertake. Such an association must not
attempt too much at once. In this respect, "hasten
slowly" is true wisdom.

It ought to be said, moreover, that this combined village-improvement work is eminently one for both sexes. There can be no dispute about woman's rights here, for this is peculiarly a work of taste and feeling; and, in matters of taste and feeling, woman's claim to a hearing and a participation none will dispute. The union of the sexes in councils about village improvement will make the consultations all the more pleasant, and the work finally done all the more satisfactory. We have in mind one village, which stands as a model for work of this kind, where the work has been done largely through the instrumentality of women. In all the councils that have led to the improvement of this village the gentler sex have borne a conspicuous part, and their suggestions have been cordially welcomed.

So it should be in all such cases. The sexes should combine in the work of improving their common home. The refining and tasteful influences of the one should co-operate with the executive energy of the other. The result will be all the more complete and satisfactory for this combination of qualities. Besides, it would be a great loss to miss the opportunities which the frequent consultations of such associations afford for the meeting of the sexes together in one of the pleasantest ways possible. Such assemblings are to be encouraged on all accounts.

CHAPTER VIII.

THE LAUREL HILL ASSOCIATION.

"Woodman, spare that tree!"—G. P. MORRIS.

A BRIEF sketch of a single successful organization for the purpose of village improvement may make the subject more clear, and prove a better incitement to action in the right direction than much more that might be said in another and more general form. Most people are more ready to work from a pattern than to originate for themselves, even when the work to be done is simple. We give a few pages, therefore, to a sketch of the Laurel Hill Association of Stockbridge, Mass., which has become somewhat widely known, and has served as the model of several like associations. And if any one would see at a glance what steady and persistent work can do, though neither large numbers nor large capital is engaged in it, let him visit the hills of Berkshire, and, after looking down upon its most beautiful village, and passing along its clean and shaded streets, let him ask some of its inhabitants to describe to him the place as it was a score of years ago.

The Laurel Hill Association had a very simple and modest beginning, showing in this that such organizations need not be started with any great formality or any plan of immediate great effects. It had its origin in the endeavor, on the part of a few sensible and tasteful persons, to preserve a well-wooded hill, situated nearly in the centre of the village, from falling a victim to the woodman's axe, and so becoming, instead of the "thing of beauty" it was, only an unsightly object. The rocky and wood-crowned eminence was purchased, and subsequently given in trust to a small company who had organized themselves for the purpose; and as the hill abounded in the *kalmia*, or laurel, this easily gave name to the association.

But it was not enough for the association simply to preserve the hill, or to add something to its attractiveness by clearing away the tangled underbrush or removing the dead or decaying trees. The securing of the hill as a matter of taste, and not because it was good for so much cord-wood, and therefore so much annual pecuniary income, naturally stimulated the proprietors, and put them upon doing something more in the direction of right feeling and public improvement. So they began by taking in hand the cemetery, which, like so many of our village burial-grounds, had been left in neglect. Accumulated rubbish was removed. Walks were cleaned up and new ones constructed. The fallen headstones were made to stand erect again. It was not long before, through the influence of the association, the town was induced to make an appropriation of money sufficient to surround the cemetery with a neat fence of iron, within which was planted a belt of evergreens. Subsequently, a stone receiving-tomb was built, where the bodies of the dead might be temporarily deposited when, on account of the frozen ground in winter, or of tempestuous weather, immediate burial might not be convenient. And thus the work has gone on from year to year until that plain country burial-place has become a beautiful and pleasant spot, and, although in the midst of the dwellings of the villagers, is not regarded as an objectionable presence.

From putting in order the cemetery, trimming and smoothing its pathways, it was easy and natural for the association to undertake to put the streets and walks of the village in better condition. The two works soon came to be carried on together. Beginning at the centre, where everybody had occasion to come for the sake of the post-office, the churches, and the stores, the inequalities and inconveniences of the principal street were corrected by proper grading and drainage; and ample gravel walks on either side were constructed in place of the narrow and devious trails which so commonly serve for paths in our country villages, the footways of the horses and cows being usually better cared for than those over which their owners have to pass. The people living along the street were also stimulated to put their premises in a clean and tasteful condition, and to keep them so. Next followed the planting of trees near the roadside wherever trees were lacking. The children, sometimes in their thoughtlessness disposed to

treat young trees too rudely by climbing them or making them turning-goals in their cheery sports, were not
only held in check, but made auxiliaries of the association in its work, and put under a beneficial culture
for themselves.   Any boy who would undertake to
watch and care for a particular tree during two years
was rewarded by having the tree called by his name.
Other children were paid a few pennies, from time to
time, for the loose papers and other unsightly things
which they would pick up and remove from the street.

Gradually this work of the association extended.   It
soon took in hand the streets connected with the main
one, and reaching out towards the borders of the town.
Year by year it pushed its walks out from the village
centre towards the remoter points.   Year by year it
extended its lines of trees in the same manner, thus
seeking to facilitate intercourse between the various
parts of the town and to make the means of travel
easy and pleasant.

In the winter season and the early spring the association, gathered in its frequent and familiar consultations
from house to house, would consider what further improvements were most needed, and then perhaps would
vote an appropriation for the construction of a walk,
or the planting of trees along some street, on condition that the dwellers in the vicinity should contribute
a like sum either in money or labor.   Thus, directly
or indirectly, a good many have been led to help on
the work who have not been members of the associa-

4

tion. And so the process of constructing walks, improving roads, planting trees and hedges, and stimulating the people generally to a more tasteful care of their premises has gone forward. Little by little, and in many nameless ways, the houses and barns, the dooryards and farms, have come to wear a look of neatness and intelligent care that makes the Stockbridge of to-day quite a different place from the Stockbridge of twenty, or of even ten, years ago.

All this has been done, too, at comparatively little pecuniary expense. Yearly subscriptions, ranging from ten dollars down to one, have been solicited, the payment of which has easily been made; and with the money thus secured from year to year, and the additional contributions made in labor, the work has been accomplished. It has really been no tax upon the town, and hardly a burden upon any one. It has rather been a source of pleasure all along, and a kind of healthful recreation. Meantime the improved appearance of the place has increased the market-value of the houses and lands by a large percentage. People of wealth and taste from abroad, from the great cities, have been attracted to the place, and have built handsome residences for themselves and made large expenditures which have gone, to a considerable extent, into the pockets of the villagers; and thus the association, though not aiming at pecuniary results, but only at those of taste and feeling, is found to be the best paying investment, even in a pecuniary view, which the people have made.

Travellers passing through Stockbridge are apt to speak of it with admiration as a *finished* place; and, compared with many even of the New England villages, it has such a look. But the Laurel Hill Association does not consider its village home finished, nor its own work completed. Still the work goes on. Committees are even now conning plans for further improvements. The association is all the while widening the scope of its action. By itself, or by suggestions and stimulations offered to others, it is aiming at the culture of the village people through other agencies than those of outward and physical adornment. It fosters libraries, reading-rooms, and other places of resort where innocent and healthful games, music, and conversation will tend to promote pleasant social feeling and lessen vice by removing some of its causes.

The monthly meetings of the association are of the pleasantest kind. Composed of both sexes, and assembling in turn at the houses of the different members, the evenings are spent in discussing whatever tends to the improvement of their common home. Something higher and more important than the fashions or the ordinary gossip of the village occupies the attention, and leaves no regret afterwards for time misspent.

Once a year the association holds its public festival, and modestly invites all who will to come and see what it is doing and what it has done. In the month of August, on some bright and sunny afternoon, you may see the villagers, together with the city guests

summering here and in the neighboring towns, making their way up the slope of Laurel Hill to a plateau
half-way from its base to the summit. Here, under the
shade of lofty oaks and elms, there is easy standing-
room for two thousand persons. Upon the eastern
side of this plateau, where the hill presents a perpen-
dicular face of rock, a rostrum of earth covered with
turf has been built, from which the eye looks out,
through the arching canopy of trees, upon a lovely
stretch of meadow, with the winding Housatonic near
by, and a portion of the Taconic range bounding the
western horizon. Here, upon their earthen platform,
gather the officers of the association, with the orator
of the occasion, and possibly the poet, with perhaps a
band of music near them, while the assembled company distribute themselves in groups on the green
grass, or on the adjacent rocks which form the galleries of this rustic theatre. Prayer is offered. The secretary and treasurer make report of the transactions of
the society during the year. The officers for the en-
suing year are chosen. Then the attention of the company is asked to an address, usually by some present
or former resident of Stockbridge who has gained a
measure of distinction in letters, in trade, or in art,
and who is willing thus to recognize his duty to the
place of abode. A poem, perhaps, follows, then short
speeches from one and another whom the president
espies among the trees, and calls upon for a contribution for the occasion. The speeches are interluded by

strains of music and pleasant neighborly talk. All is simple and unstudied. It is the village festival. People come together here who meet nowhere else. And here all are equal. Old and young, rich and poor, meet together. All feel that they are welcome; and as the sun begins to throw his slant shadows down the hill-side and along the green meadows, the groups move homeward with a kindlier interest in one another, and a stronger attachment to the place where their lot has been cast.

To complete the account of this association we give its constitution, which may possibly be of service to such as have in contemplation the formation of a similar organization.

BY-LAWS AND REGULATIONS

OF THE

LAUREL HILL ASSOCIATION.

ARTICLE I.

This Association shall be called "The Laurel Hill Association of Stockbridge."

ARTICLE II.

The objects of this Association shall be to improve and ornament the streets and public grounds of Stockbridge, by planting and cultivating trees, cleaning and repairing the sidewalks, and doing such other acts as shall tend to beautify and improve said streets and grounds.

ARTICLE III.

The officers of this Association shall consist of a president, four vice-presidents, a clerk, a treasurer, a corresponding secretary, and an executive committee of fifteen, part of whom shall be ladies. These officers shall be elected at the annual meeting (except the first election, which shall be on the 3d of September, 1853), and shall hold their offices until others shall be elected in their places.

ARTICLE IV.

The president, vice-presidents, clerk, treasurer, and corresponding secretary shall be *ex-officio* members of the executive committee.

ARTICLE V.

It shall be the duty of the president to preside at all meetings of the Association, and in his absence the senior vice-president shall preside. It shall also be the duty of the president and vice-presidents to procure addresses at the annual meetings of the Association.

ARTICLE VI.

It shall be the duty of the clerk to keep a correct and careful record of all the proceedings of the Association, in a suitable book to be procured for that purpose, and to notify all meetings of the Association.

ARTICLE VII.

It shall be the duty of the treasurer to keep safely all the moneys belonging to the Association, and to pay them over on the orders of the executive committee.

ARTICLE VIII.

It shall be the duty of the corresponding secretary to correspond with absent members, and to do all the correspondence of the Association.

ARTICLE IX.

It shall be the duty of the executive committee to employ all laborers, make all contracts, expend all moneys, direct and superintend all the improvements of the Association at their discretion. They shall hold meetings monthly from April to October in each year, and as much oftener as they may deem expedient.

They shall have power to institute a system of premiums to be awarded for planting and protecting ornamental trees, and making such other improvements as they shall deem best.

ARTICLE X.

Every person over fourteen years of age who shall plant and protect a tree under the direction of the executive committee, or pay the sum of one dollar annually, and obligate him or herself to pay the same for three years, shall be a member of this Association. And every child under fourteen years of age who shall pay, or become obligated as above, for the sum of twenty-five cents, or an equivalent amount of work annually for three years, under the direction of the executive committee, shall be a member of this Association.

ARTICLE XI.

The payment of ten dollars annually for three years, or of twenty-five dollars in one sum, shall constitute a person a member of this Association for life.

ARTICLE XII.

Honorary members may be constituted by a vote of the Association.

ARTICLE XIII.

The autograph signatures of all the members of the Association shall be preserved.

ARTICLE XIV.

The annual meeting of the Association shall be held on Laurel Hill, on the fourth Wednesday of August, at two o'clock in the afternoon. Notices of said. meeting shall be posted on each of the churches, and at the post-office, at least seven days prior to the time of holding said meeting, and a written notice sent to all non-resident members, said notices to be signed by the corresponding secretary. Other meetings of the Association may be called by the executive committee, on seven days' notice, as above prescribed.

ARTICLE XV.

At the annual meeting the executive committee shall report the amount of money received and expended during the year; the number of trees planted by their direction; the number planted by individuals, and the doings of the committee in general. Their report shall be entered on the records of the Association.

Article XVI.

Five members present at any meeting of the executive committee shall constitute a quorum for transacting business.

Article XVII.

No debt shall be contracted by the executive committee beyond the amount of available means within their control to pay it, and no member of this Association shall be liable for any debt of the Association beyond the amount of his or her subscription.

Article XVIII.

These by-laws and regulations may be amended at the suggestion of the executive committee, sanctioned by a vote of a majority of the members present at any meeting of the Association.

CHAPTER IX.

TREES AND TREE-PLANTING.

"What we lack, perhaps, more than all is, not the capacity to perceive and enjoy the beauty of ornamental trees and shrubs—the rural embellishment alike of the cottage and the villa—but we are deficient in the knowledge and the opportunity of knowing how beautiful human habitations are made by a little taste, time, and means expended in this way."—A. J. DOWNING.

"The man who loves not trees to look at them, to lie under them, to climb up them (once more a schoolboy), would make no bones of murdering."—CHRISTOPHER NORTH.

THE one natural and universal beauty of a village is in its trees, so that one can hardly think of a pleasant bit of country without them. Mountains may be grand from their very bulk and massiveness, or awful even, by reason of their sometimes scarred and naked cliffs, but they are beautiful only as they are clothed with the verdure of trees. So water, whether in the form of running stream or placid lake, is one of the charms of the country. Yet the stream must be fringed with trees, occasionally at least, and linger now and then in shady nooks, and the lake must lie like a gem in a setting of verdurous foliage, in order to produce the best effect, and make the strongest appeal to the sense of the beautiful. The water, otherwise, is valuable only as so much

4*

mill-power, or to afford means of transportation for mer-
chandise. And so every one feels that half the beauty
of the natural world, if not more, is gone when comes
the annual fall of the leaves, for then, except for the
evergreens, the trees hardly seem trees to us. They are
only so much dead wood, apparently, which we look upon
very much as we do upon that in the carpenter's shop
or the lumber-yard—valuable for certain purposes of
human art and comfort, but touching us no longer with
sentiment, nor drawing out our feeling as to living things
which have on this account some relation to ourselves.

We need no apology, therefore, after having spoken
in a general way about village life, its needs, and the
means of its improvement, for offering some more particular considerations in regard to what must bear so
important a part in the outward improvement of our
villages as trees.

A tree! What object appeals more certainly to the
universal heart of man? Its very commonness may be
a reason why very many, and especially those who have
grown up in well-wooded districts, are not distinctly con-
scious of the pleasure which they find in trees. It is
like their unconsciousness of the delight, the daily enjoyment of the atmosphere. But who, least emotional
of mortals though he be, has not, at some time, if not
often, felt a tree to be a precious thing? The tired
wayfarer, reclining by the dusty roadside under its cool,
refreshing shade! What more precious or truly human
picture than that? A party of old and young, of both

sexes, picnicking on a summer's day beneath the spreading boughs of some grand old oak! How could such a happy scene be without that tree? Yonder lofty and majestic elm, the growth of a century, standing by the side of some farm-house, which, though ample in size, it dwarfs to a cottage as it rises above it with its dome of shade, and tosses its giant arms high over roof-tree and chimney-top! What an object to fill one at the same time with wonder and admiration! How it starts deep and meditative thoughts even in the casual beholder! That lordly pine, or hemlock, refusing to be robbed of its beauty at any season of the year, but singing, like a hundred Æolian harps, with every breeze, and holding itself before us as an emblem of life and immortality, to cheer us when all around is wrapped in the chill white robe of winter, what object on earth, next after the immortal man himself, is more beautiful or more noble? "Woodman, spare that tree!" You cannot replace in a lifetime what your axe may destroy in an hour. It has taken a lifetime and more to build up that miracle of beauty.

"In what one imaginable attribute that it ought to possess," asks Christopher North, in the *Noctes Ambrosianæ*, "is a tree, pray, deficient? Light, shade, shelter, coolness, freshness, music, all the colors of the rainbow, dew and dreams, dropping through their soft twilight at eve and morn—dropping direct, soft, sweet, soothing, restorative from heaven." What a blessing to have such things around us! What a blessing to be able to place them just where we will, to plant and care for them, and see them under our hands growing into objects of beauty and delight, the adornment and one of the chief charms of our homes! Does it need any argument to show the healthful influence—healthful alike to body and soul—which they are adapted to exert upon us? There has always been a charm for the finest minds in tree-planting. It has been at the same time one of the best recreations and one of the pleasantest studies for those of the noblest powers. Scholars and statesmen, poets and philosophers, have delighted to occupy their time in producing effects by means of such planting. Says Lord Bacon, "God Almighty first planted a garden; and, indeed, it is the purest of human pleasures; it is the greatest refreshment to the spirits of man, without which buildings and palaces are but gross handiworks; and a man shall ever see that, when ages grow to civility and elegancy, men come to build stately, sooner than to garden finely, as if gardening were the greater perfection."

We know only comparatively little of what Bacon means by gardening; that is, by any practice in our own country. Gardening, in his sense, implies the planting of whole acres with trees, and the production of landscape effects by a careful and well-studied disposal of them in groups and belts, and sometimes in banks of forest almost, as well as by the judicious placing of single trees. We know little of this. Our planting is mostly confined to the arrangement of a few trees in small enclosures, or along the roadside, with occasionally something on a little larger scale, as when we lay out a city park of a few acres.

But even with the small scale on which we work, there is occasion for the production of decided effects and room for study in order to make them most pleasing.

And here let us say that no country in the world, perhaps, affords a larger variety of trees for use in planting than our own, or trees finer or more desirable in themselves. To a great extent we are ignorant of our treewealth, and not unfrequently have we sent abroad for trees when we have had much better ones at home. We might mention the Lombardy poplar, for instance, a tree very fashionable forty or fifty years ago—and the relics of the fashion are to be seen now occasionally—but a poorer thing in the shape of a tree it would be hard to find. A single one, with its tall, spiry form, as a contrast to the spreading forms of other trees, in a considerable plantation, would be admissible, and perhaps produce a good effect. But to fill one's door-yard with such, or to plant them in rows along the roadside for miles together, as has sometimes been done, is the merest caricature of tree-planting. If we want poplars, moreover, we have them in our own forests, and need not go to Italy for them, or to the nurseries. And so, also, we have scores of other trees in our forests of which we may avail ourselves for the embellishment of our village streets and door-yards. We have limited ourselves to the use of half a dozen trees, as a general thing, in our planting, when we might easily have taken our choice from half a hundred. We have upwards of forty kinds of oak alone in our country, and yet we hardly know what it is to plant an oak. What trees we have of this sort are such as have been left in the cutting-off of our forests, or those which have come up spontaneously. But there is hardly a grander tree in the world than many of our oaks. This tree, however, like all, or nearly all, our trees, needs to grow alone —to have, literally, an "open field" for itself—in order to show its true character. Our woodmen know that if they want the most serviceable tree for timber, they must seek it in the open ground rather than in the forest. The tree that grows in the forest, crowded by others, neither has the strength nor the beauty of the one that grows by itself, and consequently battles with the winds and bathes in the daily sunshine, and has room to toss its arms abroad and develop its peculiar nature completely.

In planting for beauty, therefore, care should be taken to select trees from the open ground, or those which grow upon the edge of the forest rather than in its depths. Oftentimes very fine trees will be found growing along the division fences of the farm. Choosing trees thus, we should next endeavor to avail ourselves of the great variety offered to our hand. Instead of contenting ourselves with the elm and the maple, as so many have done, though these are in themselves trees of the finest character, we should call to our aid also such as the ash, and the beech, and the birches, as well as the tulip, or whitewood, and the chestnut and hickory.* Then, among trees which have been brought from abroad, but which are now easily obtained at home, we have the horse-chestnut, a tree both beautiful in shape and beautiful for its clusters of bright flowers. And then there is the whole pine family, as we may call them, or the evergreens. We have done hardly anything with this class of trees except to cut them down for fire-wood or lumber. In this respect we are widely in contrast with the English, who often almost fill their lawns and parks with the different kinds of evergreens. And yet there is more reason why we should plant this class of trees than they. We need them in our bright sunshine, so prevalent, to tone down the too abundant light, and to give a sense of coolness to our homes and streets in the heats of summer; whereas the English are under dark-ened and dripping skies almost all the time. Then they are specially desirable in the winter, when other trees

---

* For the satisfaction of those who may not be acquainted with many of our native trees, or who may like to know the opinion of others in re-gard to the merit of different trees, we give a list of those which the Park Commission at Washington, D. C., composed of three men of high stand-ing as horticulturists, have chosen for planting on the borders of streets. They have planted nearly forty-thousand trees, which have mostly been made up of the following twelve varieties, and which we place in the order of preference given them by this commission: White maple, American linden, American elm, scarlet maple, box elder, sugar-maple, American white ash, English sycamore, button-ball, tulip-tree, honey-locust, Norway maple.

have lost their foliage and the glare of the snow is almost blinding. How pleasant and refreshing it is then to let the eye rest upon the soft yet vivid green of the pines! Comparatively few also know what a protection from the cold of winter may be secured by means of the trees. A single row of pines, planted near the most exposed side of a dwelling, will furnish a very effective barrier against the chilling blasts from the northwest; and a belt of such trees, two or three deep, will almost change a winter climate to a temperate one. This is accomplished both by the obstruction which the almost solid mass of leaves offers to the passage of the wind, and by the positive heat which the trees also impart to the atmosphere. For it has been found by experiment that the vital functions of growing trees, like the vital functions of our own bodies, are attended by the evolution of heat which is given out to the surrounding air. It is easy to see, therefore, that very much might be done by the use of the evergreens to make our village homes more beautiful, and at the same time more comfortable.

And here let us say a few words for one of our most beautiful but least appreciated evergreens. We mean the hemlock pine. We hold it to be altogether the finest evergreen that is native to our country, and rivalled by few that grow anywhere. And yet, because partly of its very abundance in many portions of our country, covering whole mountain-sides, and because of its inferiority to the harder woods, and even to the white and yellow pines, for use as lumber or fuel, it has come

to be held, among our villagers especially, as a cheap sort
of tree to be made little account of. And so it has been
very little planted, and seldom thought of as a desirable
addition to the door-yard or the street. But there is
really no such beauty in our woods, and no such adornment as it is capable of giving to our dwellings and our
villages. Whoever has had one or more of these trees
fairly established on his lawn, or has seen one that has
had a proper chance to grow in the forest, where it could
throw out its arms symmetrically on all sides and lift its
head without impediment year by year towards the sky,
has been ready to confess that there is no tree at the
same time so graceful and so grand. The elm, among
deciduous trees, alone can match it. The white and
yellow pines and the spruce fir are stiff and ugly in comparison. The Norway spruce is its only rival, but it is
of a coarser make and less attractive. Both have the
beautiful habit of drooping their lower branches till
they almost, or quite, touch the ground, and then rising
in majestic and graceful cones till they overtop almost
all other trees. But the hemlock has a delicacy of foliage and a grace in every limb which the other has not.
Its whole structure is instinct with life and beauty. Its
taper branches, ending and clothed all through with its
most delicate leaflets, sway with every motion of the air,
and toss themselves about as in a perpetual joy of life.
The Dryads surely must have this tree for their home
and temple. How its new shoots, coming out in the
spring season—and as they do in a measure even after

almost every rain in the summer—of a lighter tint than the older leaves, seem fairly to smile upon you as you behold!

"O hemlock-tree! O hemlock-tree! how faithful are thy branches!
Green not alone in summer-time,
But in the winter's frost and rime!
O hemlock-tree! O hemlock-tree! how faithful are thy branches!"

It is a pity this tree should not be made use of more than it is for the embellishment of our home surroundings; not to the exclusion of the other evergreens, but in company with them. Together they make up a very pleasant and desirable variety, while any and all of them form a fine background for the various deciduous trees. How one of our white birches, for instance, stands out against a belt of dark pines! The effect is almost magical. And not only is the landscape effect better when evergreens are mingled with deciduous trees, but both classes of trees seem to grow better in each other's company than separately. This is usually nature's own way of growing them. Abundant experiments also have proved that many deciduous trees are very much benefited by the shelter which neighboring evergreens give them. It is wise, then, on all accounts, to mingle these different classes of trees in our planting.

Some may think the evergreens specially difficult of management, but it is not so. There is just one thing to be remembered in transplanting them, and that is—that we must not allow their roots to become dry, whether by exposure to sun or wind. It is important, therefore, that they should be transplanted, if possible, in a cloudy or, better, a misty and still day, or else that their roots be covered while they are being removed from their old to their new home. If one will only thus guard their roots from becoming dry, he may transplant a hemlock or a white pine with as much ease and certainty of subsequent growth as he can a maple. Evergreens may be transplanted with this care in the warm months of July and August as well as in the early springtime. It is best commonly, however, to choose small trees, because it is not easy to find large and symmetrical ones, and because, in the case of all small trees, we are likely to take up a greater proportional share of roots than with those which are larger.

And whatever tree is handled, evergreen or deciduous, large or small, let it not only be taken up carefully, but planted also carefully. This should be the inflexible law. Careless planting is a great waste of time and timber, and very unsatisfactory. A few good trees full of vitality, and, therefore, making lusty growth from year to year, are better, worth more every way, than ever so many dead-and-alive things—mere apologies for trees—of which, alas! we see too many. Treat a tree as such a living, divinely created thing ought to be treated. A tree has rights which white men, black men, and men of all other colors are bound to respect. Do not wrench it up by force from the soil into which it has woven its very life for years; do not tear its rootlets asunder in the hasty endeavor, with rude instruments, to separate them from their hold. But with whatever painstaking may be needful, let the roots be gently separated from the soil. Remember that they are the digestive organs of the tree; the organs which are to gather and assimilate its food and convert it into tissue; and that the fine, fibrous roots are, for this purpose, of more consequence than the large ones. The tree can no more grow without them than a man can grow without a stomach. Take them up carefully, therefore; preserve them so far as possible. And if, after all, some roots are broken in the removal, let the fractured ends be smoothly pared off with the knife so that the wounds may be quickly healed and new rootlets begin to be formed; then replant the tree as carefully as it has been taken from the ground. Do not, as so many do, treat it like a post and thrust it into a hole only just large enough for it, and then ram the earth around it and leave it to take care of itself;. but be sure to make a hole as large as the natural spread of the roots, and even larger, so that they may easily push themselves out for the growth of coming years. For the same reason, make the hole of generous depth; then see that the earth is made fine and of nutritious richness. Thus, make a bed for the tree carefully, as you would make one for yourself, and then lay it therein, tucking the earth carefully about all its finest roots, and with gentle pressure bringing it into firm contact with them, settling it occasionally, perhaps, as you go on, with a few quarts of water, and finally mulching the surface with some old straw or with flat stones. It will pay, as a child well nursed pays, by a healthy growth. It will reward you with its own tree-smiles every year and every day.

It is hardly necessary to add that, as some portion of the roots is likely to be lost in the process of transplanting, even when much care is exercised, it is proper that a corresponding portion of branches should be removed in order to preserve the requisite balance between roots and branches, the two important parts of the tree-system. The necessary top-pruning should not be done, however, by lopping off at once the whole top down to a certain distance, nor by removing one or more of the lower and larger limbs, but rather by a shortening-in of all the branches a few inches, which will leave the shape of the tree uninjured and preserve the proper balance between the digestive and the breathing organs of the tree.

And now one caution in conclusion. Trees are good, but we may have too many of them, and we may not have them in the proper place. It is easy for the tree-planter to overcrowd his grounds; especially is this apt to be the case when small trees are planted. The planter is anxious for immediate effect—at least, planters in this country usually are. And so he plants a lawn in miniature, which, in itself, looks well enough. But when a few years have gone by, the impatient planter finds that his lawn has become a thicket. The trees have expanded, as it was their nature to do, until there is hardly any vacant space left. Now trees, to have their best effect, must be seen singly or in a harmonious group of two or three perhaps, and not crowded together as in a forest, where their individuality is lost. They appear at their best, also, only when they have spaces of clean turf around them, in which they are set as enamel. And when trees are allowed to be crowded, not only is their beauty and charm as trees lost, but the highest beauty of the ground is also lost, for nothing will make amends for the lack of some space of clear, unobstructed turf, on which the sun may throw its light and across which may play the shadows of the clouds. There are few things upon which the eye rests with such abiding satisfaction, from day to day and from year to year, as a breadth of clean, luxuriant grass. Neither trees nor flowers, however rich or abundant, can take its place. Then, moreover, the crowding of trees near a dwelling is prejudicial to health. Not that trees in themselves are harmful. On the other hand, science has shown us that it is the office of the trees, through their lungs, the leaves, to reverse the action of our own lungs, to inhale carbonic acid, and to throw out into the air the oxygen which we need. But there is no hygienic agency equal to that of the sun. This is the true fountain of life. Plants and animals alike, without it, have but a sickly life or die. No trees, therefore, or anything else, ought to be allowed to keep its beams from striking upon our houses and coming every day, for a while at least, into our rooms. Blinds, curtains, carpets, all ought to make way for the sun and give it welcome. Then if we want the shade of trees, let it be sought at some little distance from the dwelling. On all accounts, whether of health or æsthetic effect, there should be a clear space of some breadth around every house, where hardly so much as a shrub should break the smooth green of the turf or the clean sweep of gravel. If one can have a single elm near by, so large, and its branches so lifted up that the light can strike under them abundantly, except at mid-day, it is well. One such tree is enough almost to satisfy the most ardent tree-lover and to adorn sufficiently any dwelling-place. But if more are wanted, let them be planted farther away. They look best at a little distance, as do good pictures. Then their different forms can be best seen, and the play of light and shade upon them with every changing hour and phase of sky.

There has been much debate as to the best season of the year for tree-planting, but, like many other debates, this is, perhaps, interminable. Spring and autumn planting are advocated, one as confidently as the other. We would undertake to plant as readily in the one season as the other. The advantage of planting in the autumn seems to us to be chiefly this, that it secures so much work done, which, if postponed until spring, may not be done then on account of the many things which are pressing for attention at that season of the year.

CHAPTER X.

VINES AND CLIMBING PLANTS.

"Or they led the vine
To wed her elm; she, spoused, about him twines
Her marriageable arms, and with her brings
Her dower, th' adopted clusters, to adorn
His barren leaves."—*Paradise Lost.*

"Man, like the generous vine, supported lives;
The strength he gains is from the embrace he gives."
POPE.

AMONG the things that go to the outward adornment
and beautifying of our homes, whether in city or country, and so to the making them the more attractive and
enjoyable, few deserve a larger place in our esteem than
vines and climbing plants. Yet their very modesty
and unobtrusiveness often cause them to be overlooked, like the grace of modesty in character itself. But
there is scarcely any adornment of such universal ap-
plicability. They are a grace and charm for almost
every place. In the crowded city there is hardly anything which can do so much, in giving a touch of nature
and of beauty to a home amid walls and pavements of
stone or brick, as a single vine or climbing plant. In
the narrow space which is all that can usually be at-

tained between one city house and another, there is
seldom room for any tree to develop itself and show
what it can be or do. We have to content ourselves
commonly with mere shrubs. Yet in the narrowest
spaces it is possible to embower one's self and household amid vines, and to rejoice in a grateful seclusion
from curious eyes, while at the same time enjoying the
balm of the open air. And even when shut up to the
necessity of living in a city " block," there is no man-
sion so grand, or with walls so smoothly chiselled or so
deftly carved, but that an ivy or a wistaria can cling to
it, and give it an added grace beyond the reach of any
craftsman, and touch the heart with something softer
than stone, as it greets the eyes of the dwellers there,
or only those of the passers-by.

But the open country is the true home of the vines and
climbers, and here they work their best effects, though
they have often been greatly overlooked and neglected
amid the wealth of vegetation around them. One is
often surprised to find people who are regarded as
among the most intelligent and observing of our country villagers entirely ignorant of some of the most beautiful climbing plants which grow in profusion within
easy reach of them, perhaps within daily sight. Take,
for instance, one of our most charming climbers, the
clematis, known in some sections as " old man's beard,"
one of a dozen species, which grows abundantly along
many of our New England brooks, and hangs out its
beautiful silky tresses in autumn upon so many of the

5

hedge-rows that skirt the dusty roadway. Hardly anything is more delicate and graceful. It is a most rapid grower, covering large spaces in a single season, while it is also among our hardiest plants. Yet how many farmers have driven their cows to pasture for years through thickets of it without so much as noticing it, certainly without having any sense of its loveliness; and many a farmer's wife or daughter has seen its white, starry flowers and its silky tresses by the roadside without thinking how easily its charms might be transferred to the door-yard or the porch at home, now bare.

Nothing that grows commends itself to us more, on the score both of beauty and usefulness, than this class of plants. The grape—type of all the climbers—with its inimitable grace of form, neither needing nor admitting any touch of man to improve it in this respect, while hanging out at the same time to the sight and offering to the taste its purple and luscious clusters— what growth can equal it? Well, therefore, do the Scriptures take it as the type of all that is most beautiful and precious. Israel, God's chosen one, is a vine. A golden vine, curiously carved, we know also, was one of the chief adornments of the temple at Jerusalem. And our blessed Saviour offers himself to us, in his most endearing relation, under the figure of the vine, of which we are, or may be, branches, drinking our life from and bearing fruit with him to the glory of the Heavenly Father.

It has been well said—

"——beauty is its own excuse for being,"

and the great Maker has set around us enough of the forms and hues of beauty to show us that it has a value in itself and in his eye, and that the love of the beautiful is no unworthy feeling, but one which he would cultivate in us by every possible means. And in the vine he has shown us how closely the beautiful and the useful are linked together.

It is set down as one of the tokens of prosperity under the reign of King Solomon that "Judah and Israel dwelt safely, every man under his vine and under his fig-tree." It would be better for us if we were to become more Oriental in our habits, in this respect at least, and, in the season of warmth and leafage, were to sit more than we do under our vines, if not under our fig-trees; if, after the day's work, there were rest and pleasant talk under the grape arbor, or if the tea-table were occasionally spread beneath the vine trellis, and the flavor of the hyson were mingled with that of the blossoms or the clusters of the grape. They do this over the water, and we shall, sometime, perhaps, learn to do the same. In Germany and France especially, one may often see whole families taking their repast, and particularly the evening meal, in the open air. It is healthful—healthful not less to mind than to body. It helps to gather a tender feeling about the home. The very soil gets a more hallowed association, and the children will turn to it in after-life with a sweeter affection and a stronger attachment. It draws them into sympathy with nature herself, and tends to inspire them with her precious influences.

It is surprising what a charm is sometimes given to a very ordinary and humble dwelling by one of these climbing vines. Who has not felt, in traversing some country road, the power of a prairie rose, climbing up by the door-side and over the simple porch of a low-roofed farm-house, to dignify, and even glorify, what otherwise would have been passed by without notice, and to draw tender thoughts and feelings towards the unknown dwellers within? And then there is the trumpet creeper, aptly named from its great, red, trumpet-shaped flowers, and in respect to which one is at a loss whether most to admire its flaming clusters of blossoms or its delicate foliage. What a grand climber this is! How it mantles walls and buildings with its beauty! We carry in mind now the picture of one of these, seen more than twenty years ago in one of our Connecticut towns. It was a low stone building, erected in the primitive days, but now with its roof ready to fall in, and it was tenanted only by a couple too poor to have a better shelter from the cold and storm. But over that building, scarred and seamed by time, climbing up its sides, and fairly rioting over its long stretch of roof, and covering its stone chimney, which it almost smothered in its loving and luxuriant embrace, went that royal climber, the living sheet of green, spangled all over with crimson blossoms, so shapely withal and dignified. Why, it seemed that those walls of stone might well have been built

for no other purpose than as a scaffolding to show what
a wealth of grace and beauty the Heavenly Father had
put into one of these humble plants that run wild about
us, asking only the privilege of some support that they
may lift themselves up into our sight to bless us with
their beauty and lift up our souls with them.

And then what shall we say of the hop-vine, the *humulus* of the botanists, like humility itself drawing its
very name from the ground, or *humus?* Let us say of
it that, like humility, it has a heavenly grace. There is
a common way of speaking rather contemptuously of
this plant. Is it because of its commonness? It ought
to be so common as to find a place in every door-yard.
What a strong, sturdy grower it is! What a lusty
vitality it shows! Ready to burst from the ground at
the first approach of springtime, before most other
plants have begun to grow, this has climbed up and
is looking in at your window to greet you with its
beauty, and soon it has gone far into the air with its
twining wreaths. Give it a support, a cord reaching
up to your roof, and it will climb there in a few
weeks; or, if trained upon a pole with some cross-bars,
platform-like, at the top, so that it can hang down its
graceful stems like a canopy, there is hardly a finer
sight as autumn approaches than this common and
modest *humulus*, with its clusters of golden catkins
swaying in every breeze.

We are apt to think of the hop from the utilitarian
point of view. It suggests beer, and prosaic yeast, and

the bitter tea which many good old housewives prepare as a nervine. But apart from all these and other
domestic uses, it is an object of rare beauty, and deserves to be cultivated, if only on this account.

Then there is the *convolvulus*, or morning - glory,
which every one is supposed to know, but the wonderful beauty of which so few do really know. We
might say it is the poor man's delight, it is so commonly found near the cottages of the poor, if it were
not so characteristic of almost all this class of plants
that they are within reach of those of slender means.
There is no one who may not have his grape-vine almost for the asking, or if he will go into the woods or
hedge-rows and dig it. Even the choicest of our grape-
vines may now be had by the day-laborer in exchange
for an hour or two of his work. The ivy, the wistaria,
the Boursault roses, are equally cheap. No one need
be without them. No cottage or farm-house need be
without the charm of their luxurious beauty.

Then there is the honeysuckle tribe — graceful, rich
in color, and fragrant with odor. How easy to have
one or more of these near our dwelling! How cheap
the charms they bring, and all the more precious because they draw around us the added charm of the
bees, with their soothing murmur and promise of nec-
tar by-and-by, and of the humming-birds with their wondrous beauty of color, miniature rainbows on wings!

Last, but by no means least in value, let us speak of
the Virginia creeper, known also as the woodbine and

the American ivy, though it is not a true ivy, but belongs to the grape family. It is to be found over a
wide extent of country. But no commonness or
familiarity can lessen its beauty. Those who have
seen it encasing some tall dead trunk, where a forest
has been cut away, or completely mantling the walls
of some church, robing its tower and even its turret-
tops with its veil of green, and then seeming almost
to set them aflame when, in the autumn, its leaves exchange their green for scarlet, need no words from
any one to kindle their admiration for this most lovely climber.

Such are a few out of a large class of plants which
are adapted, in a remarkable degree, to aid us in impart-
ing outward and visible beauty and comfort to our
dwellings, and especially to dwellings in the country,
and so helping to make country life the more attractive. Besides those which have been mentioned, there
are many more of like character, which are peculiarly
adapted for culture within doors, lending us their
beauty not only in the summer season, but through
the long, cold days of winter, when all our vines in
the open air, in the Northern States at least, are obliged
to drop their leaves and their beauty together. The
English ivy and the German, and many other plants
more delicate in structure, are ready to our hand for
the decoration of the rooms we daily occupy, so that
we need, at no season of the year, to be without the
charm of these graceful climbers.

And one thing more may be said in regard to this class of plants before we leave them. They are not only most beautiful in themselves, but they are at the same time our best means of hiding from sight much that may be deformed or otherwise repulsive to the sight. A squash-vine in the garden, with its massive leaves and golden blossoms—cups fit for royalty itself —will beautify while it conceals a compost-heap. So, is the dwelling, or some building near it, bare and rude, or unpleasing in form and proportion, let a vine or a creeper mantle its side or hang along its cornice, and the deformity is hidden and beauty takes its place. And thus in many ways these rapid growers, which may so easily be trained to go wherever we will, may be made available for a double use—to offer us the charm of their own beauty and loveliness, and to shut from sight what we would have concealed.

CHAPTER XI.

FRUITS AND FLOWERS.

"To me the meanest flower that blows can give
Thoughts that do often lie too deep for tears."
WORDSWORTH.

AMONG the many divinities to whom the ancient
Romans paid honor were Flora and Pomona, the dei-
ties of flowers and fruits. And not the least worthy
of a place in the most serious regard of any people
are those products over which these fancied divinities
were thought to preside. Which of the two affords
most pleasure to man it might be difficult to decide;
for, while the fruits are at the same time grateful to
the taste and valuable as a means of sustaining life,
the flowers appeal at once to the senses of sight and
smell, and offer a more constant and varied source of
delight. But we need not discuss the comparative
merits of the two sources of pleasure, since both are
within the reach of almost every one. The more important fact to be considered is that few of us make as
much of either as we might. We neither have as
many flowers or fruits as we might have, nor do we
derive from them as much pleasure as they are capable

5*

of giving us. Why this is so it might not be easy to determine. It would seem to be by some depravity of nature, for flowers are everywhere in exhaustless profusion, and fruits follow flowers, and both offer themselves to man to be improved by his culture to an extent which knows hardly any limit. Every year surprises us with the discovery of new flowers or the development of some new beauty and grace in the old and well-known ones; while the fruit-culturist is constantly rewarded by the gain of new varieties, or the marked improvement of the old in the qualities which make them pleasurable or useful.

In the country, then, in and around our village homes, where land space is abundant, flowers and fruits ought to abound. The fairest show of these products of nature should not be found, as is now so often the case, in the city or the market-town rather than in the open country. Our villages, with their farms and cottages, ought to be rich and beautiful with these proper products of the soil.

Flowers are a sign of taste and culture, and we never see a flowering plant set in the window of a dwelling, however humble, but that we think the better of the inmates on account of it. Some of the household, we know, may be coarse; but that blooming plant, cheap and common though it may be, growing perhaps in no vase of elegant proportions, but, perchance, in some broken piece of crockery no longer able to do its duty in the cupboard or on the table, tells unmistakably that in some heart, at least, in that home—in the heart of mother or daughter—there is a real love of the beautiful, and a refinement of feeling which breaks out from the drudgeries of its surroundings and asserts itself in this way, bringing itself thus into communion with the whole outward world of nature, and with the whole realm of taste and culture.

And every such sign of taste and love for the beauty of nature is to be encouraged. Children should be incited oftener than they are to have their little flower-gardens. It is one of the commonest desires of children, as they see others cultivating flowering plants, to have some of their own. And if this desire were properly gratified, especially if they were given a pleasant and well-prepared place for their floriculture, instead of some out-of-the-way, weedy, and undesirable spot, as is commonly the case, and if they were helped to tend and watch the growing plants, and to notice from time to time the wonderful developments of their growth, there would be established in them a love of nature and a taste for the beautiful that would go with them through life, and make their life all the healthier and better.

Nor should the cultivation of flowers be thought something more appropriate for girls than for boys. We make a difference here that we should not. It would be a special blessing to our boys if, from their youngest years, they were incited to sow the seeds of various plants and then to watch and assist their growth, and thus become acquainted with the laws of nature and with the beautiful and wondrous processes of vegetable life. It would cultivate their observing faculties. It would store their minds with valuable knowledge. It would soften and refine their manners. It would give us a succession of grown-up men, more intelligent, and therefore more capable of managing the affairs of husbandry and making farm-life successful, than the mass of our farmers now are; while it would also make them more refined and tasteful, and the work of the farmer more tasteful also. Then husbands would not, as now they sometimes do, look upon the flower-beds in the garden as so much land wasted, and the time given to their care by the wife or daughters as so much time misspent or taken from more important uses; but husband and wife, and sons and daughters, would be in harmony of feeling, and all would delight to co-operate in embellishing their home and blessing their daily life with the beauty and cheer which flowers are capable of giving. Such a common and accordant employment would also tend to draw the family together and strengthen the bond of attachment to each other, and would do much to withstand those influences the effect of which is, too often, to loosen the ties of domestic life, and to make the home less precious and attractive than it should be.

But where there is a love of flowers and a desire to

cultivate them, mistakes are not unfrequently made which lessen the pleasure that flowers might give. One mistake often made is that of cultivating all sorts of flowers indiscriminately. Slips and seeds are eagerly caught up and thrust into the garden, with little thought or knowledge of their character or habits, and the result is an incongruous growth, a wild disorder of beauty, which almost turns beauty into deformity. For the best effect and the greatest enjoyment in the care of flowers, it is best, in most cases, to confine attention and expend care upon a few plants, rather than to endeavor to have many. It is better to have a few of choice character and perfect in growth than to have ever so many which are imperfectly developed. One or two roses, carefully tended, so as to bring out their completeness of form and color, will give more pleasure in their cultivation and be a richer embellishment to the house grounds than a gardenful left to grow as they may. So of other flowers. There is more pleasure in being intimately acquainted with a few than in having only a general knowledge of many. Another mistake is made sometimes in cultivating plants, whether rare or common, which bloom unfrequently, it may be only once in the year, and have no attractions except for a brief period, rather than those which bloom much oftener, perhaps blossom almost continuously. The flower-garden thus often becomes an unsightly place, a wilderness of stalks, with only occasional flowers. It is much better every way, far more satisfactory, to be con-

tent with such constantly blooming plants as the perpetual or Bourbon roses, the salvias, pansies, daisies,
portulacas, geraniums, verbenas, alyssums, asters, and
the like, with only a few of the rarer kinds.

Then, as to the embellishment which flowers give to
a village home, in distinction from the pleasure which
they give to the cultivator as he or she tends and watches
them from day to day, it is better to cultivate each kind
of flowering plant by itself than to have the various
kinds intermingled in the same bed. Unpleasant con-
trasts of color are thus avoided. The tasteful eye is
often pained by the inharmonious combination of colors,
so that flowers, beautiful in themselves and when properly arranged, now cease to give pleasure. We may add
also that flowers appear more beautiful and are more
effective as embellishments of grounds when they are
planted in masses in the green turf of the lawn or door-
yard than when set in beds in the garden. When planted in the garden, the plants will have large spaces of
bare earth visible between or around them. The more
the ground can be concealed and only solid masses of
flowers left visible, relieved against the green turf, the
more pleasing the effect; and there is no way in which
this can be better secured than by growing flowers, each
kind by itself, or at least those harmonizing in color, in
beds cut out of the closely shaven greensward. These
beds, let us also say, should not be raised up into mounds,
as is so often the practice. In our sunny and hot summer
climate most plants need all the rain which falls upon

them. But where the ground in which they stand is heaped into mounds, a large part of the rain is carried away from the plants, with the common result of a parching and withering that make the flower-garden too often anything but a pleasant object to look at. Time and labor are, for the most part, wasted which are employed in constructing mounds or beds of fanciful or elaborate pattern for the flower-garden. These may please at first by their evidence of care and good intention, but they are difficult to keep in their proper shape. The very work of cultivating the flowers, as well as the tread of feet in visiting them, tends to impair the perfectness of their shape, and unless this is preserved, they cease to please. In this case, as in so many others, simplicity is better than what is more elaborate and expensive. Our costliest things are not the most needful nor the most satisfactory. If we want flowers, we can have them; the poorest can have them. No heaping-up of mounds or elaborate shaping of ground is necessary. Flowers never look more beautiful than when seeming to spring out of the green grass; and it only requires an occasional cutting of the grass roots, so that they shall not encroach upon the space designed for the flowering plants, and these may then be left almost to themselves. With a mass of flowers of one color, or of harmonious colors, bedded in the green turf, and here and there another, differing somewhat, it may be, in size and shape, and a climbing rose or honeysuckle perhaps over the doorway, what a charm may be given to almost any dwelling-place!

But shall we confine the cultivation of flowers to the open ground and the open season of the year, or shall we have them with us at all seasons, and in the house as well as in the garden or on the lawn? This is somewhat a question of expense as well as of taste. Throughout the northern portion of our country, flowers are a forbidden thing out of doors for half the year. During the long winter months we must resort to the florist if we would have them, or we must create an artificial summer in our houses, or in some apartment specially arranged for the purpose. Happily, in these days, our improved methods of warming afford us the ready means of supplying that protection from the cold which flowering plants demand. By the use of our self-feeding stoves, in which we can keep a continuous fire during the entire winter, or by means of a furnace, we are able to maintain such a temperature in a single room, or throughout the whole house, that it is quite practicable to protect even tender plants from the severest cold, and to have their bright colors and fragrance with us all the year. It would be a great accession to many of our country houses if better appliances for warming them were introduced, so that the presence of flowers might be had there at all seasons of the year. Our farmers and villagers would find it a cheap expenditure. Saying nothing of the gain on the score of health and general comfort from having a warmer and more uniform temperature secured throughout their rooms, the cheerful effect of bright blooming plants here and there about. the house, and their refining influence, would be worth much more than their cost every year. They would make the house more inviting and more satisfying to all the inmates, and tend to the production or the confirming of a spirit of contentment. It would be one of the things that would help to attach the children to their home, to make them feel that it is a *home*, and not a place merely for shelter and food, and so to make them less disposed than they now often are to forsake it for something pleasanter. Everything that increases the comforts and attractions of the home makes other places less attractive in comparison with it. Make the surroundings of the house pleasant and healthful, with green and graceful lawns, bright flowers, and intermingled and properly balanced sunshine and shade; with proper drainage and shaping of grounds, so that no unwholesome damps or noxious matters shall hang about the premises to offend the senses or threaten the health.

Make the interior arrangements of the house cheerful and pleasant. Let there be sunshine within as well as without. Let there be no best room, never to be used except on state occasions, but all the rooms good and ready for use. Let all be well furnished, though it may be inexpensively, and the children have rooms which they can call their own, fitted up with some care, and warmed for them, perhaps, in the cold winter nights. In such homes children will grow up with strong roots of attachment to hold them there. There is enough wasted on many farms and country places to make them very palaces of comfort and beauty if it were saved and properly applied in practical use. The Bible tells us that God has made everything beautiful in its season. And if he has made things beautiful, we may be assured it is for a good purpose, and that we do well to love the beautiful, and to bring ourselves into contact with it wherever we can. The gospel of beauty needs to be preached as well as the gospel of goodness; and, indeed, it is preached wherever a blossom unfolds itself to the sight. The flowers are God's messengers, designed to touch us with the sense of something more and higher than the merely useful, to lift us above the narrow questions, "What shall we eat? or, What shall we drink? or, Wherewithal shall we be clothed?" "The life is more than meat." The life is more than food. It consists in thoughts and feelings, and these are closely connected with the sense of the beautiful. And if the Creator has made the flowers to be especially the types and ministers of beauty, we shall do well to surround ourselves with them, and to cultivate their fellowship in our grounds and in our dwellings.

Closely related as they are, after what we have said of flowers, we need not say much in respect to fruits. That we might have more of them, and of better quality and more desirable than what we now have, is clear. What a few in every town and village have might be had by almost every owner of a few acres, or even a few rods. There are usually two or three persons in every farming community who are noted for the abundance and quality of the fruits which they cultivate and send to market. They are a class by themselves, thought to be of a somewhat higher order of farmers and cultivators than those who limit themselves to the growing of corn, potatoes, and the like. They are of a higher order, inasmuch as they include in the range of their work what the others are either too ignorant or too lacking in enterprise to undertake.

But what the few have is clearly within the reach of the rest. The cultivation of fruit requires care and attention, as does the cultivation of anything else. Trees bearing desirable fruit do not spring up spontaneously and grow luxuriantly of their own accord. The original crab-apple, perhaps, did so ; but the Baldwin or the Spitzenberg does not. So with the many other fruits which we prize. But, with a reasonable amount of care, these fruits may be had by almost any owner of the soil. They may be had with such care as almost any cultivator can give without detriment to his other work. A great deal of this care can be given when such work is not pressing, and in the odd moments or odd hours of time which otherwise would very likely be lost. Most of our fruits, probably, have been raised in this easy and inexpensive way, and yet the value of our fruit crop taken together is even now quite noticeable. The census report gives the number of acres devoted to vines and fruit-trees as 4,500,-000, and the estimated value of fruit products is as follows :

Apples.............................	$50,400,000
Pears..............................	14,130,000
Peaches...........................	56,135,000
Grapes............................	2,118,900
Strawberries......................	5,000,000
Other fruits......................	10,432,800
Total.........................	$138,216,700

This amounts in value to nearly half that of our wheat crop, one of our great staples. Great as this amount is in the aggregate, it is only a beginning of what our fruit crop might be, and with advantage to us in every way. On the score of health, a larger consumption of fruit is desirable. It is probable, also, that the agreeableness of fruit to the taste will cause the use of it to keep pace with its increased production. The modern processes of preserving fruits by canning, drying, and otherwise, and the use of refrigerator cars and ships, by which they can be transported long distances, tend, also, to increase their consumption. By these means the evils of unequal production in different years are avoided. The excessive product of a favorable year, instead of being largely wasted, is carried over in part into a less favorable one, and thus an even supply is secured. By the same means, also, a large European market is secured for our fruits. So, practically, the market for good fruit is now unlimited, and there is abundant encouragement for the fruit-grower. Ninety thousand barrels of apples are reported as having been sent to Liverpool alone in the month of December, 1877. The exports during the whole year amounted to nearly

$3,000,000. In 1871 they were only $509,000. This shows a rapid increase. Our exports of dried fruits for the year 1876 to 1877 amounted to 14,318,052 pounds. Thus we are beginning to send our apples, peaches, and other fruits abroad in exchange for the figs, oranges, and grapes which we have so long imported from the countries across the sea. But this is only the beginning. The exportation thus begun will increase many fold.

And how pleasant it is to the cultivators of fruit to have it in variety and abundance, none know better than themselves. How agreeable fruit is to the taste, what a contribution it is to the enjoyment of life, we all know, in a measure at least. We might enjoy it much more than we do, and find it contributing more largely than it does both to our comfort and happiness. On the score of health alone, we should find in the greater abundance and more common use of fruit an ample compensation for the cost of its attainment.

Let the flowers and the fruits, then, receive more attention. On all accounts such attention is desirable. It will repay us in more ways than one. It will add at once to the charm and to the profit of village life.

CHAPTER XII.

THE COUNTRY DWELLING-HOUSE.

"Until common-sense finds its way into architecture there can be but little hope for it."—RUSKIN.

"Houses are built to live in, and not to look on; therefore let use be preferred before uniformity, except where both may be had."—BACON.

WHAT should be the structure in which our village residents may find the most fitting home? The question implies that not every structure called a dwelling is appropriate for those whose home is in the open country. A house is not simply a contrivance for shelter, or something a certain number of cubic feet in dimensions, and therefore capable of containing a given number of animals, and furnishing them with the needful conveniences for eating and sleeping. It is the home of human beings; it is the nursery and abode of all those feelings and sentiments which distinguish the human creature, and which are so different from all that belongs to the mere animal. Every house should have supreme reference to this in its plan; and when we see so many structures occupied by man which were manifestly built with no such reference to the peculiarly human elements of our nature, we have only to say that they are buildings, and not properly houses at all.

But even when the attempt is made to provide for these inner wants of the man, his spiritual and æsthetic nature, there are certain limitations to our work, arising from various sources. Not to discuss these here, which is unnecessary, it is enough to say that the less available space for building in the city or populous town will necessarily modify the character of the structures there as compared with those in the open country. There cannot be that freedom and variety of arrangement, nor the same choice of material or position, which there is in the latter. We expect in the city a certain uniformity of style in building, because the excessive cost of land obliges the generality of house-builders to construct their houses upon a very limited ground-space. Hence we have, and are content to have, because we deem it an inevitable necessity, whole streets and blocks where the houses are indistinguishable from one another except by the street numbers upon their doors. Were it not for these, one would be as likely to go into his neighbor's house as his own. In the country we are happily able to avoid this tiresome uniformity, this merging one's self in the mass, this loss of individuality.

Here there is room for each one to house himself as he will. He may fit a house to himself instead of fitting himself to a house, as he is obliged to do in the city. And this is as it should be; for where there are no forbidding limitations, each person or family ought to indicate its own character somewhat by the structure in which it dwells. The house is for the man, not the

man for the house; and in the ideal state of things the
house of an intellectual and refined family should as
certainly indicate by its very exterior that it is not the
abode of the coarse and sensual, as the shell of the nau-
tilus tells us that it is not the home of the periwinkle or
the clam. And though we may not hope to reach this
ideal, we may and should approximate towards it more
nearly than we do. At present it is only here and there
that we see a dwelling having a character of its own,
and indicating the character of those who occupy it. To
a great extent our country houses are mere imitations
of one another, or they are so many cubical structures
having as little meaning as a like number of magnified
dry-goods boxes. The imitations, moreover, are usually
without reason—mere whims or conceits. Some one has
perchance added a new feature to the former customary
house of the place, and forthwith every new house must
be a copy of his, or at least a copy of that particular
feature. It is amusing to see how far this copying disposition will go, and what little and meaningless things
seem to satisfy it. You may go into some of our most
respectable and well-built villages and find, for example, the conceit of painting that part of the house-wall
which is under a piazza-roof of a different color from
the rest. The house will be white, of course, but this
little piazza bit will be yellow perhaps, or green, or blue,
it matters not which, only for some reason, or want of
reason, it must be of another color from the general
mass of the house. And this petty conceit will run

perhaps through the whole village. In another village a different but equally meaningless conceit will be seen to be characteristic of the place.

For all good country building, for all good building anywhere, the first requisite is, as Ruskin intimates, common-sense. Let there be a reason for everything; and if one has a reason for everything he does in the way of building, he will not be likely to go far astray. The question to be asked all the while and at every point is, "For what use is this or that to be done?" Putting this question of use foremost, it will at once be seen that the house of the farmer will call for a different sort of rooms or a different arrangement of them from what will be called for by the mechanic or the professional man. The dairy-farmer, again, will need a house somewhat varying from that of one whose farming processes are different. Then, in addition to these reasons for building one kind of a house rather than another, there will come in the size of one's family, the pecuniary ability and the peculiar tastes and habits of the family. All these things are to be considered, and all have a legitimate influence in deciding what the house shall be. But there are still other considerations to be regarded.

Prominent among these are climate and the natural features or peculiarities of one's place of abode. One would not build in the same style amid the rugged hills of New England as upon the smooth plains of the West or the savannas of the South. The heavy snows of the

6

former region call for a high-pitched roof that will carry their burden or slide it speedily to the ground. The very lines of the hills also, and the tapering evergreens which so commonly meet the eye, demand, if the house is to be in keeping with them, that its lines should tend upward. For the same reason a level region will suggest as appropriate a style whose lines tend in a horizontal direction. Speaking architecturally, the Gothic, or Pointed, and the Italian styles represent these upright and horizontal lines; and these styles, or modifications of them, will be chosen accordingly as one's place of abode is assimilated in its prevalent outlines to the one or the other. That style will be best, in any given case, which produces a structure so in keeping with its surroundings that it seems to have grown out of the ground rather than to have been placed there artificially or by construction.

The question is an important one—"Of what material shall we build?" The abundance of wood hitherto in most parts of our country, the fact that almost every householder could gather the material for his house upon his own land, and get it ready for the carpenter at little cost to himself, except his own labor, has led to the almost exclusive use of this material in the construction of our country houses. Coupled with the abundance and cheapness of wood, there has been a prejudice in the villages against the use of stone and brick. Houses built of these latter materials have been frequently damp and unwholesome. But this has been owing to a faulty method of construction. Usually no provision has been made to prevent dampness from coming up and filling the walls of the house from the cellar below. Then, in addition to this, the plastering has commonly been placed immediately in contact with the walls, and thus the moisture has been constantly and directly brought into the various rooms. All that is necessary to prevent such a result is that just above the level of the ground there should be a course of stone in the walls of a slaty character, which will prevent the dampness from being carried up by capillary attraction; or that a few courses of stone, or brick, if the walls are of that material, should be laid in cement, which will intercept the moisture. Then, as a protection from the dampness which might be absorbed from the rains or the damp atmosphere, let strips of wood an inch in thickness be nailed to the walls at suitable intervals, and the lathing be applied to these instead of being placed directly upon the brick or stone. This will form an air-space between the outer wall of the house and the inner wall of plastering, which will effectually exclude all dampness. Many of our old houses which have long been unwholesome on account of moisture arising from the faulty mode of construction just adverted to, have been renovated and made wholesome by simply applying strips to the old walls, and putting a new surface of lath and plaster upon these, thus creating the requisite air-space.

The advantages of brick and stone over wood as ma-

terials for building are so great that we are disposed to
say that nothing but great difficulty in procuring them
should make one willing to build of wood. The first
cost may be somewhat more than if the latter material
is used. But as an offset to this, brick and stone are
much more substantial and durable. A building constructed of these, when completed, is finished once for
all. On the other hand, a wooden structure is never
finished. It is all the while subject to decay. It is only
by covering it with pigments, encasing it in lead every
few years, that we are able to preserve it for any considerable length of time. The cost of these frequent
paintings, and the repairs which come in spite of painting, will soon make the cost of the wooden building
equal to one of stone.

But in many cases it would cost no more at first to
build of stone than of wood, did we but take counsel
of common-sense. There are multitudes of places in
New England, and in other parts of the country, where
there are rocks lying on the very ground where one
would wish to build, ready to be broken to pieces and
wrought into walls for the dwelling; or where, by
quarrying only a few feet below the surface, the builder may often find an abundance of stone. Now, if
he will only be content to lay the stone up in a
rough but solid manner, not expending labor and money to dress it to a smooth surface, but leaving the un-
hewn pieces in their native form and honest beauty,
his walls need cost him but little. If he wants orna-

ment, let him seek that also, as he may legitimately, in a cheap way and from a source close at hand, and better than any craftsman's chisel can give him. His rough wall is just what the vines of various kinds love to cling to. Let him plant them on this side and that, and allow them to run over his house, chimneys and all, without fear of their injuring it. Nothing adds such a charm to the exterior of a house in the country, or, for that matter, to a house in the city, as one or more vines climbing up its sides, and holding it in their tender, loving embrace; and one of the difficulties with our prevalent wooden houses is that we cannot allow the vines to run upon them freely, as we would often like to do, because we must tear them down every few years in order to paint the houses; or if they are suffered to cling to them, they promote their decay. Nothing can be better, nothing in the long run more satisfactory, than one of these simple, rough, and solid structures, vine-clad and mantled year by year with their garniture of leaves and blossoms. It harmonizes completely with nature around it, and year by year the touches of time, instead of threatening its decay and destruction, only mellow its hue, and make it more attractive. Such a house seems a living thing, a growth, in which one may have perpetual delight, and with which he may live in a constant sweet fellowship. In this it differs from any painted wooden structure whatsoever. Such a house may be elaborate in finish within, or it may be as simple as its exterior, and so is adapted to the use of those differing greatly in fortune. To those of restricted means it will suggest a correspondingly plain and simple furniture in many rooms, much of which perhaps the helpful hands of the household will construct. It will be a home of taste and frugality rather than of show or extravagance. It will be within and without a true village home.

Next in value to stone as a building material are bricks; but inferior, as being artificial, and, as commonly used, by no means as expressive. But we might put this material to better use than we do. In Europe, some of the finest buildings are constructed of bricks. By moulding them of various forms, and combining different colors, we can obtain very fine effects in brickwork. The last few years have given us some illustrations of what may be done in this way; and it is to be hoped that our monotonous and meaningless red-brick structures will give way to something more pleasing. Well-burned bricks are a much more durable material for building than many of the softer stones; and for color nothing can be better than that of the so-called "Milwaukee brick," for example, which is made in many places in our Western States. This color, ranging from a cream tint to almost a positive straw color, is one of the best for its general harmony with objects around; and, varied in its effect, as it may be by combining with it stones or bricks of a different hue, it is all that can be desired. For use in the country, it is better to seek the effect given by color and plain but decided mouldings and projections in ordinary rough bricks than to expend money in building with the carefully pressed bricks and with the nice and elaborate finish which they require. Their place is the city rather than the country.

But whether stone, bricks, or wood be chosen as the material with which to build, there are some considerations equally applicable to all. As to site, the utmost care should be taken to fix upon a spot which can be effectively drained, and which is not in the vicinity of standing water. The researches which have been made within a few years by physicians and sanitary commissions have abundantly proved that the permanent presence of water in the soil upon which a dwelling is built, or the presence of standing water near it, is a source of some of our most fatal diseases. The aim, therefore, should be to secure a site free from this danger. The bottoms of valleys are also to be avoided, not only on this account, but because any dampness or miasmatic influence engendered upon the hills around is likely to flow down into them. The summits of high hills, however, are to be shunned, on account of the trouble involved in climbing to them, and because of their exposure to winds and storms. One should build under the shelter of a hill, upon its southern, sunny slope, rather than upon its summit. In the larger part of our country the advantage of such a situation will be felt during the greater part of the year, and amid the heats of summer such an exposure will be more favored by the grateful and mitigating breezes than almost any other. If one can build his house near a

wood, so that he may have that as a screen from the
cold winds, let. him do so. He will find the trees a
charming background for his dwelling, and a source
of comfort and pleasure in many ways. A little care
will enable one, in most of our states, to establish himself on some wooded or partially wooded slope, where
all the demands of healthfulness shall be met, and from
which he may look out upon a pleasant landscape. In a
country of so much natural beauty as ours, it is a pity
that so many have fixed their homes, seemingly, with
so little reference either to comfort or pleasantness.

We have said if one can build near a wood, let
him do so. *Near* a wood, but not *in* it. It is a
great mistake for one to bury himself in a forest. We
need sunshine more than shade, and can better dispense with the latter than the former. Woods are desirable for a screen, and to give certain pleasant effects
to the surroundings of a home, but this does not require that we should be under their shadows or the
drippings of their branches. They are better farther
away. Their effectiveness as a screen from winter
blasts is as complete when several rods distant as when
they are close by us, and for all effects of beauty and
embellishment a little distance is quite desirable. If
one can have two or three well-grown trees in the
immediate vicinity of his house, it is enough. But
sunshine he must have, and he should have it in every
room of his house, even in pantries and store-rooms, for
they are the sweeter for a sun-bath every day.

On this account our houses should not be made to face, as they usually do, the cardinal points of the compass, but rather be set diagonally in reference to them; in other words, the corners of the house, and not its sides, should face those points. For the same reason our streets should not run in north and south, east and west, directions, but diagonally to those courses. Then at some time in the course of the day the sun would shine upon all sides of the house, and therefore into every room in it, whereas now the rooms upon the north side of our houses, during the winter months, are unvisited by the sun, and every one knows that they are the least comfortable and least pleasant rooms.

Our country houses have too commonly been either of the shabby or the showy sort, rather than homes of comfort and taste. They have been either cheap and ill-built structures, destitute of every sign of human taste, mere barns almost, or they have been pretentious, built more for show than for convenience and daily use and comfort. What is wanted is a style of buildings which, while differing among themselves in minor features, even as persons and families differ in look and character, shall yet have a common appearance of having been made for human beings to dwell in, and to be the home of tender and refined feelings and tastes. On the one hand, simplicity will be adorned and dignified by taste and refinement, and, on the other, the most elaborate structure will be elaborate only for purposes of utility and comfort, and not

6*

for show or display. We want no show-rooms in the country, no rooms to be opened only on company occasions. City style and manners may, perhaps, call for these. But in the country house no room and no furniture should be too good for the daily use and enjoyment of the household. We are not called upon to treat our neighbors and visitors better than ourselves. There is no sufficient reason why the largest and pleasantest chamber should be kept in reserve for a chance visitor to occupy only once or twice a year, and the well-furnished parlor be opened only when "we have company." It is a wrong to ourselves to do so. Those who occupy the house three hundred and sixty-five days of the year ought to have the best of it rather than the visitor of a day or an hour. We want the refining influence of the best surroundings. It is barbarous in tendency for a family to spend the larger part of its time in the kitchen and in small and scantily furnished bedrooms. The children need the culture and refining influence which come from familiarity with the best things that can be put within their reach; and to be brought up within sight of show-rooms and nice furniture, which yet they must not enjoy, gives them false ideas of life, teaches them to put show for substance, and prepares them to grow up with a double character, a feeling that it matters little how or in what spirit they habitually live, if only they can put on the proper appearance when occasion demands.

Let the best, then, be used—used by all the household.

Let the amplest rooms, the best furniture, and the finest prospects from windows be the daily enjoyment of all. If visitors come, let them have that truest and pleasantest welcome, a share with the family of those things which they daily use, rather than special privileges and attentions, which latter would keep them all the while from being at ease. We are persuaded that if many of our village families would move forward from their rear offices and cramped bedrooms so as to occupy the ampler apartments now so often closed for the greater part of the time, devoting the abandoned rooms to conveniences which now they lack, making them into wash-rooms, bath-rooms, and store-rooms, a new life would dawn upon them, and they would soon wonder how they could have lived as they did, when the means of better living were all the while at hand. Such a removal would lift the whole family life to a new and higher plane. It would make it more dignified and more tasteful. It would inspire it with new ideas and feelings. It would cultivate and intensify the home feeling. It would form new ties to hold the family together and give a new meaning to the word *home*.

This is not a treatise on architecture, or we might say much more on the construction of the country dwelling-house. We assume that one about to build a house in the country will call in the aid of a competent architect, or, if we may not assume this, we urge it upon all as the best means of securing a satisfactory result.

Every dwelling, as we have said, ought to be to some extent an expression of the character of its occupants. It should indicate by its appearance, its site, its form, its surroundings, what sort of people have it for their home. Therefore every house should be planned by those who are to live in it. They know best what they want a house for, and, consequently, what kind of a house they want. On this account, they should determine its general and many of its particular arrangements. Yet, even in these an architect may often make suggestions of the utmost importance, which will essentially modify the plan of the builder. It is the business of an architect to deal with the various details and modifications of structures. He is conversant with the possible alterations of plan, and the adaptations of means to uses. He has thought of them, and made them familiar to his mind as they cannot be to any other class. Few persons about to build have anything more than a rude idea of what they want. The proper adjustment of rooms to one another, so as best to serve the purposes of the building and the comfort of the occupants, they are quite incapable of determining, while in regard to the proper architectural form of the structure, within and without, they know almost nothing. And this is simply because it is not their business to know these things. It is the part of true wisdom, therefore, for every one who is about to build him a house, to consult an architect from the beginning. Nor let it be thought that where the contemplated

structure is to be of the humbler sort, because there
is little money which can be expended for its construction, the services of an architect can be dispensed
with, and a saving of cost be secured thereby. On the
contrary, it is in the case of the smaller and cheaper class of structures that the greatest advantage is to
be secured by the services of the architect. His taste
and knowledge of his art will enable him to put the
money and materials placed at his disposal into the
most serviceable and tasteful shape, and procure for his
employer that which will be permanently satisfying.
But let no one mistake the mere carpenter for an architect. The one who contemplates building a house will
have to go to the neighboring town or city, probably,
to find one who can fitly be called an architect, for no
village can furnish sufficient employment to induce
one to make his residence there. But it will be worth
one's while to go twenty-five or fifty miles, or even more,
if need be, in order to secure the services of an architect.
If he had a suit at law pending, or a legal question
to be settled, involving only a small amount, he would
not hesitate to travel as far and to be at any expense
necessary to secure proper professional advice. So let
him take his case or question of building to the architect and tell him what he wants, and then leave it with
him to make a plan for him and a contract, with proper
specifications, just as when any one commits his case to a
lawyer he leaves its management with him. In the case
of the building the result involves, not the gain or loss

of a small debt or the recovery of a piece of property, but the construction of that which, by its tasteful form, and convenience of arrangement, and substantial quality, is to be a life-long comfort and pleasure, or, for want of these, a continual source of disappointment and regret. The commission paid to a good architect for his services is probably the most profitable expenditure incurred in building a house.

But some will not take the trouble to seek the advice of an architect, or will not deem it expedient. Let us make a few suggestions, therefore, for such and for any who may heed them. They will be in the main such as any good architect would make.

Having fixed upon a proper site for the building, one sheltered rather. than exposed, withdrawn somewhat from the street and the noise and dust of the passers-by, rather than thrust conspicuously upon the view, if there is not absolute exemption from dampness resulting from standing water in the neighborhood or from a wet and springy subsoil, the first thing to be done is to thoroughly underdrain, by means of tiles, or ditches four feet in depth and partially filled with stones at the bottom, the whole vicinity of the house. Let these drains lead the wet away from the house, and let one, at least, be connected with the cellar, and at such a depth that no water can by any possibility find standing-place there. Let there be no mistake or neglect in this matter of drainage. There are many pieces of ground which appear dry upon the surface, but which, owing

to a tenacious subsoil or to the abundance of springs
near at hand, are saturated with moisture.   One who
has not tried the experiment will be surprised to see
the quantity of water which will escape from drains
properly constructed in such ground, and how constant will be the flow.   It is only by such drains that
moist land can be made a healthful place for a dwelling, or be brought into the best condition for tillage.
It is safe, indeed, to presume that almost every site
chosen for a village residence will be improved, both
as to healthfulness and profitable cultivation of the
ground, by being thoroughly underdrained.

The site being thus properly chosen and prepared, let
the contemplated building be planned consistently and
intelligently as a whole.   Let its outward shape, and
color, if possible, be in harmony with the site and its
surroundings.   A house in the country, where land is
usually abundant and one is not limited in ground-
space, should spread out laterally and rest broadly upon
the soil, rather than be lifted high into the air upon a
narrow foundation after the manner of city houses.
It should seem to grow out of the ground almost,
and to rest solidly upon it, bidding defiance to any
storms that may sweep along; and as one family
need or convenience after another may call for more
room here and there, let this be gained by proper
additions on the one side or the other, and thus let
the house ramble out on the ground as though a live
and growing thing.   It will be all the prettier and

better for so doing, for thus freely moulding itself to the wants of its occupants.

Of course, as already intimated, we should prefer to build of stone, hoping to find it near at hand, and thus to build solidly, and make the house, though but the simplest cottage, all the more a part of the solid earth itself; and we should choose our stone so as to get not only solidity, but a pleasing tint of color, if possible in harmony with objects around. On the one hand, we would avoid a very dark-colored stone, as giving a too sombre effect to the house; though even then, if the walls are laid up in a rough way, and with stones for the most part of small dimensions, the mortar will serve to lighten up the color. On the other hand, if we were building in the vicinity of a quarry of marble of purest white, we should prefer to go some distance in order to secure stone of a different color. Nature, in all her bouquet of colors, does not give us white except in bits, as in the flowers. She does not give us white in masses. Even her marble is white only when freshly broken open, and then she hastens to cover its surface again with a softer and more pleasant tint, toning down its glare and bringing it into harmony with surrounding objects. The winter snows, to be sure, are white, but there are special reasons for this, and we all know how disagreeable the whiteness is—how, oftentimes, we have to hide it from our eyes by veils and colored glasses. It is strange, in view of these facts, that our people should have chosen white so extensively as they have

done as the color for their houses. It throws them out
of all harmony with objects around, and breaks up, oftentimes, what would otherwise be a very pleasant picture.
A white house, especially in the glare of the full sunlight, is a blot upon the landscape. It is tolerable only
when almost surrounded and hidden by trees, and so
has its color really changed.

Equally out of taste, though not so disagreeable, is
the custom of covering our houses, no matter what their
color, with patches of vivid green in the form of blinds
to the windows. Why the blinds of a house should be
of a different color from the house itself it would be
difficult to assign a reason, while it is not at all difficult
to see that by this arrangement what would otherwise
be the solid bulk of the house is broken up into patches
—the house loop-holed, so to speak, and all dignity and
massiveness of effect utterly lost.

Where stone is not used for building, but wood takes
its place, there is a somewhat wider range of choice in
respect to color. Some one has given as a rule by which
to secure proper harmony of the house with its surroundings, to pull up a piece of turf, growing in the vicinity,
and paint the house the same color as that of the bottom
of the turf. Whether this rule be a good one or not,
one cannot go amiss, in choosing a pigment for his house,
if he copies the tints which he may find on the bark of
the trees close around him, or if he takes almost any of
the grays, or drabs, or neutral tints which are so easily
made by a mixture of the more positive colors.

One can hardly be too careful to have his contemplated house thoroughly planned in all its parts, and in
their relation to one another, before beginning to build.
With a well-digested plan, the work of building is half
done. From cellar-floor to chimney-top the house should
form a consistent whole, its parts all mutually dependent.
The method of warming and ventilating the house, for
instance, will modify the construction of the cellar. If
a furnace is to be used, then a chimney-flue must be carried up from the cellar, and a cold air box and other
appliances must be provided for in the very laying
of the foundations. So if water is to be carried freely
throughout the house, this will necessitate certain arrangements which should be provided for at the outset.
All such things as air-ducts and water-pipes are more
easily arranged, and more cheaply, when the house is
contrived and is in process of building than afterwards.

A cheap and effective method for protecting houses
from the excessive cold of winter, and equally from the
heats of summer, ought to be adopted in every house.
This consists in interposing a space of air between the
rooms of the house and the outer walls and roof. This
is easily done in the case of a stone or brick building by
means of what is called "firring out." Strips of wood,
an inch in thickness, are nailed to the walls, and the lathing fastened to these. Air, when confined, being one of
the best non-conductors of heat and cold, a thin space of
this kind is sufficient to prevent the cold or heat from
penetrating rapidly the rooms thus protected. Hence a

house so treated will be warmer in winter and cooler in summer than it would be if built in the ordinary way. In the case of wooden buildings the same effect is secured by filling in the spaces between the studding with bricks set upon edge and laid in coarse mortar. The cheapest bricks can be used for this purpose. Or a partition of lath and plaster may be placed half way between the outer wall, or weather boarding, and the ordinary plaster wall of the rooms. This will leave two air-spaces, each an inch and a half wide. When houses are built so that the chambers have their ceilings formed wholly or in part by the roof timbers, it is necessary that this double plastering should be extended to these as well as to the side walls of the house. The expense of this arrangement is so small (not more, probably, than fifty dollars for a house of ample dimensions) that no one should neglect so effective a protection against the discomforts of heat and cold.

The place of ornament, and the extent to which it should be used, is an important matter of consideration for every builder. It is a safe rule for one's guidance that no ornament is to be allowed for its own sake alone, but only as it is an embellishment of what is useful. And the embellishment should never go to the extent of attracting attention to itself, to the exclusion of attention from that which is sought to be embellished. A veranda, for example, is a desirable feature of a house. It affords opportunity for sitting or walking in the open air while protected from sun and storm. But

when such a structure is placed upon the northern side
of a house, where there is always abundant shade, and
where no one would wish to be during the storm, and so
is seen to have been built because it was thought to be
a pretty thing in itself, then it is at once an offence to
good taste and shows itself a useless expenditure of
money. The roof of a veranda, again, needs, of course,
supporting columns. They may be plain and simple,
and not conspicuous by their size, for the weight they
have to carry is small. But when they are expanded,
as they not unfrequently are, into a maze of elaborate
wooden lace-work cut out of thin boards, one cries
"away with them" at once. This principle of judgment
may be applied to all ornamentation, whether of the exterior or interior of the house, as also to that of furniture and dress. Whenever ornament attracts the chief
attention, as though existing for itself, we may well
consider it out of place, and a violation of good taste.
In general, the style of building in the country should
be characterized by simplicity; and ornaments, whether
within or without, should be of a simple rather than an
elaborate character. They should partake of the severe
simplicity of nature rather than the intricate nicety of
art. And so doing, they will be really more beautiful
than anything which art alone can give.

But especially let all dishonest ornamentation be
avoided, as also dishonesty of any sort. The prevalent
custom of painting and graining pine and other cheap
woods, so as to resemble those more beautiful or costly,

is not only in bad taste, but bad morality ; and, like all bad taste and bad morality, it costs more than that which is good. These imitations never really deceive one. No one, unless it be a child, thinks the painted pine is oak or mahogany. But they pretend to be what they are not, and so have a constantly debauching effect upon those who see and tolerate them. From seeing such pretences approved, children may easily grow up with the belief that pretension may be indulged in anything and anywhere. And yet we have these misrepresentations and false representations, these base imitations, these falsehoods in wood and paint and plaster, not only in our dwellings, but in our churches, the very temples of Truth. Falsehood may be said to be ingrained in us thus. What wonder that the world is so full of shams and falsehoods in character, when it is so full of shams and falsehoods in carpentry !

And then, if we want the effect of the beautiful grain of woods, why not have it in an honest way, by using various woods just as they are, and as they are furnished us by nature, instead of first covering up her beautiful work with paint, and then upon that dead leaden surface endeavoring to make a poor imitation of what is beyond all imitation ? Our common pine has a beautiful grain. By a little care in the selection of boards with reference to the development of the grain, and simply oiling or varnishing them after they have been wrought into doors and the various finishings of a room, we may have, at little cost, a room more beautiful than any grainer's brush can give us. Then we have the maple, the ash, the white-wood, the birch, the catalpa, the walnut, and a hundred other woods, which only need to be treated in the same way, and they will give us, used separately or in combination, an almost infinite variety of effects. Every room in the house may thus have a character and expression of its own, and almost all needed embellishment may thus be had in a natural and honest way, and at no inconsiderable saving of the cost of paint and carpentry mouldings, to say nothing of the saving of much labor needed for the scrubbing and cleansing of the latter.

Such, it seems to us, should be the common country house. Wealth may indulge in more elaborate, costly, and highly finished structures; but for the mass of those whose residence is, and is to be, in the country, tasteful simplicity should be the characteristic of their dwellings. Their houses should be homes rather than show-places, and their chief embellishment that of the beautiful life lived in them. What money is at command in our villages should be expended for purposes of education, and for the social improvement of the community rather than for display in architectural construction. A rich man in a village had better found a library or endow a school of high order than build a palace for himself. The library and the school will live and impart benefits to many generations to come. His palace he does not know that any son of his will occupy when he is gone.

In village life let show and parade be discouraged, and let the endeavor be, on the basis of industry, frugality, and simplicity, to carry the general culture in intelligence, taste, morals, and virtue as high as possible.

CHAPTER XIII.

FENCES AND HEDGES.

"The hedge was thick as is a castle wall,
So that who list without to stand or go,
Though he would all the day pry to and fro,
He could not see if there were any wight
Within or no."—CHAUCER.

AMONG the things that have much to do with the
good appearance of a village are the fences by which
the grounds are divided from one another, or which
serve as boundaries of the roads. In most cases certainly they are anything but pleasing objects in themselves, while they often do much to detract from the
beauty of the country where they abound. In general
they may be regarded as an evil, though sometimes,
perhaps, a necessary evil. Boundaries and divisions of
lands to some extent we must have. Divisions of farms
into separate fields are also necessary for the best car-
rying-on of the work of agriculture. The pastures must
usually be separated from the cornfields by some effective barrier. But a great deal less of this is necessary than many think; and every unnecessary fence
taxes the proprietor with a needless expense, while it is
a disfigurement to house or grounds, perhaps to both,

and to the general aspect of the vicinity. In many parts of our country the subdivision of lands and the consequent expenditure for fences has been carried to a lamentable extreme. It is not unusual to find single acres of land, or several pieces of only a few acres each, severed from a large farm and enclosed by themselves. This not only involves a great expense for the construction and maintenance of fences, but oftentimes the waste of much time in opening and shutting gates, in the passage from one portion of the farm to another. Added to this, also, is the loss of time in the cultivation of such small enclosures occasioned by the necessity of frequent turnings of the teams and machines employed. Then there is a loss of ground involved also wherever there are fences, the cultivation never coming quite close to them; and in the case of the very common zigzag or Virginia fence, the loss of ground for cultivation is very considerable, while this unused space becomes a nursery of weeds and bushes, at the same time unprofitable and unsightly.

The expense of fences is not considered as it should be, and especially the fact that this expense increases in proportion as the divisions of our farms are multiplied. For instance, if we enclose a piece of ground measuring ten rods by forty, equal to two acres and a half, it will require one hundred rods of fence, which at one dollar a rod makes the cost of fencing forty dollars an acre; whereas to enclose ten acres, or forty rods square, requires only one hundred and sixty rods of fence, mak-

7

ing the cost in this case only sixteen dollars an acre. In the same way it is seen that if we enclose forty acres in one field, the cost will be only eight dollars an acre, and if we enclose a hundred acres, the cost will be reduced to four dollars and four cents an acre. The great disadvantage, as to cost, when lands are divided into small fields, is thus seen at once. But the whole story is not yet told. These fences need to be renewed in from seven to ten years. Now, if we reckon seven per cent. interest on the original cost of the fence and ten per cent. for depreciation or annual repairs, we shall have, in addition to the great disparity of original cost, as already shown, an annual cost of six dollars and eighty cents an acre in the case of the field of two acres and a half, and a cost of only eighty-five cents an acre in the case of the field of one hundred acres. The economical advantage of large fields is thus seen yet more strikingly. We are persuaded that this cutting-up of farms into small fields might be much lessened and thereby a great burden be taken off from our agriculturists. Enough might be saved in this one way to make the difference often between a pecuniarily successful and thriving farmer and one who is running all the while towards bankruptcy. The saving in this item alone would furnish books, pictures, music, and numerous other things to many a farmer's house where now they are not found, because they cannot be afforded. And why should there ordinarily be any other divisions on our farms than those which will separate pasture ground from that used for tillage? Why should not the corn, oats, rye, and grass be allowed to grow side by side in the same general enclosure? They will not quarrel or trespass on each other's ground.* And then how much better the land looks when the eye can range over large surfaces, with the graceful curves which nature always gives them, unbroken by any unsightly and stiff cross lines of fence! Besides, if smaller divisions are needed, as they may be temporarily, it is easy to make them by means of movable structures of wood or wire. These must come into use more and more, as we realize the cost and inconvenience of the old mode of enclosure, and the wire fences have the great merit of being comparatively invisible, and therefore not being a blemish to the landscape.

The cost involved in the construction and repair of fences on a single farm may not be readily estimated, partly because such cost accrues not all at once, but gradually. Yet it is a real cost. And when we multiply

---

* If our farmers and village residents could generally visit Europe, they would think fences less necessary than they now do. Throughout England they are seldom to be seen, hedges taking their places. In Belgium and France there are very few fences, the farms stretching side by side for miles with no visible barriers between. In Lombardy and Northern Italy fences are hardly known.

The comparative scarcity of timber in some parts of our own country has happily led to views of the fence question which are in accord with what we have been saying. In Illinois and Iowa, and perhaps others of our Western States, the farmers are fencing only comparatively small portions of their lands, relying upon herdsmen to watch their cattle and keep them from the growing crops.

this cost by that of the number of farms in an entire state, the sum becomes impressive. A few years ago Mr. Dodge, the statistician of the Agricultural Department at Washington, from reports received from intelligent observers in all parts of the Union, compiled a statement from which it appears that the whole cost of fences in the United States amounts to $1,700,000,000 ; and the cost of annual repairs to $198,000,000. The matter is one of so much interest that we append Mr. Dodge's tables.

AMOUNT AND COST OF FENCES IN THE UNITED STATES.

States.	Acres Fenced.	Rods of Fencing.	Total Cost of Fencing.
Maine...................	4,377,925	31,214,605	$31,214,605
New Hampshire..........	3,288,117	28,771,023	34,525,227
Vermont................	4,164,917	32,278,106	42,929,880
Massachusetts...........	2,481,767	21,095,019	36,916,283
Rhode Island...........	448,988	4,489,880	9,877,736
Connecticut.............	2,185,000	19,883,500	33,801,950
New York...............	20,549,909	169,536,749	228,874,611
New Jersey.............	2,736,251	25,310,321	40,496,513
Pennsylvania...........	16,374,641	156,377,821	179,834,494
Delaware......	963,770	6,023,562	7,228,274
Maryland...............	4,112,936	25,911,496	32,389,370
Virginia...............	8,165,040	40,825,200	36,742,680
North Carolina..........	8,902,909	49,856,290	37,392,217
South Carolina..........	5,284,224	26,421,120	21,136,896
Georgia................	11,035,877	60,255,888	45,191,916
Florida................	736,172	3,415,838	2,459,403
Alabama...............	7,536,947	45,975,376	36,780,300
Mississippi.............	6,437,137	27,035,975	25,954,536
Louisiana...............	2,045,640	8,182,560	8,182,560
Texas.................	6,822,757	30,020,130	33,022,143
Arkansas...............	3,294,189	19,435,715	18,463,929
Tennessee.............	10,027,762	65,681,841	62,397,748
West Virginia..........	4,067,289	36,605,601	32,945,040
Kentucky..............	13,381,978	80,291,868	76,277,274
Ohio..................	18,090,776	155,580,673	155,580,673
Michigan............... ..	7,558,040	60,464,320	57,441,104
Indiana................	14,111,963	95,961,348	100,759,415
Illinois................	22,606,406	107,380,428	128,856,513
Wisconsin..............	8,807,332	46,238,493	39,302,719
Minnesota..............	1,857,681	7,430,724	6,539,037
Iowa..................	7,517,173	31,572,126	34,729,338
Missouri...............	12,274,766	64,442,521	64,442,521
Kansas................	1,576,802	6,701,408	7,371,548
Nebraska..............	517,624	2,070,496	2,174,020
California..............	4,974,504	24,141,642	29,598,298
Oregon................	1,116,290	5,023,305	5,274,470
Nevada................	74,115	296,460	444,690

COST OF REPAIRS OF FENCES.

States.	Cost per 100 Rods.	Total Cost.	States.	Cost per 100 Rods.	Total Cost.
Maine.........	$3.06	$955,166	Ohio...........	$5.25	$8,167,965
New Hampshire.	3.80	1,093,298	Michigan.......	4.00	2,418,572
Vermont........	4.00	1,291,124	Indiana.........	5.40	5,181,912
Massachusetts.	4.50	949,275	Illinois	9.50	10,201,140
Rhode Island...	5.75	258,168	Wisconsin......	4.55	2,103,851
Connecticut	7.50	1,491,262	Minnesota......	5.10	878,966
New York......	7.06	11,969,294	Iowa...........	9.80	3,094,068
New Jersey.....	9.80	2,480,411	Missouri........	4.90	3,157,683
Pennsylvania....	6.32	9,883,078	Kansas.........	6.75	452,345
Delaware	7.50	451,767	Nebraska.......	8.50	175,992
Maryland.......	7.80	2,021,096	California.......	8.50	1,797,039
Virginia........	3.51	1,432,964	Oregon.........	7.50	376,747
North Carolina..	3.40	1,695,113	Nevada.........	9.00	26,681
South Carolina..	4.00	1,056,844	Total cost of an-		
Georgia........	4.00	2,410,235	nual repairs....	......	$93,963,187
Florida.........	3.80	129,801			
Alabama........	4.65	2,137,853	Interest on the		
Mississippi......	5.26	1,422,092	original cost at		
Louisiana.......	6.51	532,684	6 per cent.....	......	$104,852,995
Texas..........	8.50	2,551,712			
Arkansas.......	5.92	1,150,594			
Tennessee......	5.00	3,284,092	Grand total, ex-		
West Virginia..	4.50	1,647,252	clusive of re-		
Kentucky.......	5.15	4,035,031	building fences.	......	$198,806,182

In the closely settled portions of our villages, of
course the grounds will necessarily be in rather small
enclosures. But even here a good deal of fencing may
be dispensed with, and where this cannot be done the
fences can be made less obtrusive and less positively
ugly than they usually are. Anything almost would be
an improvement upon the generality of our fences.
They are unsightly things, for the most part. Nothing
can be less tasteful than our common picket fence, for
instance, with its stiff array of pikes set up as a barricade around our dwellings, as though every passing

man or beast were accounted an enemy against whom we must entrench ourselves. And then when we give up the picket or palisade fence, it is usually to replace it with something as repulsive in iron, or some elaborate gingerbread extravagance of the carpenter, altogether incongruous and uncalled for and a great waste of money.

As we become more civilized and tasteful we shall feel less need of these barricades between us and our fellow-men, and shall be unwilling to mar the sweep and beauty of the lines which nature has given to the surface of our fields, as we now so often do by these stiff and tasteless structures. Many a house of respectable look, taken by itself, is now dwarfed and half hidden by a huge and expensive fence stretched across its front, useless because not enclosing ground enough for the cultivation of flower or shrub, and not needed to prevent any unwelcome intrusion, but which, if removed, might give place to a beautiful sweep of lawn stretching down to the very edge of the travelled roadway and adding at once dignity and beauty to the dwelling. Such a lawn is the best possible setting for a house, be it large or small. It is the best possible setting also for a few flowers or flowering shrubs.

And if any one interposes the objection that without fences cattle will trample the flowers, or look in at the windows, the ready answer is that it ought no longer to be thought possible that any village will allow swine or cattle to make pasture ground of its highways, or even

go upon them without a keeper. It ought to be understood, also, as it very frequently is not, that the roads
really belong to the proprietors of the adjacent lands on
either side of them, and not to the town or the public
generally. A villager, if he is the owner of a plot of
ground, owns to the centre of the highway in front of
him. All the right the public have in the road is the
right to travel over it, and that too not where they
please, but in the particular path designed and prepared
for travel. The adjoining proprietors own and have as
much right to the grass or the fruit which grows on the
road in front of them as to that in their pastures or
their orchards. Hence the man who pastures his cattle
on the road is a trespasser upon his neighbors who own
the road, and may be prosecuted as such. His cattle
may be taken and impounded.

And as a man may take away the barricade fence in
front of his house, in most cases with manifest improvement to the appearance and pecuniary value of his
premises, so he ought to be at liberty to remove his
farm fences by the roadside to any extent without sub-
jecting himself to any damage from cattle running at
large. In one state, at least—Connecticut—no man is
obliged to build a front fence, and if cattle come upon
any one's premises he can take possession of them and
hold them for the payment of damages. This ought
to be the law in every state.

We are so accustomed to see fences everywhere that
the suggestion of their disuse is very unwelcome to

many, who yet are quite ready for anything which will improve their residences. They have become so used to their barricaded enclosures that they feel at first a sense of vacancy and loss without them. But it only needs the actual experiment for a few days or weeks to convince almost any one of the improvement thus made. And we have now some fine examples on a large scale of the advantage resulting from the absence of fences, especially from the fronts of dwellings. Individual instances are to be found in very many of our towns and villages, all over the country, as far West even as Colorado. The village of South Manchester, Conn., the seat of the silk-mills of the Brothers Cheney, is a notable illustration of what may be done by not doing. This village covers seven hundred and fifty acres of land, and has a hundred and fifty houses; but not a wall or fence of any kind is to be seen between these houses and the various roads along which they stand. Each house has its lawn in front, dotted with flowers and shrubs. An unmistakable look of comfort, neatness, and taste pervades the village, and every visitor is charmed by its appearance. Another illustration of the effect of open grounds may be seen at Williamstown, Mass., where the fences along the principal street have been taken down one by one until, finally, under an impulse of general improvement the present year, aided by the pecuniary generosity and personal influence of Mr. Cyrus W. Field, nearly all have been removed, and the entire street, a mile in length, presents the appearance of a park. There is the unmistakable look of good neighborhood and kindly feeling thrown over the whole place. The adjoining proprietors have also, by this means, practically enlarged their premises. The eye of each one, as he looks out from his windows, sweeps along a ground surface far beyond what he owns. He has, it may be, a legal title to a plot only fifty or a hundred feet in width. Yet he seems to be living on one of many times that extent. To look upon, his neighbor's trees and turf and flowers are as much his own as they are his neighbor's. So all gain by this practical enlargement of their possessions. They gain, also, almost of necessity, some enlargement of heart and feeling, a closer and kinder fellowship, a deepening interest in each other.

Why should not this, or something approximating this, be realized generally in the villages of our land? Why should they not thus seem to be, what they ought to be, communities—places of a common life, of common as well as individual feelings and tastes, where all flow together as having common interests, hopes, and joys, a real partnership in each other?

Hedges are of three kinds—those designed for screens, those designed to take the place of fences, and those for decorative purposes. As yet they have come into use but to a moderate extent in this country. In England they are in very general use for the separation of fields, and they form a conspicuous object in the landscape, so

7*

that English hedges have become quite famous. With us hedges have been used thus far mainly on small grounds, like those of our cities and their suburbs, rather than in the open country and upon large farms.

There are two classes of plants suitable for hedges: the thorny shrubs like the buckthorn, and the Osage orange, or maclura, on the one hand, and on the other the evergreens, like the arbor vitæ, the Norway spruce, and the hemlock. The former have an advantage, where a barrier is needed which will effectually turn cattle, in the fact that they have thorns against which cattle are unwilling to push, and because they occupy little space. The evergreens, on the other hand, have greatly the advantage of beauty, and for all places where they are needed simply as division boundaries, or for screens, or for ornament, are much to be preferred. In the northern portions of our country especially, where for six months of the year the trees are leafless, and the ground is brown or covered with snow, there is ample reason for choosing evergreen hedges wherever they can be used. Near a house, particularly, such hedges should be chosen, for the ordinary thorn hedges during the half-year when they are leafless are by no means pleasant objects to look at. For screens, also, none but evergreens are of any account, while these are all that can be desired. Whether to shut off the cold winds from the house or from the cattle in the barn or barn-yard, or to hide from sight some undesirable objects, stables or other outbuildings, nothing better than the Norway spruce or the hemlock could be wished for. As a protection for a garden, excluding the cold winds of early springtime, as well as intrusive poultry and other animals at all times, evergreen hedges are most desirable, while they also aid materially to make a garden an object of beauty. For tall hedges or screens the Norway spruce and the hemlock are equally well adapted. For hedges that are to be kept low the hemlock is preferable, being a plant of finer and more delicate foliage, and bearing the shears well, while in many parts of the country it is so abundant that cheapness will be in its favor.

But, whatever plant is adopted, it needs to be borne in mind that in securing a hedge one must proceed very much as in building a house. The first thing is to have a good foundation. In other words, the beauty and the utility of a hedge consist in a good thick growth close to the ground. Consequently the upward tendency of the plants must be repressed by topping them until bottom shoots are started in sufficient abundance. It will require four or five years to grow a hedge in this way to the height of four feet; but when this is once done, the work remains, and you have something of abiding beauty and usefulness.

In growing such a hedge it is also necessary, certainly very desirable, to prepare the ground by deep spading or ploughing, and by the proper intermixture with the soil of some fertilizing material. Let the plants

then be set therein in two rows—the rows themselves
six inches apart and the plants twelve inches asunder
in the rows—the plants of the different rows not opposite each other, but alternate, thus:

This will make a hedge the more impervious to small
animals at the bottom, though we have grown hemlock
hedges in single rows, the plants a foot apart, which
would effectually shut out poultry. For evergreen
hedges plants should be chosen not more than eighteen
inches or two feet in height, and such, if possible, as
have well-developed lower branches. These, when
planted, should be cut down to a uniform height of
one foot. The next year one half of the first year's
growth should be cut off. And so from year to year
the top should be pruned or shortened in, and the
hedge thus built up in proper form and with the desired thickness or density. If the pruning is not continued until the proper growth at the bottom is secured,
no subsequent care will remedy the defect. But with
this precaution, in a few years one may surround himself with a wall of living green that will rob the winter of half its chill and irksomeness, and furnish a pleasant object for the eye to rest upon at all times.

CHAPTER XIV.

LAWNS.

"Nothing is more pleasant to the eye than green grass kept finely shorn."—BACON.

"The peculiar characters of the grass, which adapt it especially for the service of man, are its apparent humility and cheerfulness. Its humility, in that it seems created only for lowest service—appointed to be trodden on and fed upon. Its cheerfulness, in that it seems to exult under all kinds of violence and suffering. You roll it, and it is stronger the next day; you mow it, and it multiplies its shoots as if it were grateful; you tread upon it, and it only sends up richer perfume."—RUSKIN.

THE two things that will do most to make a piece of ground attractive and pleasant to look upon are trees and grass. And this is true whether the ground be large or small in extent; whether it be a house lot on the edge of some city, or a gentleman's park of thousands of acres. These, then, are the most desirable outward adornments of our village homes, as they are the cheapest. Yet how slow we have been in our country to apprehend this fact! We have filled our grounds with trellises and Chinese pagodas, and various conceits of carpentry, with mounds and hillocks covered with flowers and flowering shrubs, with plaster Floras and Dianas, and with cast-iron deer and dogs, until we have often been buried in a wilderness of incongruous and

misplaced decorations. It is only within a short time
that we have come to understand what Lord Bacon
saw nigh three hundred years ago — that Nature has
provided for us in the very grass of the field something
more beautiful than anything which we can put in its
place. It would seem as though our farmers would
have been so struck with the beauty of their hay-fields
when newly shorn by the scythe that they would have
made the attempt to secure something of the same effect, but more permanently, in the immediate vicinity
of their dwellings; but this they seldom have done.
The value of grass with them has been simply in its
yield of hay and pasturage for the cattle. That there
was also a pleasure in it for themselves, a gratification
of the love of the beautiful — something, likewise, to
nourish pleasant thoughts and tasteful feelings in their
children—does not seem to have often come into their
minds. And so our farm-house surroundings have been
greatly lacking in a beauty and adornment easily within reach. On one side there has been, perhaps, a plot
fenced off for a garden, which has only been an apology
for a garden, after all, so neglected has it been, the
rampant weeds choking the proper growths of the
place. In front there has been what has borne the
name of a "door-yard," it may be, into which the door
is never opened except on the rare occasions of a funeral or a wedding, the usual entrance to the house
and exit from it being by a side or rear door, and probably through a varying mass of plantains and mallows

near the road, and the chips and dirt of the wood-pile farther back; well if carts and other agricultural implements have not also obstructed the pathway leading to the house.

How easily might all this be changed! Sweep away those picket fences, which in most cases are no protection against the intrusion of cattle, inasmuch as the gates are usually left open. Remove the garden to some ampler spot on the farm, where, planting the seeds of his vegetables in long rows and in the open field, the farmer can cultivate them easily with his plough, as he does his field crops. Put the wood-pile, with its attendant rubbish, in some place out of constant sight, and the wood, when cut, snugly in the wood-house. Let carts and wagons, ploughs and harrows, be sheltered in their proper store-room. Then let the ground thus made vacant be laid down to grass, and planted appropriately with trees singly and in clumps, with here and there a bed reserved in the midst of the turf for a few choice flowers, massed so as to give the full effect of their bright colors; and the farmer or villager has spread before him "from morn to noon, from noon to dewy eve," a picture of ever changing yet abiding beauty. It will be something to satisfy him. He will delight in it more and more the longer he looks upon it. It is really wonderful what effects may be had in connection with a bit of grass and a few trees. As the light changes every hour, and the tone of the atmosphere, so a lawn takes on a new look from hour to hour; and then, as the shadows of the clouds pass over it, it offers perpetually new phases and combinations of light and shade, so that so simple and seemingly fixed a thing as a piece of grass becomes a source of infinitely varied and surprising pleasure.

But not every piece of grass is a lawn. It must be green, velvety turf—not rank stalks of grass showing the bare earth between, as is so often the case. The latter will do for a mowing-field, perhaps, but not for a lawn. For this, we want a turf short and thick as the pile of an Axminster carpet; and we want a turf that will keep its emerald greenness all through the year, except in the frosty months, when, of course, we cannot expect it. Every one knows that such lawns are not common among us; and some who have endeavored to secure such have declared, after making much effort to obtain them, that the thing is impossible. Nor is it easy to have in this country lawns like those which are so common in England, and which are so charming. Our hot summer suns are very severe upon grass, as upon other things. England, with its sky so often overcast with clouds and its frequent rains and fogs, enables its people to have the luxury of the best lawns with little care; but with us, while the grass looks well in the spring months, it is apt to look very brown and uninviting in July and August.

The first need, therefore—the essential condition of success—in our country, in the production of a fine lawn, is a good, deep, well-drained soil. Grass needs for its full development a deeper soil than do some trees. Give them a well-pulverized soil, and some of our grasses will send their roots into it to the depth of between three and four feet. Roots which have reached such a depth are, of course, little affected by drought. No sun or want of rain will trouble them, but they will go on pumping up their supplies of nutriment from these cool, moist depths for the sustenance of the plants above, making them quite independent of outward circumstances. Whoever, therefore, would have a lawn which will not fail him at the very time when its beauty would be most desirable should see to it that the ground is thoroughly broken up by the trenching spade or subsoil plough to a depth of two feet, while at the same time he should see that it is sufficiently underdrained to carry off any superfluous moisture. Let him not trouble himself much about grades. To get ground exactly level, or smoothed evenly into inclined planes, is only a mechanical contrivance. It may be desirable for a croquet-ground or the rampart of a fort; but the flowing lines which nature gives to the ground, the gentle swells and corresponding hollows which succeed each other, the ever-varying turns of the surface which are to be found everywhere, except in the flattest prairies of the West, are far more pleasing to the eye than all the smoothing of art. They give opportunity for that play of light and shade which is productive of the highest beauty in landscape.

But, having secured a proper depth of soil, sufficiently but not highly enriched, thoroughly pulverized and cleared of all surface stones, so that the scythe or the lawn-mower may do its work without hindrance or obstruction, the next thing needed is a proper seeding; and here the two things to be chiefly considered are the kind of seed and the quantity. No single kind of grass seed will make a good lawn, however adequate it may be for the production of a good hay-field. What we want in a lawn is not a tall rank growth *above* ground, but a fine, thick growth *upon* the ground. What we want is not a crop of hay, but a carpet. It is an established fact, also, that any one sort of seed will not cover the ground with verdure; but that, after you have given the soil all the seed of one kind which it will sprout, you may sow another kind which will take root in the vacant spaces that are left; and yet another kind of seed will occupy the places which still remain. Only by a variety of seeds, therefore, can we cover the ground with that thick mat of green which we speak of, appropriately, as a "velvet" lawn. In Europe, as many as a dozen different kinds of seed are sometimes mixed for the purpose of seeding a lawn; and great care is taken in adapting the kinds of seed to special soils and situations. In this country the grasses which have proved most satisfactory for lawns are the common red-top, or bent grass, the white clover, and the Kentucky blue or June grass. To these is sometimes added the sweet vernal grass. These grasses are mixed in different proportions by different cultivators. A mixture frequently used consists of Rhode Island bent—a variety of red-top—eight quarts; creeping bent, as it is called, three quarts; red-top, ten quarts; Kentucky blue grass, ten quarts; and white clover, one quart. Some use for lawns a mixture of three fourths red-top and one fourth white clover.

But whatever seed is used, let not the quantity be stinted. From three to five bushels should be used to the acre, according to the richness of the soil; and in the same proportion for a larger or smaller extent of ground.

Having sown the seed, of proper kind and in proper quantity, and rolled it in well, the beauty and continuance of the lawn will be secured by frequent mowing and occasional rolling. If the lawn is not cut frequently, it will soon become like any hay-field, and certainly its principal beauty will be lost. About once in twelve days or a fortnight the scythe or the lawn-mower should go over the ground, and the grass cut should be left upon the field to act as a mulch to the roots of the grass, to protect them from our hot suns; and, finally, by its decay, to keep the ground properly enriched. Treated in this way, with perhaps an occasional top-dressing of ashes, a lawn will last a lifetime, and longer. The durability of such a lawn makes the labor needed at the outset for its establishment a cheap expenditure, whether of care or money.

The trouble and expense of frequent cutting may seem an objection to the establishment of a lawn on a

large scale, except to people of considerable wealth.
The farmer may also think that the cutting and leaving
the grass involves the loss of some hay. But it is not
necessary, in order to have a lawn, that a large piece of
ground should be devoted to it. Only let there be a
proper depth of soil and sufficient space kept clear of
trees or shrubs to give some effect of breadth—enough
to give room for a solid mass of sunshine to fall somewhere on the ground—and even a city door-yard may
become a lawn. But in our villages and on our farms
we may make beauty and practical economy go hand in
hand by carefully and frequently mowing a limited portion of ground near one's dwelling; while the rest, separated, perhaps, by an invisible wire fence, may be past-
ured by a few sheep, with some handsome Jersey cows
for companions. These creatures are among the best
of lawn-mowers, after all; and while they keep the
grass short and the ground in good heart, they are also
storing up wool and butter for their owner. At the
same time, they add beauty and life to the lawn itself,
and make it additionally attractive; they add the only
thing possibly lacking to its completeness and our perfect satisfaction with it.

CHAPTER XV.

WATER.

" For fountains, they are a great beauty and refreshment; but pools mar all, and make the garden unwholesome, and full of flies and frogs. Fountains I intend to be of two natures — the one that sprinkleth or spouteth water; the other a fair receipt of water, of some thirty or forty foot square, but without fish, or slime, or mud. For the first, the ornaments of images, gilt or of marble, which are in use, do well; but the main matter is so to convey the water, as it never stays, either in the bowls or in the cistern."—BACON.

Says John Ruskin, to whom the English public are indebted more than to any other writer, not to say than to all others, for the stimulus that has been given to the observation and the love of nature, " Of all inorganic substances, acting in their own proper nature and without assistance or combination, water is the most wonderful. If we think of it as the source of all the changefulness and beauty which we have seen in the clouds; then as the instrument by which the earth we have contemplated was modelled into symmetry, and its crags chiselled into grace; then as, in the form of snow, it robes the mountains it has made with that transcendent light which we could not have conceived if we had not seen; then as it exists in the foam of the torrent—in the iris which spans it, in the morning mist which rises from it, in the deep crystalline pools which mirror its hanging shore, in the broad lake and glancing river; finally, in that which is to all human minds the best emblem of unwearied, unconquerable power—the wild, various, fantastic, tameless unity of the sea; what shall we compare to this mighty, this universal element for glory and for beauty, or how shall we follow its eternal changefulness of feeling? It is like trying to paint a soul."

A substance of such glory and beauty must have, of course, large and important relations to life in the open country, where streams and clouds abound—relations which it cannot have in the pent-up town or city. The æsthetic value of water is something which belongs peculiarly to country life. It is only as the city snatches some bit of soil from the encroachments of the constantly extending lines of streets and buildings, and thus imports, so to speak, a piece of the country within its precincts, and establishes some " Central Park," where the water can find room to shoot into the air as a fountain or expand into a miniature lake, that it takes on anything of beauty or appeals to the finer senses. Your Croton Aqueduct is only a mechanical contrivance for securing what will quench the thirst of men and beasts, or wash the city streets, or preserve the city itself from destructive conflagrations. It may be a triumph of engineering and very admirable as a piece of masonry. Yet hardly anything makes less appeal to the æsthetic faculty than such a contrivance.

But go back into the open country, whence the water comes to suffer imprisonment for the vulgar uses of the town, and you come upon it at once in a new character. The brook or river goes winding at its own will, in sweeping curves of grace and beauty, through the meadows, brightening all the adjacent fields with a luxuriant verdure, or babbling with sweet music over the pebbly bottoms, or leaping down the hill-sides in wild and foaming cascades that are a joy to the eye and ear at once. The cattle take on an added look of beauty as they stoop to drink by the brook-side, such as they never could have at a watering-trough in the barn-yard; and the birds never seem so charming as when flitting along some stream, or mingling their songs from the branches above with the liquid song of the brook below. And then, is water ever quite so refreshing and so welcome to the thirsty lips as when it is caught fresh from some spring that bursts from the turfy bank or from some cleft in the rock near the old farm-house? The children hasten to catch it in their hands, making cups of them, or, perchance, of some grape leaf, rather than drink from the daintiest silver that adorns the table.

But while this element, water, is so abundant, covering three fourths of the earth's surface, and the whole soil full of it, so that it is ready to shoot forth from innumerable springs, and while it is in itself so beautiful and capable of ministering to our love of beauty in so many ways, it is remarkable that we derive so little benefit from it, compared with what we might, either in the way of use or pleasure. It is the more remarkable that this should be the case in the open country— the very home of the brooks and springs. Taking it on the side of the most practical utility, how many of the dwellers in the country live without any adequate supply of water for even the necessary uses of life. They will content themselves often with a well, and that perhaps inconveniently located, and with such inadequate and clumsy appliances for raising the water to the surface that to "bring a pail of water" is considered one of the hardest tasks of domestic life. And so the pail of water is drawn only when absolutely necessary; and a drink of fresh water, instead of being accessible as the air, is oftentimes one of the most difficult things to procure. For a large portion of the time the inmates of the dwelling must, if they drink at all, accept a stale draught tinctured with the rust of the tin pail or the white-lead of the wooden one. And then the poor cattle, in the long season when they are not in pasture, must be left without any supply of their want, except as they are driven, once a day, perhaps, through the snows and storms of winter, to some distant brook, where only with difficulty, and with manifest danger to their limbs, they can manage to quench their thirst through some hole in the ice. What a shame and cruelty is this in a country such as ours, which, like the promised land held out as an attraction to the Israelites of old, is "a land of brooks of water, of fountains, and depths that spring out of valleys and hills."

Then, also, for the demands of cleanliness and health, how inadequate is the provision often made! In how many of our country houses is there such a thing as a bath-room, or water enough, easily accessible, to supply it if there were one? Perhaps there is a small cistern receiving the water from the house-roof, but, through lack of proper protection against the intrusion of toads and other animals, or the infiltration of noxious matters, the water is rendered so repulsive that it is an unpleasant thing to bring it near the face. Or the only storehouse for water may be—how often it is so!—a barrel at the corner of the house, with perhaps a board slanting down under the projecting eaves of a portion of the roof to serve as a conductor of the precious rain into this generous receptacle; and the scanty supply by this means secured suggests the necessity of washing hands and face as seldom as possible, while the ablution of the whole body is not to be thought of, and so the less said about personal cleanliness the better.

Happily this is not a correct picture of all our country homes. But it represents so many of them, approximately, at least, as to warrant the conclusion that there ought to be a far better supply of water for our villages than there now is. For the common uses of life, for the common needs of a household, there is no one thing more desirable than an abundant supply of this element. To have it in unlimited amount, to have

8

it convenient and easy of access—this is the oil which makes all the wheels of domestic life run smoothly. If, as has been said so often, cleanliness is next to godliness, then water is the first physical need of existence; and there are few of our farms and country homes which might not be abundantly supplied from springs near at hand, or, by the associated enterprise of the village, from copious streams not far away. Everywhere, almost, in our country, the water is waiting to be used, waiting to bring us its blessings of health and manifold comfort. The valleys and hills are full of springs ready to pour their refreshing and healthful streams through our dwellings. It requires a comparatively small outlay, in most cases, certainly, to secure an ample supply of this most necessary element. The saving of steps for the busy and often overburdened housekeeper, the diminished lifting and carrying, the great amount of time as well as labor saved in accomplishing the work of the household, these, in a single year, and frequently sooner than that, would more than pay for all the cost involved in securing for our country dwellings an abundant supply of water. And then its importance in promoting health and the increased comfort and pleasure of living thereby insured to all the inmates of the house, who shall estimate this, who measure the value of this by any figures of pecuniary cost? There is no virtue in drudgery—though not unfrequently men and women live as though there were—and wherever we can save labor or lighten it, it is not only our privilege, but our duty to do so. The tone of life is thereby elevated; opportunity, at least, is given for the higher life to assert itself.

We have spoken thus far of water mainly in reference to the utilities of life. But a proper consideration of country living and what is needed to make our village life more attractive and satisfying requires something to be said of the æsthetic qualities of water. There is no perfect landscape where the eye cannot, somewhere in the sweep of its vision, rest upon water. Whatever else may be had, be it the most beautiful contour of hill and vale, be it lofty crag or lawn-like meadow, be it amplest sweep of forest and field, or densest and richest verdure, there is a want felt so long as the gleam of water is not seen. Nor is the needed effect measured by mere quantity. A little stream, across which you can almost leap, is worth as much sometimes as a whole ocean. How such a stream, shooting its silver thread through one of our green meadows, will often light up the whole landscape! Who does not feel the beauty of water at times? In the tumbling cascade or in the expanse of a little lake, what child even does not find something that touches a fount of feeling within and calls out his admiration? What dullest son of toil is not stirred by such a sight, and made sensible of something within him that is above the drudgery of toil? The jet of water, throwing up its silver drops and its feathery spray from some door-yard fountain, what passer-by does not have his steps arrested and his soul refreshed by the sight? It has a power of universal appeal. Old and young, the rudest and the most cultured, are alike, though not, perhaps, equally, touched by it. Why should we not have these sights and their resulting pleasures oftener than we do? There is hardly a village, we may say hardly a farm or cottage-yard, which might not have its plashing fountain to gladden the sight. And nearly every village might easily secure for its adornment some stretch of water, with the accompaniment of one or more fountains, around which the villagers might gather at will, and which would be a constant delight to all. These pleasures need not be costly. There is no necessity of great outlay for cast-iron basins and bronze dolphins and naiads. These may be left for those of abundant wealth and scanty taste. Their absence is commonly more desirable than their presence. If the villager can command though but a small stream from some spring, with sufficient head to give a moderate degree of pressure, all that is requisite is to scoop out a shallow basin of earth in his door-yard six or eight feet across and coat it with hydraulic cement, which any. one can do, having first brought his supply-pipe up through the bottom with a waste-pipe leading out from the basin, near its margin, into a tank near by. A sunken barrel filled with stones will answer for this purpose. Now let him procure a stop-cock, and two or three different jets, which he will find very cheap in any city or large town, and he has at command not only a perpetual fountain of water, but a perpetual fountain of delight. It is really wonderful the many effects and the constant yet ever-varying pleasure to be derived, for old and young alike, from such a simple and inexpensive source. Once possessed of such a source of enjoyment, no one would be willing to part with it for many times its cost. And then there are many little streams running through our meadows or down our hill-sides which we might, with only a little labor, lead into new channels, and so cause them to flow where the sight of them would be pleasantest, or across which even the children might throw dams sufficient to make them expand into little lakes that might be made the home of fish and fowl, and a place for many a pleasure and sport.

These are but hints and suggestions, when very much more might be said. But these are enough to indicate the great addition to the comfort and pleasure of life in the country which might be made by the judicious use and management of the simple element of water. Our country homes, of all places, ought to have it in abundance. Its streams should be ready to flow at house and barn and wherever else it would be useful or pleasant. The bath-room should not be only a city luxury, but should be deemed as necessary to the equipment of a country house as is the kitchen. Health and comfort demand it. The Mohammedans are as careful to erect baths as they are mosques. Ought not Christians to be as thoughtful of cleanliness as they?

CHAPTER XVI.

SANITARY ASPECTS OF COUNTRY LIFE.—DRAINAGE.

"It is not enough that we build our houses on beautiful sites, and where we have pure air and pure water ; we must also make provision for preventing these sites from becoming foul, as every unprotected house-site inevitably must—by sheer force of the accumulated waste of its occupants."—GEORGE E. WARING, JR.

IF any advantage has been generally conceded to the country as compared with the city, it has been that of its healthfulness. The "*healthy* country ;" how stereotyped is that expression! It is on every lip. The narrow and close streets of the city or large town, the densely compacted population, the filthy dwellings in great numbers, and the accumulation of many noxious matters in streets and yards, have been regarded as certain and prolific sources of disease. And so, also, the great cities of the world have been notorious for the prevalence in them, from time to time, of great plagues and epidemics of virulent character, while they have been the almost constant homes of fevers and other destructive diseases.

But the difference between city and country in respect to healthfulness is not so great as it was. A change in this regard has taken place within the last twenty-five, certainly within the last fifty, years. This has been occasioned by a better knowledge of the principles of physiology and hygiene and the diffusion of that knowledge among the people. The laws of health are not only better known than they were within the memory of those living, but the knowledge of those laws is not confined to the few, and they chiefly of the medical profession. It has become, to some extent, the property of the masses. Popular text-books on physiology are in our schools and on our tables. These are supplemented also by lectures on the subject adapted to the popular understanding, while newspapers and magazines are doing not a little in the same direction.

Of this increased knowledge the cities and towns have reaped the benefit more than the open country. This might have been expected. The former, having been the greatest sufferers from the ravages of disease, would naturally be the first to consider the means of escaping them, and to apply the discoveries of science for the promotion of health. The very necessities of the case, and the greater promptness and energy of action which mark the people in towns, as compared with those in the open country, would lead to the earlier adoption, by the former, of measures for the improvement of their sanitary condition. This would be stimulated, also, and made more effective by the urgency of the medical profession, who would be more likely to speak out in the city and act vigorously in behalf of sanitary measures than in the country. Their numbers, their facilities for combined action, and their probably superior knowledge would lead to this.

For these reasons, not to mention others, it has resulted that very decided and systematic measures have been taken, in many cities and large towns, for the purpose of lessening or removing the prevalence and power of diseases. The earliest and most efficient movements for this purpose were made in the city of London, which brought to its aid in this work a commission established by the British Parliament. The results of the investigations made by this commission have led to similar inquiries in other cities and to many discoveries in regard to certain diseases, their causes and remedies.

Attention has been specially called to what are termed the preventable causes of disease. In consequence of this, some diseases, which have been among those most dreaded, have lost much of their terror, and are now regarded as being quite within our control. Typhoid fever, for example, is found to have such an established connection with the contamination of drinking-water, or of the air, by means of the decomposition of organic substances, that it is quite within our power to prevent its existence. Indeed, Dr. Rush anticipated the knowledge of the present day by declaring, nearly a century ago, that he was so well convinced that fevers are subject to human control that he looked for the time when the law would punish cities and villages for permitting any sources of malignant or bilious fevers to exist within their jurisdiction.

The effect of proper drainage and ventilation upon the health of places using these means of preventing the contamination of the water and the atmosphere has been quite remarkable. It has reversed the relations of city and country to the existence of fevers. Whereas these were formerly regarded as the special pest of cities, they are now most prevalent in the country. As the result of what has been done in cities for the removal of known causes of disease, the death-rate of the population has been reduced in a measure that is very noticeable. An English writer shows that by the sanitary measures already adopted, imperfect as they are, the average mortality has been reduced from five to more than thirty per cent. below what it was previously, and the reduction of the typhoid-fever rate has been from ten to seventy-five per cent. Colonel Waring, one of our best authorities on this subject, tells us that when the improvement of sewerage was actively undertaken in London, about twenty-five years ago, it was found that the death-rate was so much reduced in some of the worst quarters that, if the same reduction could have been made universal, the annual deaths would have been twenty-five thousand less in London, and one hundred and seventy-seven thousand less in England and Wales; or, by another view, that the average
8*

age at death would have been increased to forty-eight, instead of being, as it then was, twenty - nine. As further evidence that the causes of disease are largely within human control, we have facts like the following. In 1790 the death-rate in the British navy was one in forty-two, and the sick were two in every five. In 1813, when measures had been taken to secure to vessels better conditions of health, the death-rate was one in a hundred and forty-three, and the sick only two in twenty-one. Careful examination in Philadelphia at one time showed that two fifths of all the deaths taking place there were from diseases arising from want of cleanliness. More than seventy-five per cent. of deaths in New York, it is stated, are among the population living in tenement-houses — which are notoriously the abodes of filth—and in neglect of the ordinary means of cleanliness. A drainage law was passed in the city of New York in 1871, and under its operation a section of the city east of Fifth Avenue and above Forty-fifth street was drained. In two years diseases of a typhoidal and malarial type, which had prevailed there for more than twenty-five years, almost disappeared. Such facts show how healthy such a city as New York might be, if all its people were living as those in the better portions of the city live—in clean streets and clean houses.

All investigations show, and by an overwhelming mass of proof from cases of every description, that typhoid fever stands in close connection with the amount of neglected filth allowed to poison water or air. The question of the prevalence of fevers, and of pythogenic diseases generally, resolves itself, therefore, very much into the question of the tolerance of filth, whether in city or country. Dr. Derby, who has investigated the subject with much care, says, " The well are made sick, and the sick are made worse, for the simple lack of God's pure air and pure water." The water and the air may be contaminated in various ways, and often when we least suspect it. There is a general conviction that water taken from wells is wholesome. Most persons probably would prefer the water from wells to that taken from cisterns or from springs. That is, if they were to think at all of the purity of the water and its consequent healthfulness, apart from the consideration of pleasantness to the taste, most persons would probably regard the water of our wells as being more free from contaminations than that flowing from springs or that collected in cisterns. But there is no water so pure as that which falls as rain upon our house-roofs, and is gathered thence. There is nothing to injure it, except the foreign matter which collects upon the roofs in the intervals between the rainfalls; and that, in our villages and in the open country, must be very little. On the other hand, many of our springs may be injuriously affected by noxious matters in the soil or upon the surface near which they flow, and our wells may easily be little better than receptacles of what is most threatening and harmful to us. A well is not necessarily

a good thing. Unless we know that it is in the midst
of clean surroundings, extending for a sufficient distance, and that it is protected from the intrusion of
deleterious matters, we have no assurance but that it
may be a storehouse of poison and death. Wells are of
the nature of drains, collecting water which filters from
the surface of the ground somewhere. They are, in
this respect, like springs; and if the water flowing into
them passes through decaying animal or vegetable matter, there is great danger that it will be rendered unfit
for use as drink. The earth, indeed, possesses a certain
cleansing property. Dirty and unwholesome water,
filtered through it, is rendered clear and wholesome.
There is abundant proof of this. But another thing is
equally sure. Earth, long exposed to deleterious matters, and having them washed into it by rains, becomes
so saturated with them at length that it loses its purifying power. The noxious matters then pass directly into
the water of the well without being cleansed. Now,
this is the case, to a great extent, in cities, and often in
the open country. The wells are frequently situated
where a great deal of noxious matter is deposited near
them. Sinks, cesspools, and privies are often in close
proximity to them. In the country, wells are often
placed, for the convenience of supplying water to the
cattle, near, if not actually in the barn-yard. And yet
people, instead of remembering that everywhere else
they expect liquids to settle down through the soil, and
disappear, act in these cases as though the earth were a

solid and impervious barrier between the filth on or near the surface and the deposit of water below from which they draw their supplies. In London, in a given instance, fever was generated all along a district where milk was taken from a dealer who was accustomed to dilute it with water from a particular well. On investigation it was found that this well had some connection with a cesspool not far away. Similar instances abound in our own country where the proof has been abundant and incontrovertible that fatal diseases have been occasioned by the pollution of wells in this way. The fact has been put beyond all question by cases where, when the cause of pollution has been removed, the disease has been checked ; and when the pollution, for some reason, has been allowed to take place again, the disease has returned, and then has been suppressed once more by another removal of the source of pollution. This is not a treatise on sanitary matters, or it would be in place, and extremely interesting, to cite some of the cases recorded in our medical and sanitary journals. It is enough to say that too much care cannot be taken to insure that all deleterious substances are kept at a proper distance from wells. That distance will vary in different circumstances, but it is safe to say that no such matters should be allowed to accumulate or be deposited upon the ground within a hundred feet of a well.

It is a quite common practice in the country to throw the sink water from the kitchen door, or to allow it to flow from the sink-spout directly upon the surface of the ground near the house. The result is usually a pool of greasy, decaying matter in close proximity to the windows and doors of the dwelling. This is doubly dangerous. In the first place, the gases generated from the kitchen waste find easy access to the house, especially in the warm seasons of the year, through the open windows and doors; and some of the most hurtful gases do not betray their presence by an offensive odor, which might put us on our guard against them. To a certain extent, foul substances emit a foul smell, and so give us warning of their presence; but it is not always so.* The germs of fever and meningitis, and even consumption, give no such warning of their presence or approach. And so, also, when these germs are washed down from the kitchen-drain or sink-spout, or from the cesspool into the well, which is likely to be not very distant, they may give no perceptible taint to the water. Neither the eye nor the nose may detect the fatal poison. The water may be clear and sparkling, and even

---

* The superintendent of the water-works in one of our cities, in reply to some inquiries of ours in regard to drainage, after giving some facts on the subject, makes the following statement: "A short time since, it was necessary for an examination to be made in one of our main sewers. I entered it, and passed about six hundred feet, when I perceived a fulness in my face; my forehead felt as though receiving blows from some flat substance. I knew the cause and at once backed out, but none too soon, as I could scarcely stand when in the street again. Now, there was no odor except near the entrance; but, you see, the poison was very active. I felt thankful at my escape, I can assure you.

"This is a subject that people must be educated to, and must be appreciated before we can say good-bye to typhoid fever and diphtheria."

havc an enviable reputation in its neighborhood for pleasantness to the taste ; yet it may be deadly. It is only by its effects that its really poisonous character will become known. And when the drinking of such water docs not generate fevers or other diseases at once, it very often induces a slow poisoning of the system, revealed by a certain low tone of life, a chronic invalidism, a general debility and incapacity for work of any kind, and many unpleasant but perhaps unnamable feelings and ailments—a sort of good-for-nothing condition of the whole being, which is ready to issue in diseases of various kinds whenever the proper exposure comes or the appropriate conditions arise.

The evil effect of almost all polluted waters is very much lessened by heating them to the boiling-point. It is owing to the fact, doubtless, that so much of the water which we use for drinking purposes is thus heated—as in the making of tea and coffee, and in many culinary processes—that we do not experience more disastrous results than we do from the foul and effete matters which too often have access to the sources of water supply.

As an illustration of the effect of heat upon the impurities of water, may be cited the case of one of the prisoners at far-famed Andersonville, the dreadful mortality at which has been largely attributed, and, without doubt, justly, to the foul water which the prisoners were obliged to drink. But one of the first prisoners sent there, and who remained there until the end of the war,

came from the prison without having had anything of
the so common disorder of the bowels. He never drank
the water without boiling it. Being often detailed to
bury the dead, he was enabled to gather roots and sticks
sufficient to make a fire that would enable him to boil
what water he needed. Other evidence of a like character might be adduced.

Most persons have a reasonable or unreasonable fear
of epidemics, and when these break out are aroused to
take measures adapted to stay their ravages and prevent
their recurrence. But epidemics are, at the worst, un-
frequent, while other diseases of fatal character are an
abiding presence with us; and the loss of life by epidemics is by no means equal to that from other causes
constantly in operation. Even when that most dreaded
scourge, as we call it—cholera—is rife, there are more
deaths from many other diseases, to which we pay little
attention, than from that. During the epidemic of
1849–50, there were reported thirty-one thousand five
hundred and six deaths from cholera in the United
States. During the same period, there were more than
the same number of deaths from other diseases of the
intestinal canal, and more from fevers alone.

It is the constant dangers, rather than the occasional,
against which we ought most to guard. The cardinal
health formula of old Hippocrates ought ever to be
kept in mind—"Pure air, pure water, and a pure soil."
We seem, to a great extent, to have forgotten the importance of the latter, if not of the former, of these.

How long we may escape fatal results from the poisonous matters draining into our wells from sinks and cesspools, or coming back in gaseous form into our dwellings from drains or the putrescent house-slops thrown
under the kitchen window, we cannot tell. But this
we know, or ought to know, that whenever we are living under such circumstances, we are living under the·
constant threat of disease and death; and when death
occurs in such cases, instead of saying that one died by .
the act of Divine Providence, as we are so accustomed
to do, we ought rather to say, he died as the result of
human improvidence. It ought to be recognized as a
first duty to remove, as far as possible, or to a safe distance, all sources of danger from the pollution of the
soil. It should be a fixed principle with every householder to see that all the waste substances of the house
—waste food, waste matters from the body, decayed and
decaying vegetables, and organic substances of every
kind—shall be removed from the house, and not allowed to get back to it again, whether in solution in water
or mingled with the air we breathe. The wash of the
house should by some means be carried rapidly away,
and either made useful by being returned as fertilizing
matter to farm or garden by means of the compost-
heap, or conducted into some stream by which it shall
be washed away. At any rate, and at any cost, it should
be put at a distance from the dwelling.

Many of the drains used for the purpose of carrying
waste matters away from the house are worse than use-

less; they are positively harmful. They are causes, rather than remedies, of danger. Instead of removing, they
often keep near us the foul and festering matters in
which are the seeds of disease and death. Who has not
been troubled with drains and sink-outlets filled up, so
that the wash of the house would no longer pass through
them? Who does not also remember the sickening effect when the drain has been fully uncovered, in order
that the accumulated filth might be removed? But the
sickening shock of such occasions is only the empha-
sized report of what has really existed every day for
weeks—it may be months—before. It is only the reve-
lation or uncovering of what existed, and was doing its
poisoning work unseen; all the while breeding, slowly
if not swiftly, disorders of mild or malignant type, or
bringing on those nameless debilities and local affec-
tions which are ready to issue at any time in fatal
disease.*

---

* Even while writing this chapter, the papers have brought to us several illustrations of the results of defective or improper drainage. We copy
the following, not as being more remarkable than many others, but only
as an example of what is taking place all the while:

"The shocking story of the death, in rapid succession, of six children of
Patrick Murray, of Newport, R. I., by diphtheria, was telegraphed at the
time, with an account of the frenzy of the father, whose grief had almost
crazed him. The mayor of the city requested Colonel George E. Waring,
Jr., one of the most accomplished civil engineers in the country, to investi-
gate the case carefully, and the report is now published. It is condensed
in one word—filth. That was the patent cause of the trouble. The drain-
pipes all led to a 'leaching cesspool' in the ground which had not been
touched for ten years. There were virtually no traps in the pipes, and the
vilest gases flowed into the living room as easily as—indeed, more easily

As usually constructed our drains carry off the waste and wash of the house so sluggishly that the greasy matters, by themselves perhaps innocuous, become chilled before they are carried far, and adhere to the sides of the drain, serving also to fix other and more deleterious matters with them. Thus there gradually accumulates a festering mass, which, occasionally at least, sends back its polluting gases into the house, even though there be a sink-trap ; and finally gives notice of its presence in a way to be no longer disregarded, by a complete stoppage of the drain.

---

than—pure air. Besides this, out of the 'living-room' of the family there opened a sort of L, one room through which was the back entrance to the house. Under this L, which had no cellar, ran the main outlet sewer-pipe on its way to the cesspool. The pipe had recently broken ; filth had oozed out and covered and permeated the sea-weed packing that had been put over the pipe to keep it from freezing in winter, and with the first warm weather deadly gases from the decomposition spread at once. The first victim was the oldest child , her domestic duties kept her at the sink, and the air she inhaled there, contaminated by the untrapped sink outlet, had so weakened her that she went down first. The closing words of the report should be read everywhere. Colonel Waring says :

" 'Murray's children are gone—past recall ; but other children in Newport, and all over the land, are being subjected to unsuspected dangers of the sort above described ; and I cannot close the record of this deplorable calamity without entreating all physicians who may be called to cases of filth-born disease to insist on an immediate and most searching scrutiny of all possible sources of contamination ; and, if contamination is found, *upon the immediate removal of the whole family* away from the infected premises. If Patrick Murray and his family had been removed into Mr. Cushing's stable, into a tent, or into a wholesome house, on the first development of the disease, there might have been a chance of saving them. Left where they were, they fell one after another before an unremitted assault, which the simplest examination would have discovered.' "

A mistake is often made in the construction of drains by making them too large. A drain five inches in diameter is large enough for any house. When larger than this, the liquids passing through them are spread over a wide surface, friction is increased, consequently the waste matters move slowly, and there is the greater danger of adhesion to the sides of the drain, and of consequent accumulation and the generation of gases, if not of final stoppage. The smaller drain has less surface exposed to the deposit of offensive matters, while the swifter flow of the current tends to sweep them all away to their place of ultimate deposit. Our hydraulic engineers have found it advantageous to use pipes of smaller size than those which were considered necessary for the same service a few years ago.

Drains should be made of tile or of metallic pipe rather than of wood or bricks, on account of smoothness of surface and the consequent readiness with which the contents of the drains will flow away. They should not be of porous material, nor have loose joints which will allow the leakage of either gases or fluids. The cement or the vitrified drain-tile is probably the best material we have for this purpose, if it is carefully fitted at the joints. To make the work of drainage entirely satisfactory, however, there should be either such an abundant supply of water flowing through the drain all the time, from some spring or aqueduct source, as to wash everything of waste nature quickly away to a safe distance, or there should be some means by which, at

frequent intervals, the drain can be flushed and so be
swept clean of all waste and deleterious substances.   An
excellent contrivance for the latter purpose, known as
Field's Flush-tank, has been in use for several years in
England, but is little known as yet in this country.   It
consists essentially of a tank—a barrel or hogshead will
answer the purpose—with an inlet for the house-waste
at the top through a grating, and a siphon tube, the bent

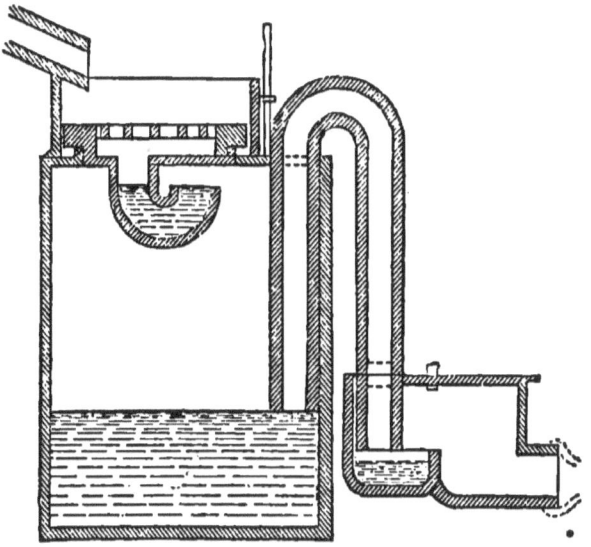

part of which is near the top of the tank.   One foot of
the siphon is near the bottom of the tank, and the other
is so connected with the drain that when the siphon is
thrown into action by the filling of the tank to the top
of the siphon, the entire contents of the tank are at once
drawn off, and flow through the drain with such force
that nothing lodges by the way.   The peculiar merit of
this tank is that the waste-water, and whatever may be

contained in it, instead of being allowed to flow into the drain in small quantities, as is so commonly the case, and therefore to flow with so little force that greasy and other matters may easily adhere to the sides of the drain and finally obstruct it, is now discharged only when the tank is completely filled, and then all at once and with a strong and rapid flow. The accompanying cut, for the design of which we are indebted to Colonel George E. Waring, Jr., who is an authority on the subject of drainage, will explain the construction and working of this tank.

Care should be taken to secure such a slope in constructing a drain that its contents may readily flow off. This should not be less than thirty inches in a hundred feet; a slope three times as great would be better, as producing a more rapid and effectual flow.

But with the best arrangement in other respects, great mischief may be wrought, and when we are least aware of it, unless care be taken to cause all drains and waste-pipes to be well ventilated, and so arranged by proper and sufficient traps that the gases generated in 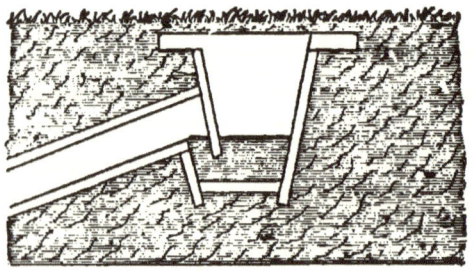 them shall not be allowed to enter the rooms of the dwelling.

Here is given an illustration of a common form of trap for a drain, the entrance to which is out-of-doors.

If such a trap is placed within the house, there should be a ventilating-pipe extending from the trap, or from the drain near it, to a point in the open air, which will convey any possible noxious gases to a safe distance.

Too much care cannot be taken with all traps and drain-pipes, whether within doors or without, to see that they are properly ventilated, and that no noxious gases can escape from them into the apartments of the house. The overflow pipes of our wash-basins, for want of properly constructed traps and proper ventilation, have often been overflows of foul gases into our rooms.

With any arrangement there will be more or less of effete matter adhering to the sides of the sewer and of the drainage pipes, and this will give origin to deleterious gases ready to penetrate our houses and rooms whenever opportunity offers. To prevent this, it is desirable, in the first place, to give the sewer and the sewerage pipes, if there be any within the house, as free communication as possible with the outer air. The atmosphere is the great oxidizer of all foul matters—that by which they are consumed. The more and the sooner we can bring all foul and waste matters into contact with the atmosphere, the better. Hence, in the case of the flush-tank of which we have spoken, there ought to be a ventilating-pipe extending from the top of the tank to some point considerably above it, so that the gases which will inevitably be engendered in it may pass off to a place of safety. So, likewise, sewers should have similar ventilating-pipes or openings; and the soil-pipe connected with sinks or water-closets should be carried from the drain or sewer to the top of the house in a straight and unbroken line, and be three or four inches in diameter, so as to admit abundance of air. It should be of cast-iron, with joints effectively cemented, so that no gas can escape through them. It should extend some distance above the roof, and its extremity be covered with a hood, as shown in the accompanying cut,

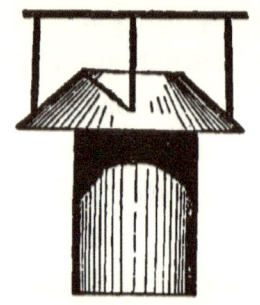 so that whatever may be the currents of wind, there may yet be a clear upward and outward draught. All water-basins should empty into this main upright pipe by side pipes protected by traps, so that no gas may be able to get back through the water-closets into the house apartments. And then, finally, there should be such a supply of water as will effectually wash away all effete matters, and carry them as speedily as possible from the dwelling and to their ultimate destination. Only thus can the work of drainage be effectually done.

The management of drains is attended with difficulty at the best; but their proper management is the price of life and health, the latter of which is, in many instances, more important than the former. Says Professor Brewer, of New Haven, writing upon this very subject, "Let us not forget that the evil of *death* is not the greatest one. A man dead may be a loss to a family or a community, but he is not a burden. A *sick* man is no longer a producer; he is a burden, often a heavy one, on his friends." It is estimated that for every case of death there are five cases of severe sickness; and how many cases are there of chronic, life-long ailments and debilities of one sort or another? A large part of these are believed to be connected more or less directly with the improper disposal of the waste matters of our dwellings and the consequent pollution of the water and the air. Here, then, is the point where we should be willing to expend most freely our care, and, so far as may be needful, our money; every interest of man and society demands it. Stagnant water near houses; damp cellars arising from a soil from which the water does not readily find an outlet—these evils should be remedied by thorough drainage, and, in connection with these, all household wastes should be put at a safe distance.

9

CHAPTER XVII.

SANITARY ASPECTS OF COUNTRY LIFE (*continued*).—
VENTILATION.

" Man's greatest enemy is his own breath."

"It is not too general an expression to say that every thought and act•·
of man, as well as every action within his body, is accompanied by the
consumption of oxygen and deterioration of the surrounding air."—DR.
EDWARD SMITH.

IN considering the sanitary aspects of country life, as
indeed of life anywhere, drainage and ventilation are
of paramount importance. It is difficult to decide
which of the two is the more important. They are
closely linked together, and often it is hardly possible to
separate them. Ventilation may be said to be the sewerage of the atmosphere; the one implies or necessitates
the other. Drainage is imperfect without a proper system of ventilation, as a proper system of ventilation
cannot be carried out without a corresponding system
of drainage.

It is because of the imperfect arrangements for ventilation connected with them that many modern plans for
underground drainage have been pronounced inferior, in
a sanitary point of view, to the old plan of carrying away
the filth and slops of houses by means of open surface

drains. The sight of the foul mass in the latter case is not pleasant; but it is better to have the sight of it and feel that in the open air there is some probability that the waste matters will be rapidly oxidized and so rendered innoxious, or that the various gases engendered will be rapidly dissipated by the free winds, than to have these gases arising in a close drain where, for want of proper outlet, they may be driven back into the various apartments of the house to work their mischief there.

Nearly all are ready to admit the importance to health of pure water and pure air. Comparatively few, however, will take the pains necessary to secure the one or the other. People will take it for granted that they have both pure air and pure water, without any sufficient consideration of the facts on which their purity depends. That one lives in the country, and not in the city or densely populated town, is thought to be, of itself, the sufficient guarantee that he will have these vital elements in a state of purity. If the water is not turbid, and if there is no absolutely foul smell in the atmosphere, it is supposed that both are in the proper condition for the promotion of health. But modern science has proved that while the senses of taste and smell have an important office in warning us of many things which are or would be prejudicial to health, they are not sufficient to secure us against some of the greatest dangers which threaten us on this score. Water, as we have seen, may be poisonous when it is altogether pleasant to the taste, while, on the contrary, it may be all that health demands, although so turbid that the eye regards it with suspicion. So, also, the air may be unfavorable to health when none of the senses can detect the hurtful ingredient in it. It is not the foul-smelling gases which mingle with the air that are the most harmful. Carbonic acid and carbonic oxide, which are so fatal, frequently give no sign of their noxious quality to the senses. The former of these is even very grateful to the taste. It is what gives the sparkle and the pleasant tingle on the tongue to our most agreeable drinking-waters, whether from the native spring or the so-called "soda-fountain" of the shops, which, however, has no trace of soda about it.

The air which we breathe, it hardly needs to be said, is composed mainly of three ingredients in gaseous form. One of these bears so small a proportion to the others that the atmosphere is often said to be composed of the latter alone, there being little more than a trace, or from four to six parts of carbonic acid in ten thousand parts of the atmosphere in its normal condition. In general terms, and for ordinary purposes, the air may be regarded as composed of oxygen and nitrogen. The former constitutes about one fourth of the atmosphere in weight and one fifth in bulk, the latter being three fourths of it in weight or four fifths in bulk.

It is the oxygen of the air which supports life. The nitrogen seems to be important, so far as respiration and the support of animal life are concerned, chiefly as a medium for the dilution of the oxygen, or a vehicle for its proper conveyance into the body. In an atmosphere of oxygen alone, life would go on too fast and end too soon, as the familiar experiments of the chemists show us that candles and other combustible substances burn with increased brilliancy and increased rapidity in oxygen. Respiration, we now know, is a true combustion, as much so as the burning of wood or coal in the stove, and resulting, as that does, in heat. It is the oxygen we breathe which is the source of our animal heat, the carbon and hydrogen of the blood, derived from our food, being oxidized, as the wood or coal is oxidized or burned in the stove. The chief difference between the combustion going on in the human body and that of a lamp or a fire is, that the former goes on at a lower temperature and at a slower rate than the latter; just as in the rusting of iron, which again is a simple combustion, the combustion goes on at a still lower temperature and a still slower rate.

We take in, or inhale, the air we breathe for the purpose of bringing oxygen (or vital air, as it was formerly called, because life is so dependent upon it) into contact with the blood in the lungs, and through that into contact with the contents of the blood throughout the body. The oxidation of the carbon and hydrogen in the blood gives origin to carbonic-acid gas and watery vapor, which are thrown out from the body at every expiration along with the nitrogen which we have inhaled. "The body," says Dr. Edward Smith, "is a great oxidizing apparatus by which it sustains its bulk, produces heat, and modifies the composition of the atmosphere; and when it has cast off that which, having been used, is no longer useful to it, it not only deteriorates the atmosphere, but renders it impure."

In the natural arrangement of things, the oxygen of the air is supplied in the proper proportion for the best support of life and health, and provision is made for removing from us at once the noxious products or waste material thrown off by respiration. Gaseous substances have a remarkable property of diffusibility. As the result of this, the carbonic acid thrown out from the lungs, though heavier than common air, tends at once to spread through the great ocean of the atmosphere above and around, and so does not remain in hurtful proportions near us to be inhaled in place of, or mingled with, the pure oxygen. So, also, where there are trees and plants, these perform an important sanitary function for us. They breathe through their leaves, as we do through our lungs. But there is one very important difference between the breathing of animals and that of plants. While the former inhale oxygen and throw out carbonic acid, which is poisonous to them, the plants greedily absorb this gas by their leaves or lungs, and, decomposing it in their laboratory, add it to their own structure in the form of solid carbon, while they set free, or pour out into the air, the oxygen of the carbonic acid, fit to be used again by man.

Thus we see how the animal and vegetable kingdoms

stand in most beautiful and important relation to each other, the one built up out of the waste of the other. And so, if men lived in the open air along with the trees, and did nothing to pollute the atmosphere except to pour into it the products of respiration, the trees would keep the air pure for them.

But as we live in houses, and shut ourselves close in them so that the trees can help us little, what shall we do? What, of course, but see to it that our houses are so constructed as to secure the needful supply of oxygen for our lungs, and the removal to a safe distance of the poisonous matter which our lungs are all the while throwing off. This is the simple dictate of self-preservation.

Every person, if he would breathe as good an atmosphere as that ordinarily found out-of-doors, requires about a thousand cubic feet of pure air every hour. This would be sufficient to fill a room ten feet square and ten feet in height. Some have said that the hourly demand of air for a state of health is three thousand cubic feet; but careful experiments have shown that this is not necessary. But on the lower estimate which we have given, it is easy to see how rapidly the air of our public and private rooms must become vitiated unless some means be taken to avoid the danger. "Man's greatest enemy," one has said, "is his own breath." By the very processes of life, we are threatening ourselves with death. Shut one in a close room, and he will soon die, as certainly as though he were to place by him a brazier of burning charcoal. Every time we breathe we make the air about us less fit to breathe. Our only safety, therefore, is in having the air around us in motion, so that what we expire—the noxious gases, the effete matter poured out of our bodies by means of the lungs—may be carried away and a supply of wholesome air may be brought to us. Hence movement of the air is essential to life. Still air is virtually death.

And yet, as though we were bent on suicide, what pains we take, with our double windows, window-stops, and weather-strips, to shut out the pure air from our rooms and imprison that which we have fouled and made unfit to be breathed, and to imprison ourselves with it! It is worse than substituting greenbacks for gold, for it is debasing the currency of life. Then think how the student often sits hour after hour absorbed in his studies, with door locked fast against any possible opening; or how our wives and daughters, busy with needle or book, sit the whole morning or afternoon in some small apartment through whose closed doors no one comes or goes for hours together! Think also of the mere closets, called bedrooms, in which so many sleep, or try to sleep, commonly with doors and windows shut, as though all we need were space for a bed and possibly a wash-stand! Is it to be wondered at that the brain of the student grows dull and refuses to work, or that mothers and daughters have aching heads, or that so many wake in the morning not rested or refreshed, and with a good-for-nothing feeling and a general lassitude?

And, to make the matter worse, during the season when windows and doors are kept constantly shut, we also frequently place in sitting and sleeping rooms a stove, which is itself a ravenous consumer of oxygen, lives upon it, in fact, just as we do, and for the same reason; and this stove probably pours out from its various joints a large amount of carbonic acid and carbonic oxide. Thus the supply of vital air needful for us is still further lessened.

The quantity of carbonic acid exhaled from the lungs of an adult is estimated to be two hundred and fifty gallons every twenty-four hours. In addition to the vitiation of a close sleeping-room or sitting-room from this cause, four pounds of moisture are in the same time given off by perspiration, contaminated with various minute organic and deleterious substances. "If," says Prof. C. E. Joy, "the air of an occupied room loses one per cent. of its oxygen, respiration becomes difficult; the loss of four per cent. renders life nearly insupportable, and death arrives when the loss reaches five or six per cent." Think, then, what is the condition often of our family apartments; still more, what is the condition, in regard to health, of our schools and churches and other public buildings, where for every thousand persons there will be thrown off, by the breath and by insensible perspiration, from two to five hundred pounds of fetid vapor, and two hundred pounds of carbonic-acid gas every six hours. Can we wonder that we have dull and disorderly schools, drowsy listeners to

9*

drowsy sermons, or headaches by day and by night, or corrupting and fatal diseases of the lungs from corrupt air constantly inhaled?

But the story of the lack of proper ventilation in our country homes is not yet fully told. Who does not remember the stifling atmosphere when he has been ushered into the best room of some farm-house, the sickening, musty smell, making him think of fever in spite of himself, and the mingled odors of decaying turnips, onions, cabbages, and potatoes, coming up through the crevices of the floor from the cellar below? But what is thus in the best room, and reveals itself so pungently, because that room is shut perhaps for weeks together, is equally present in the other rooms, only not so perceptibly, and is working its mischief all the while. And this is the atmosphere in which many of the people of our villages live from year to year. Our modern hospitals and jails are palaces of purity in comparison with many a stately country house. We make ourselves fit for the hospital in our dwellings, and then perhaps go to the hospital to learn how a building should be arranged to secure health.

Thus, in the matter of ventilation as well as in that of drainage, the villages have become more defective than the towns and cities, for in these necessity has at length compelled attention to both of these subjects, while in the country they are as yet very generally neglected.

It is a curious fact, also, stated on the authority of

Professor Joy, that attention was first drawn to the subject of ventilation in a practical way, not with a view to
benefit human beings, but brute animals. "It was not
for the sick in hospitals that new devices were introduced, but for the silk-worms in the spinning of cocoons.
Observation showed the necessity of fresh air to the
preservation of the worms, and it was carefully introduced; and, after it was done, the same apparatus was
pronounced to be equally useful for man." So it was
because a man had successfully ventilated a stable in
New York that he was asked to apply his invention to
a public building.   It was first the horses, then the men.
And to-day the hall in Paris in which meets the French
Institute, the first scientific body in the world, is said
to be the worst-ventilated room in Europe.

The first principle in regard to ventilation, or the
preservation of the air of our houses in a fit condition for
health, is that there must be opportunity for its free circulation in the house and in every room of the house.
It is not necessary, however, that this circulation should
be attended with strong draughts, or currents, unpleas-
antly perceptible or dangerous.   If there is a ventilating-flue in the house, or a properly arranged furnace by
which the house is heated, and the windows and doors
are not fitted close or sealed with the so-called weather-
strips, a sufficient change of air will be secured, the fresh
warm air from the furnace pushing out the vitiated air
through the crevices of doors and windows, or through
a flue designed expressly for the purpose of carrying off

the impure air. Only care must be taken to avoid two dangers—first, that of having a furnace so imperfectly constructed as to permit the gas from the burning coal to get admission to the hot-air pipes; and, second, that of taking the air to be heated from the cellar, and not from without the house. For want of proper precaution in regard to these dangers, many furnaces have been prolific sources of disease. They have been but so many contrivances for pouring poisonous gases into our rooms. Too much care can hardly be exercised on both these points. Cast iron, of which most furnaces until recently have been constructed, has been proved to be permeable by gases when it is heated to a high temperature. Preference should be given, therefore, to furnaces constructed of wrought iron. Care should also be taken to have as few joints and seams as possible around the fire-pot and flues, and to see that these are so made that no gases from the fire shall pass through them into the apartments above. Then it should be remembered that the air of no cellar is pure, or fit to be used as the source from which the supply of heated air is to be drawn for the purpose of respiration. It is simply a violation of the laws of health to use it. No one should think of using a furnace without having connected with it an air-box of large size reaching a point outside of the house, and considerably above the level of the ground. Steam and hot-water heaters are, in some respects, preferable to hot-air furnaces; but there can be no simpler or more effective way of supplying an abundance of fresh

air to a whole house than a properly constructed furnace.

· It ought also to be remembered that every furnace
or heater should have as an essential part of it an apparatus for evaporating water. The cold air from without has less capacity for moisture than it has after it
is heated. If this increased capacity is not satisfied by
an evaporating-dish, the warmed air will take its desired
moisture from our lungs, or our furniture, or wherever
it can get it. Many housekeepers know that doors
shrink and chairs and tables open their joints when
the furnace fires have been in operation for a while.
They do not always understand the reason of it or the
remedy for it. Nor do they always consider that the
too dry air is as bad for us as it is for our furniture.

But the best of all ventilators within ordinary reach
is an open fireplace. Nothing has ever equalled the
old fireplace of a century ago as an instrument at the
same time of good cheer and good health. That old
fireplace, of which hardly more than the tradition now
remains, was the centre and glory of the country house.
The kitchen was the family living-room, and large
enough to be such with both comfort and decency. It
usually occupied the entire width of the house, with the
exception of a small portion reserved for pantry or bedroom. In the centre of one side was a huge fireplace,
into which almost a cart-load of wood might be emptied
at a time, and where there was room besides for the
children to sit literally in the chimney-corner. Such

logs were laid there for the foundation of the fire as no man alone could lift. Tradition says they were some-times drawn in by cattle. And then, when the armfuls of lesser logs, and limbs of oak and hickory and maple, were piled high and had become fully ablaze, how the flames danced and went roaring up the wide chimney! How the great mass of coals glowed upon the broad hearth! What pictures were, in imagination, painted, and what castles were built among them! How the very music of the forests, like that hidden in old Cre-monas, came out of the burning logs and limbs! It would have been pardonable, almost, if our Puritan ancestors had become fire-worshippers.

With such a torrent of heated air rushing up the chimney, and no weather-strips on doors or windows, there was a pretty strong pull upon the outside air, and it came in with such force sometimes as to give unpleas-ant sensations of cold to the back when the face was hardly able to bear the heat in front of it. But there was health and good cheer around those old-time fire-places. There was no chance for foul air in those old living-rooms. The carbonic-acid and every other foul gas had to go up the chimney, whether it would or not. Oxygen was plenty and fresh all the time, and it show-ed itself in the glow of the cheek and the healthful sparkle of the talk as the family sat around the blazing fire. Think of the change to air-tight stoves and weath-er-strips of India-rubber—demons of darkness and death! And yet our country people, with forests all around them,

elaborating for them, by the subtle chemistry of their
leaves, the life-giving oxygen, and offering them the
amplest supply of the best fuel for the promotion of
health, for a little seeming saving of present expense
and trouble have shut up the fireplaces which their
fathers built; have drawn the carpet over and hidden
the sacred hearth-stone, on which were nurtured the
best virtues of family and social life; have shut out the
air and the sunlight of heaven from their houses; and
sit, sodden in mephitic vapors, over their close stoves or
furnace-registers.   In working out the petty problem of
saving heat, we have done not a little to destroy health.

It is time for a reform in this matter.   It is time that
our fires were so managed as to be sources of health as
well as of heat, as they easily may be.   Better add ten
or twenty dollars, if need be, to the cost of the winter's
fuel, and secure the positive pleasure and benefit of the
cheerful open fire than pay twice or thrice that for the
services of the doctor.   One room in the house at least
ought to have such an arrangement for the health and
daily enjoyment of the household.   The old open fireplace, or, what is next to it, the Franklin stove, should
be in every house.   Then every chimney, where there
are no such open fireplaces, ought to have a ventilating-
flue—a part of the chimney separated from the rest by a
thin partition of slate or some other like material, so
that the heat in the smoke-flue will be readily commu-
nicated to it, and cause a strong upward draught.   By
means of openings into the ventilating-flue from the

rooms adjacent to the chimney, a healthful change of air may be secured at all times, and little will be wanting on the score of ventilation.

We are not accustomed to think of the air as a food; but the highest authorities now class it as such. And if this is its true character, then who can fail to see the importance of securing this in its purity and free from all contaminating mixtures? Moreover, the air is far from being uniform in its quality. It varies in this respect as do the other foods which we use. Hence the need of daily, constant care, in order that we may obtain that which is best. There is all the more need of care, also, because the air is not a food which we take only occasionally, a few times daily, or for which we may substitute some other kind of food. We feed upon this constantly, by day and by night, when we wake and when we sleep. Nothing can take its place. This we must have. This we must have constantly, and of wholesome quality, or we perish.

Where is the chemist or philosopher who will invènt for us some apparatus which, in addition to the thermometer, which shows us the temperature of the atmosphere, and the barometer, which gives us its weight, will show us at a glance the condition of the atmosphere in our rooms or elsewhere in regard to purity or impurity? The world is waiting for science thus to come to the aid of practical life. Is it too much to hope that we shall not have to wait long for what we so much need?

CHAPTER XVIII.

SANITARY ASPECTS OF COUNTRY LIFE (*continued*).—
THE CARE OF THE SICK.

"Life hath its mission, fit for all and each:
˜It may be thine this lesson to secure,
What angel-whispers in thy sick-room teach,
'Learn thou to wait and patiently endure.'"

MRS. BARRETT.

HAVING spoken of drainage and ventilation as means of promoting health and guarding against the preventable causes of disease, it may be in place now to say something in regard to the treatment of those who become sick. It is not to be concealed that in the care of the sick the advantage is, at present, on the side of the city or town as compared with the open country. In the first place, as to physicians and medicines, the towns are better supplied than the villages. The most skilful physicians, those conversant with diseases in the greatest variety and with their various treatment, are naturally to be found in the larger places. The benefit of their united wisdom is also to be had there at any time, while in the country the patient is often at an inconvenient distance from any medical help whatever. In the case of severe or peculiar disorders, therefore, the pa-

tient in the country is at a disadvantage compared with
one in the city. The poorest sufferer in the city is not
far from a hospital, where he may have the best medical
advice combined with the best nursing which modern
science and art combined can give. Indeed, hardly anything is more noteworthy in regard to our city life than
the improvement which has been made in all that properly constitutes the care of the sick. And what is particularly noticeable is, that a great increase of attention
has been given to the nursing of the sick, in distinction
from mere medical attendance.

After all, the former is of more importance than the
latter. Not in all cases. But the majority of our ailments are not those for the cure of which we are dependent upon the scientific or professional skill of the
physician. There is a power of self-recovery in the human constitution which is simply wonderful. The *vis
medicatrix naturæ* is the greatest power which we
have at command in overcoming the assaults of disease.
And it is often astonishing to see through what forlorn conditions and desperate straits this will take us.

In most cases of disease the chief thing to be done is
to let this latent power of self-recovery have a fair
chance to act, and every sensible practitioner is ready
to recognize in a good nurse his most effective ally. It
is the lack of such a helper that the physician finds the
most frequent hindrance to his own success in the treatment of a disease. It is easy enough, for the most part,
to see what is the appropriate medicine to give, and to

have it given; but that it shall be given at the right time and in the right way, and that all the circumstances of the patient shall be what they ought to be, so as to favor the action of the medicine given, and facilitate and encourage the reactions of nature, this is not by any means easy to secure. There may not be any neglect, in one sense, yet in another there may be the greatest, and sometimes the most fatal. Many sick ones, doubtless, are literally killed by kindness. Friends must be doing something for them, and, in their ignorance, often do the wrong thing. They must be doing something, when perhaps the thing most needed is that they should just do nothing, but give the patient a fair chance to fight the battle with disease out of the armament which his own nature has given him. What is needed most commonly is that we shall stand out of the way and let nature do her own work. If we will only stop infringing her laws, and our friends will keep from their infringement to our harm, it will be quite surprising how soon we shall ordinarily get the better of our ailments and come up into a condition of health again.

We have, perhaps, been taking too much food, or food of an improper character. The system has been burdened with a load which it could not carry and go on with the ordinary functions of life. We have been long breathing an impure and noxious atmosphere, it may be, taking in for food (for air is food in the highest sense) some foul gases, and these have poisoned us. Now, what is chiefly wanted is that we should stop in this

destructive course of living, give the wearied body—
the digestive organs especially—rest for a time, and
let the lungs take in only pure air. Not a grain of
medicine, oftentimes, will be needed.

But now anxious and truly loving friends will be very
likely to come in with all sorts of herb drinks and ap-
plications; and this nice thing and that will be forced
into the stomach, when the faint appetite is nature's
own indication that rest for the digestive organs, and
not food, is what is needed. And then, in addition to
this abuse, the patient is very likely to be shut up in
some small room at the best, and, as though this were
not bad enough, every door and window will be kept
closed as much as possible for fear of "exposure to the
air," as it is called, when the very thing wanted above
all else is a free exposure to the pure air of heaven. It
is simply marvellous to one who goes into many of our
sick-rooms from the open air, and scents the foul atmosphere in which the sick are literally imprisoned, that
they ever get well again. It is astonishing, also, that so
many of our physicians allow their patients to be kept
in such an atmosphere. Whether it is that they have
not yet attained proper convictions as to the importance
of purity of atmosphere, or think it no part of their
function to look to this in the treatment of their patients, there ought to be a great change in this respect.

When sickness comes, especially if it is of a sort in
which recovery is to be slow, as in the case of fevers
and many nervous disorders, the sick one should have,

if possible, the largest and pleasantest room in the
house. Something more is needed than just space
enough for a bed or an easy-chair. Yet how often is
it thought that this is all that is necessary. How many
of our good and kind country housekeepers would be
ready to give up the spare bedroom to an invalid?
How many would even think of such a thing? But
the confinement of the sick-room is irksome and severe,
at the best. Think of the change from the freedom
which allowed one to go all about the house from room
to room at pleasure and abroad in the street, to the seclusion of a single room. Any one who thinks of it, or
who has had the experience of severe and protracted
illness, will feel that too much care cannot be taken to
give one who is sick a room of ample dimensions, and
as pleasant as possible in all respects. It should not be
on the shady side of the house, but by all means where
the sun can shine into it freely. The sunlight is not
only pleasant to the sight and cheering to the spirits,
and thus indirectly beneficial, but it is in itself a medicine in the strictest sense. Then the furniture should
be pleasant; the windows should have an agreeable
drapery; flowering plants should lend their healthful
presence, and the walls should have some cheerful pictures for the eyes to rest upon. In the time of health
it does not matter so much by what objects we are surrounded. We are busied with other things, to a great
extent. But in sickness the eye and the mind are filled with the things nearest us. Every chair and table,

every thread in the carpet, every figure and line on the wall-paper, is known and noticed. And how weary the poor invalid often is with the sight of things which are uninteresting, if not positively disagreeable! It is a great relief, sometimes, simply to change the arrangement of the furniture in the sick-room, putting the chairs and table and bed in new positions. It breaks up the old association of one with another that has become so wearisome. It is like going into another room.

It is very desirable that an invalid's room should have an open fireplace. In the colder seasons of the year, this is especially desirable as the best means of securing proper ventilation. But there is hardly a month in the year when a fire will not be serviceable to the invalid by its pleasant warmth. And then, apart from these uses, the sight of the blazing fire is almost always very pleasant to the ailing one. It is one of the most cheerful of companions, a most welcome and valuable nurse in itself.

One of the simplest and best contrivances for securing the admission of fresh and pure air, whether into the rooms of the sick or the well, is to have a strip of wood—as long as the window is wide, and from one to two inches in thickness—placed beneath the lower window-sash. This lifts the sash just far enough to admit the air at the junction of the two sashes, but in such a way that no draught or blast is felt, even though the wind may be blowing freely. This may be a permanent fixture of the window, and with it, especially in connection with the open fireplace, one is sure of good air at all times, and without any harmful exposure to the most delicate and feeble. One has only to try it to see how effective is this simple arrangement.

As we are coming to understand better the importance of proper care or nursing of the sick as compared with the mere administration of medicine, it becomes apparent that we need to make some provision for the training of nurses, so that we may have at command those who may with confidence be intrusted with the care of the sick. A large field of usefulness is open in this direction, and there will be an ample demand for those who will qualify themselves for this work. A beginning has been made by the establishment, in some of our cities, of training-schools for nurses. But it is only a beginning. One of the great wants of our country villages is proper care for the sick. You may search many of them through in vain to find a nurse in time of sickness, one who is at once competent to have the charge of the sick, and sufficiently disengaged from other service to be available for this.

And so the sick are left to the haphazard attention of friends and neighbors already burdened with cares and duties; and while there may be abundance of kind feeling on their part, there may be such a lack of knowledge, judgment, tact, and proper sensibility that it is often difficult to tell whether the sick one is bene-

fited by it all or not. It is much to be desired that in
almost every village there could be two, three, or
more nurses, trained either at some school established
for this purpose, or by the village physician, and having such knowledge and experience that they could
be trusted by the physicians and by the friends of the
sick. They should have some knowledge of physiology. They should have an intelligent discernment of
symptoms. They ought to know something of the nature and working of medicines. They should be able to
comprehend and carry out the wishes of the physician
in charge. And then they should have such an intelligent and appreciative understanding of the peculiarities and wants of the patients intrusted to their care,
and such a proper sense of the needs of the sick, that
they would make their every act, and every thought
even, to be somehow a ministry of benefit to them.
There are times in every physician's experience when,
if he could put such a nurse in charge of his patient
for only a single day, he would feel confident of his
passing the critical point and beginning his recovery
of health; whereas, for want of ability to do so, he is
obliged to see the life go out, notwithstanding his own
skill and all the care and ministry of loving friends.

CHAPTER XIX.

CEMETERIES.

"'The boast of heraldry, the pomp of power,
And all that beauty, all that wealth e'er gave,
Await alike the inevitable hour.
The paths of glory lead but to the grave."

GRAY.

A RESPECTFUL regard for the bodies of the dead seems to be characteristic of mankind everywhere and in all ages. The first use of money, so far as we know, was for the purpose of a burial, and the first purchase of land was that of a cemetery. Whether the final disposal of the dead bodies of friends is by burial or burning, whether by mummification, as among the ancient Egyptians, or by exposure upon stages or shelves in the open air, as practised by some Indian tribes, each and all of these methods of treatment spring from the same common feeling of respect for the departed, which evidences itself in a care for the bodies which the departed once inhabited.

Burial has been by far the most common method of treating the remains of the dead. The ancient lands of Assyria and Egypt show us the remains of vast burial-places—cities of the dead, as it were, removed from, yet

10

near by, the cities of the living. And if the Pyramids of the Nile were constructed for the burial-place of the Egyptian kings, then no palaces of kings in their lifetime have equalled in grandeur the resting-places of their bodies when dead.

Among the most impressive items of early history as given us in the Old Testament Scriptures is that interview of Abraham with Ephron, when the former purchased of the latter the cave of Machpelah for a burial-place, and then, by the interment of his beloved Sarah, consecrated it as a family burying-ground. And what a scene was that when, years afterwards, the vice-regal Joseph led that grand funeral procession, composed of his brethren and the high dignitaries of Pharaoh, as they went up from Egypt to lay the body of Jacob in that same rural cemetery of Machpelah! The world has seen few sights as imposing as that.

But all along the course of human history, from age to age and from nation to nation, we find the cemeteries and monuments of the dead holding a conspicuous place, and cherished with the greatest respect. From the early days of Christianity the custom has prevailed of burying the dead in the immediate vicinity of churches. For a long time the "God's acre," as the English people call it (the plot around the church thickly studded with headstones), has been a familiar sight. Considered in a purely religious aspect, it was fitting that the bodies of Christian believers should be laid down in the immediate neighborhood of the church, the ever-present symbol of the believer's faith. The Christian idea of death is pre-eminently that of sleep—a sleep from which one is soon to awake to a higher realization than he ever had before of the glorious and eternal verities of his faith. It was fit that the body, whether to be literally raised or not, should pass its brief sleep close by the place where those verities had been so constantly proclaimed, and that burial-places should take the name of *cemeteries*, or sleeping-places. But in a sanitary point of view and æsthetically considered, the custom was objectionable, and on the former account interments within cities and within and around churches have come to be more and more forbidden by law, while good taste has chosen to make its burial-places where they can be rendered more pleasant in themselves than is possible within the limited space that can be given to them in the crowded area of the city or in the narrow bounds of the churchyard. Accordingly, there have sprung up in the vicinity of our cities and large towns, within the last thirty or forty years, many cemeteries or burial-places which have combined, with proper respect for the dead, a beauty and tastefulness in themselves which have given them a character of their own and made them objects of general attractiveness. They have served to remove some of the repulsive associations of death, to bring the living into pleasant communion with the departed, and to link the present life attractively to the life beyond. Vanity and pride will sometimes reveal themselves in the elaborate and overwrought monuments erected over the dead, as where will not vanity and pride lift up their foolish heads? But, on the whole, the tone of these cemeteries is subdued and at the same time tasteful, and the impressions which they tend to make upon those who visit them are of a healthful character. Mount Auburn, near Boston, and Greenwood, near New York, are types of what, with only minor differences in extent and style of development, may be found near a large number of our cities and most populous towns.

And the country villages are beginning to ask why they may not have something approximately like these, and some have answered the question in a very satisfactory way. The old square or rectangular plot of ground, chosen for convenience of access and the ease with which its friable soil could be excavated and laid out, garden-like, with its stiff, straight rows of human bodies, crowded together as though land in the country were too precious to be wasted even for affection's sake, is giving way to something better and altogether more pleasant. The level, rectangular, monotonous, and crowded burial-place is exchanged for one ampler in extent, and having varying contours of lines sweeping in different directions, and offering pleasing surfaces and attractive views to the eye continually.

There is often no better place to begin the work of improving the outward aspect of a country village than the cemetery. It has this advantage as a starting-point, that it is something in which all are interested. A good deal is thus gained at once for village improvement, by having something proposed or undertaken in which all can be enlisted. If you propose at first a road, or a park, or an aqueduct, you are apt to have a minority against you, because, perhaps, the road or the park is not to be in their immediate vicinity. But the cemetery is equally for all; and if any are not moved to activity in the work of improving an existing burying-place or providing a new one, you have, at least, their acquiescence. Opposition, if it comes at all, can only come as against methods and plans, not against the object itself. If the existing cemetery is in a neglected condition, a strong appeal can be made to all through their respect for departed friends. Perhaps there is only a rude wall around the enclosure, which in process of time has been thrown down in different places, so that the cattle have free access and pasture at will on the sacred graves of ancestors. Or the headstones have been tilted by the frost or have been broken down. Or the paths have become overgrown, and the whole place is the home of wild weeds. It will not be difficult, in such cases, to make an effective appeal which will enlist the entire community in the work of improvement. And then, having thus fortunately got the great mass moving together for one desirable object, it will be comparatively easy to enlist them in a combined movement for some other good end.

The very fact of their having acted together once

prepares them to act together again. They feel the pleasure which always comes from fellowship and co-operation. Having done one good thing, and being able to see what they have accomplished, they will even be eager to set about something else. Perhaps the desirableness of good roads and footpaths will be suggested, or the planting of trees along the village streets, or a park or fountain may be spoken of as calculated to improve the appearance of the village; and so one thing may easily and naturally lead on to another, till in the course of a few years the whole appearance of the place may be changed for the better. And then it will be found that not only has the outward aspect of the place where they live been improved, but, what is best of all, the villagers themselves have been greatly changed and improved by this coming together and working together for common and worthy purposes. What intermingling of thoughts and feelings has it produced! What a breaking-down of barriers of distance or of timidity has it occasioned! How this gentle attrition of society has rounded off the sharp edges of asperities, and smoothed away many an uncouthness! How this intermingling has removed shyness, and encouraged confidence, and promoted true knowledge of one another! And so there has been going on continually an improvement of society, which is the highest and most valuable sort of village improvement.

In regard to the subject of cemeteries much might be

said, but in a place like this only certain hints can be given. A difficulty in many of our country towns may arise from the fact that there are several places of burial, perhaps as many as half a dozen in some towns. This may have come from the fact that the people are settled somewhat in clusters instead of being distributed evenly throughout the town limits, or it may be the result of local and family feeling in the absence of any common feeling and interest. The consequence often is that none of these places of burial are properly cared for; and because the interest of the people in them is so divided, it is not easy to arouse the feeling needful to bring them all into fitting condition. It may be difficult to decide in such cases just what to do. It may be best to endeavor to concentrate interest upon a single one, protecting the others from utter neglect, but seeking to make the one as pleasant and attractive as possible. Or it may, perhaps, be best to abandon all and lay out a new one. In such a case the old ones should be suitably protected by fences or walls, and family affection may be relied on to some extent to see that no injuries or depredations are committed.

In laying out a new cemetery, care should be taken, not only to secure a pleasant site, but a sufficient extent of ground. Most of our rural cemeteries are mere garden-plots for size, and consequently cannot be made objects of beauty. If trees are planted, they soon overgrow the whole space, and make it gloomy and for-

bidding as well as very inconvenient. It is hardly possible to get any pleasant landscape effect on less than
ten acres of ground. This amount, therefore, should
be secured, and, if possible, where future enlargement
will be practicable. Of course, land having an undulat-
ing surface should be chosen. Then the paths and
burial-lots should be laid out somewhat in conformity
with the natural shape and sweep of the ground, and
by no means in straight lines. Human beings should
not be buried by square feet and inches. The separate
burial-plots should be of unequal size, adapted to the
uses of families unequal in numbers; but all should be
large enough to allow the planting of trees and shrubs
without having them seem crowded or becoming an interference with the pleasantness of the place. In short,
the cemetery should be laid out on such a broad scale
as to secure something of a park-like effect. If water
is at command, let it be made to play here and there in
fountains, with their pensive, soothing music. Let
bright, blossoming shrubs and plants enliven the dark
and sombre tone of the evergreens which are appropriately planted in such places. An evergreen hedge
may properly enclose the whole. And so, by all that
art and taste can do, let our burial-places be made
pleasant places of resort, moving to quiet meditation,
and at the same time to hopeful trust and heavenly as-
pirations.

A most valuable appendage of a rural cemetery, of
any cemetery, is a receiving-tomb or vault, where the

bodies of the dead may be temporarily deposited, when for any reason immediate burial is not desirable or not practicable. As they have commonly been conducted, funerals in the country have frequently been attended by great inconveniences and unnecessary exposures of health. Often the company gathered at the house where the funeral services are held is so large that the doors are obliged to be held open, and through them, if the weather is cold or stormy, come blasts of air which are the fruitful causes of colds, if not of more serious maladies. Then often follows another and even worse exposure at the grave, where sometimes there is a second service of a somewhat protracted character. How much better would it be if, except in pleasant weather, this second service were dispensed with, and the body were quietly taken by a few friends and deposited in a receiving-tomb, to be taken thence for final burial at a convenient and pleasant season. There is no sufficient call of duty which requires us, out of respect for departed friends, to expose life and health in a country cemetery in a northern winter. To do so is little less than an act of barbarism. We can show our respect for the dead and our sympathy with the living in other ways than by facing tempests in order to effect a hasty burial. And now that we have come to feel that our burial-places should be made tasteful in appearance, is it not time that our burial-services should lose some of their harsh and even harmful features, and be brought more into keeping with the cheerful, hopeful spirit of
10*

that Christianity which teaches us that death is only a
sleep preparatory to a glorious awakening and a never-
ending life to come ?

> "Secure from every mortal care,
>   By sin and sorrow vexed no more,
> Eternal happiness they share
>   Who are not lost, but gone before."

CHAPTER XX.

ROADS AND BRIDGES.

"The road is that physical sign, or symbol, by which you will best understand any age or people. If they have no roads, they are savages; for the road is the creation of man and a type of civilized society. . . .

"If you wish to know whether society is stagnant, learning scholastic, religion a dead formality, you may learn something by going into universities and libraries; something, also, by the work that is doing on cathedrals and churches, or in them; but quite as much by looking at the roads. For if there is any motion in society, the road, which is the symbol of motion, will indicate the fact. . . .

"Nothing makes an inroad without making a road. All creative action, whether in government, industry, thought, or religion, creates roads." —BUSHNELL.

"Every judicious improvement in the establishment of roads and bridges increases the value of land, enhances the price of commodities, and augments the public wealth."—DE WITT CLINTON.

THE legislatures of our states are not more certain to assemble at the designated time than they are to appoint among their standing committees one on "Roads and Bridges." This indicates the important place which these are recognized as having in our practical and social life. They are at the same time the signs and the instruments of our civilization. Without them we should be barbarians. There could be no advancement in the arts, no advancement in culture; and so

.

the quality of our roads indicates very well the progress
we have made in civilization, in culture, in refinement.

Roads and bridges—for the latter are strictly roads,
and best considered as such—are, in their essential character, means of communication between mankind, instruments by which man comes in contact with his fellow-man, and so produces, or enlarges and improves, society. In the rudest and most primitive stages of society, a simple footpath like the Indian trail is all, perhaps, that is necessary. But as intercourse increases the
desire of intercourse, and there arises a disposition or a
need for the exchange of commodities, the trail or the
bridle-path will gradually give place to something better; and so as the lines of intercommunication lengthen,
and the demands of trade and commerce increase, and
culture advances, the roadways will necessarily be improved. The wheels of transit, instead of being left to
roll over the ground at each one's convenience or inconvenience, will have a definite path provided for them by
a common agreement of those in the vicinage. Then
the larger public composing a state or municipality will
recognize the general interest of all in the roads; and,
as a consequence, laws will be enacted to regulate their
construction and use. This will result in securing a
certain uniformity and excellence in the roads. And
yet there will still be room left for each particular country or province to go beyond the mere requisitions of
the statute or of usage, and bring its roads up in quality to the demands of highest usefulness; as when some

Rome, in the glory of its universal power, and as a means of preserving that power, stretches out its highways of stone to Scotland on the north, and to Asia Minor and Spain on the east and west—roads that have outlasted the empire which constructed them, and are the wonder of our day, unexcelled, as they are, even by our boasted Telford or MacAdam roads.

That there is abundant room for the improvement of our village roads no one can doubt. Comparatively few of them meet the demands of the time. Most of them are even a shame to our civilization. The more pressing necessities of life in a new country, the sparseness of our population, the great spaces to be traversed, and the scanty capital available for the construction of good roads, have been an excuse for our past neglects in this direction. But the time has come when these excuses are no longer valid. Instead of being content with the poor roads to which we have been accustomed, it is time for us to make them what they ought to be. We cannot, indeed, expect the best macadamized roads to be constructed in our sparsely settled villages; but our main country thoroughfares certainly ought to be far better than they now are, and many of the minor roads might be greatly improved, and with manifest pecuniary advantage as well as with gain in other respects.

Frequently the location of our country roads is bad; and it would be the plainest economy to abandon many of them and construct others in their place, rather than continue to use them. Many of our roads have been

laid out carelessly, and almost by accident. Old foot or
bridle paths have often grown into carriage-roads. In
cases not a few, a road has been laid directly over a hill
or through a swamp, when it might as easily have been
made to pass around such an obstacle; or it has been
carried over a hill at a very steep incline, when, by a
little care, it might have surmounted it by a more easy
slope. The mechanical laws affecting transportation
were imperfectly understood until recently, except by
comparatively few. The effects of friction and gravity
upon the traction of loads, both on levels and inclines,
have been little taken into account in the construction
of our roads. Our railway building has taught us some
important lessons in regard to the grading and construction of common roads. We have learned, among other
things, that any but a very moderate grade obliges us
either to lighten our loads or to move them at the expense of a great strain upon our vehicles and the beasts
that draw them. Experiments of the most thorough
character, made in England and France, give us the
following conclusions on this subject. Calling the load
which a horse can draw on a level 100,

On a rise of 1 in 100 he can draw only 90 per cent.
"   1 " 50   "   81 "
"   1 " 44   "   75 "
"   1 " 40   "   72 "
"   1 " 30   "   64 "
"   1 " 26   "   54 "
"   1 " 24   "   50 "
"   1 " 20   "   40 "
"   1 " 10   "   25 "

On a slope of 120 feet to the mile, a horse can draw only three fourths as much as on a level. On a slope of 220 to the mile he can draw only one half what he can on a level; and on a slope of 528 feet to the mile, only one fourth as much. This latter slope is that of one foot in ten; and if we take a board, for instance, and set it at that angle to represent the incline of a road, it will seem a hill of easy ascent, whereas it is really quite steep. Many of our roads have a much sharper pitch than that. We are able to surmount them after a fashion, but it is at the expense of a great strain upon our animals and vehicles, and with much useless expenditure of power. For very short distances we can avail ourselves of what may be called the reserve force of our horses and other draught animals; and, by stimulating them to the utmost, we can draw considerable loads up quite steep ascents. But these must be very short, so that the team can soon reach a level and rest. And even on short ascents, how frequent is the sight of the poor animals straining themselves to the utmost, and then not being able to accomplish the work to which they have been put, but falling victims to the heavy load behind them, and dragged back by it, despite all the shouts and blows, perhaps, of a cruel driver who has no mercy upon his beasts. How frequent is the sight of loads stuck fast upon some ascent, the strength of the animals attached to them completely exhausted, and no possibility of moving the loads onward until additional men and animals are brought to the spot at considerable expense of time and money. How often do we see parts of loads lying by the roadside as proofs of the unavailing strength of teams to surmount the neighboring grade until a portion of their load has been thrown off! The strength of a chain is proverbially equal only to its weakest part. So the weak part of a road is a hill. If we have a road ten miles in length, and there is only one hill of any steepness in its course, we can draw over the level part of the road only such a weight as we can draw up the hill. The amount that can be drawn up the hill is the measure of available power for the entire road. Nine tenths of the road—ninety-nine hundredths of it, perhaps—may be level and smooth almost as a railway, so that one horse might draw ten tons upon it; but a steep incline upon the remaining one hundredth part of it may practically limit the loads to be drawn over the road to a weight little more than that of the vehicles themselves. There has been—there is—a great overlooking of this stern fact. There is an enormous waste of time and strength, and of vehicles, in our country for want of a proper construction of roads as to grades as well as in other respects. In many cases, a road which goes over a hill might have gone around it without being any longer. And even if a road around a hill were necessarily longer than one going over it, it has been proved by the most careful investigations that a road may profitably avoid an ascent, even when it has to go twenty times the height of the ascent in order to get around it. Let it only be remembered that where there is a grade of one foot in twenty extending for any considerable distance, it requires two horses to draw the load which one could draw upon a level road; and that it practically doubles the number of horses or cattle needed to do the work of the region where that ascent has to be frequently passed, and we may, perhaps, get some impression of the loss incident to the improper grading of many of our roads. It is a most silly and short-sighted feeling, also, which will sacrifice the grade of a road to its straightness, as is sometimes done, as though straightness were the highest excellence of a road. The grade is the first thing to be considered. The weight of load to be carried over a road, and the speed with which it can be carried, both depend upon this more than upon anything else; though, of course, other things being equal, straightness or directness is desirable. Says Professor Gillespie, in his admirable treatise upon roads—a work which ought to belong to every town library, not to say to every road-maker—"Roads should be so located and constructed as to enable burdens of goods and of passengers to be transported from one place to another in the least possible time, with the least possible labor, and consequently with the least possible expense." This should be taken as an axiom on the subject. Only a little calculation, also, would show that it is the truest economy to make large expenditures, if necessary, in order to secure for our roads as little deviation from a level direction as is consistent with the proper drainage of water from them. For this purpose English engineers allow a slope of one foot in eighty, and the French that of one in one hundred and twenty-five, or forty-two feet to the mile.

Grade being properly regarded, the next thing to be considered is the material of which the road is constructed. And here again we are often greatly at fault. On a well-made road of broken stone, smooth and hard, a horse can draw three times as much as on a road made of gravel, and ten times as much as upon many of our roads. As a matter of economy, therefore, we ought to aim to secure roads as nearly as possible of this quality. Two thirds of the expense of transportation may often in this way be saved, to say nothing of the increased pleasure of travelling where roads are of this character. Yet what roads do we content ourselves with? Rather, what roads do we tolerate? Often they are little more than pathways over fields or through sand, or they are rough and uneven, abounding in loose stones and deep holes and ruts, covering the traveller now with dust and now with mud—according as the weather is dry or wet —and threatening him and his vehicle not unfrequently with wreck. If there is any attempt at what might be called making a road, it is usually thought sufficient to scrape up the surface soil, be it sand or loam or clay, with whatever stones may accompany such materials; and, having rounded it up a little in the middle, leave it to the wear and tear of vehicles until it becomes so bad that it can be endured no longer, when the selectmen or sundry other citizens proceed to "mend the road," as it is termed, which means that they scrape back into the centre of the road the material which the passing vehicles, aided by the rains, have pushed off upon the sides, and finish up the business by taking a quantity of soil from near the adjacent fences and applying it as a sort of top-dressing. The result is, for a time, a worse road than before, and then a gradual decline from a passable condition to one that is unsafe and intolerable, when the "mending" process is renewed.

One of the most important requisites for a good road is, that it shall be kept dry; that no water shall flow upon it from the bordering lands, and that the rain which falls upon it shall quickly pass off. For this purpose, it is very important that the road should be higher than the adjacent land through which it passes, and that there should be ditches on either side of it of sufficient depth to carry away all water that might penetrate the road from springs beneath it, or which might fall upon it, as rain or snow, from above. These side-ditches should also have such a slope as to carry off at once the water that flows into them. No standing water should be allowed by a roadside.

Proper drainage having been secured, the endeavor should be made to construct as smooth and hard a road as possible; for this economizes labor in the transportation of goods or passengers, and at the same time makes travel pleasant. Such a road is also kept in repair at less cost than a poorer road. The best material with which to construct roads is broken stone. What is known as trap-rock is the best, being at the same time the hardest and toughest of our rocks, and breaking into angular fragments, which pack well together. When this stone is not to be had, a softer may be used; and we are persuaded that it would be the truest economy for our villages to make their main roads of stone, even when it has to be drawn a considerable distance. The expense at first might seem large, but roads once made in this way would be durable and require but little outlay to keep them in repair. The construction of such roads might also be made so gradual that the expense would not be burdensome. Let a village begin with a small section of road—that most travelled, for instance—and make that of proper material and in the best manner first; then let another section be taken in hand the next year, and so on. The villagers would be surprised to find how soon all their principal roads had been made good roads, and at what an increase of pleasure and comfort to themselves. In many parts of our country, stone is so abundant that enough might be taken from the surface of the adjacent fields to make a good hard road, while at the same time benefiting the fields for tillage purposes.

Where stone does not abound or is too expensive to be used, gravel is the next best thing to be sought; and where this is not to be had, of course common earth must be used. In the latter case the coarsest and hardest that can be obtained should be chosen. The subsoil is better than that of the surface. Turf is bad for road-making, and should be avoided; it is better for the compost-heap. In these days, when anthracite coal is so largely consumed in the country, the ashes may be used with advantage on the roads. They are, perhaps, as good as gravel. At any rate, and by whatever means are necessary, let the best attainable materials be used for the construction of the roads. There is little danger that any expenditure in this direction, however great, will be regretted. The economic advantage of a well-built road is illustrated by the fact, stated on good authority, that for want of properly constructed roads the Spanish Government, on one occasion, was obliged to use 30,000 mules and horses for the purpose of transporting about 500 tons of grain from Castile to Madrid, when with good roads the work might have been done by 300 horses.

We have spoken of the two most important requisites of a good road—a proper grade and proper materials for its construction. Some other things, however, are to be taken into consideration as having an important bearing upon the subject. Among these may be mentioned the width of the road and the form given to its surface. We should have better roads, in many cases, if we did not undertake to make them so wide as we often do. It is better—cheaper—to make a good road of fifteen or eighteen feet in width than to make an inferior road thirty or forty feet broad. Wide roads waste land which might be used more profitably for other purposes, and the cost of their construction and repair is greater than in the case of narrower ones. If the road is well made—that is, so as to have a smooth, hard surface—there will be no need of rounding it up, as is so often done. The surface may be nearly level. A slope of three or four inches each way from the centre, in a road twenty feet wide, is ample for the purpose of carrying off the water; and only what is sufficient for that purpose should be allowed. On such a road, vehicles would pass over all parts of it with equal ease and with equal comfort to travellers, instead of being confined to the centre, as they now are, so far as possible, because the excessive slope commonly given to the roads makes it unpleasant to ride upon the sides, the wheels on one side of the carriage being necessarily so much lower than on the other. Roads used thus equally, or almost equally, upon all parts of their surface will be less likely to be worn into ruts and holes, to the discomfort of the traveller and the strain of vehicles, than roads as ordinarily made. The very fact that the centre of our roads is commonly the only portion that approaches a level, and the disposition to drive on that portion in order to keep the vehicles upright, leads to an excessive trampling of the road in that part, which soon wears it down so as to make it lower than the portion upon either side of it, and gives occasion to standing water, which tends to put the road out of good condition for travel sooner than anything else. The wheels of the carriages, for the same reason, being rolled mainly on the same line, tend to wear the road into ruts, in which, at every fall of rain, the water collects and flows along in streams that soon get volume enough to tear the road and break up its smoothness. If a road is only well made as to material and shape, and properly drained, there will be hardly any need of water-bars, as any rain falling upon the road will run off at once into the side-ditches without wearing or injuring the road-bed. Water-bars are often made so large and high that they are a serious inconvenience. They are little else than hills piled upon hills, increasing the amount of ascent to be made, while, by the sudden checks and jolts which they create, they often result in the breaking of harnesses and vehicles and the serious injury of persons. If water-bars are to be made at all, they should be made as slight as possible, and of stone rather than earth.

The following cut shows a section of road as often made, rounded up so much that travel is unsafe upon

the sides, while the centre soon gets worn lower than the parts adjacent, and consequently becomes a depository for water, to the speedy and permanent injury of the road. The cut on the following page shows a cross-section of a road as it should be. It consists of two inclined planes with a slope of seven and a half inches from the centre of the road to the ditch on either side. On a road of

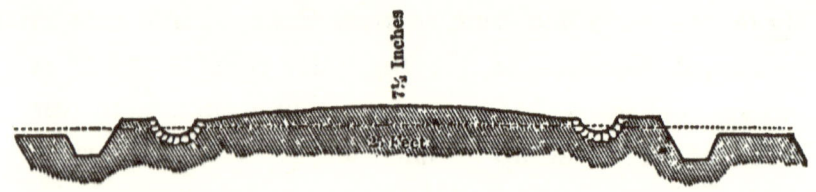

good material this slope is ample for the carrying-off of water, and renders driving easy and pleasant on all portions of the road.

But a good road-bed is not all that we want; for mere transportation this is enough—certainly it is the prime requisite. But in so far as roads are the means of facilitating the intercourse of human beings with each other, they ought to be pleasant in every way, and even minister to our sense of the beautiful. If I am going to see a brother man, or only going on some errand of business, let me go in as pleasant a way as practicable. Let my road take me through agreeable scenes if it may. Let it be sheltered, if possible, from the scorching heats of July and the sweeping blasts of December.

On the island of Jersey, off the coast of France, the roads are bordered with trees, so that the traveller passes under an almost continuous arch of cool and living green; while all along the border upon which the trees are planted—which is a mound formed by casting up the earth from the ditch on either side of the roadway— the loveliest ivies and other vines constantly greet the eye. Managed in this way, the roads on that island constitute one of the chief charms of a charming piece

of country. Why should not our roads be made pleasant in some such way oftener than they are, instead of
being so frequently mere strips of mud or sand through
which we flounder in summer heat, and where we are
smitten and swept by the winter cold, dreading the
passage over them, and undertaking it only as a necessity? In the island of Jersey the land is so limited in
extent and so valuable for cultivation that most of the
roads are only wide enough to accommodate a single
vehicle, with occasional wider places or turnouts where
carriages may pass each other. But with the broad
roads which we often have in this country, especially
in many of our New England towns, it is an easy thing
not only to have pleasant highways for travel, but to
make the roads at the same time most effective village
embellishments. All that is necessary is to construct,
in place of the driveway which ordinarily meanders
along such streets, without much regard either to convenience or beauty, a narrow but sufficient roadway
upon each side of the street, and rather near to the
houses, for the purpose of giving easy access to them,
together with diagonal roads now and then crossing
from side to side, so that there may be ample facility
of intercourse between neighbors living upon opposite
sides of the street. Then let the intervening space be
made into a lawn-like surface, with trees and shrubs ju-
diciously planted, and a fountain here and there throwing up its silvery jets. How easy it would be for those
living along such a street, by their combined efforts, to

11

convert it thus into a beautiful park which would be a daily delight to them and the admiration of the passing traveller! How many of our old roads, which are now little more than dreary expanses of weeds and wild grasses, might thus be made objects of beauty and the means of a most desirable social culture! Any one who has traversed the wide village streets which stretch along the valley of the Connecticut; who has visited old Hadley, Deerfield, Longmeadow, Enfield, and Windsor, to say nothing of other places in various parts of the country, will at once perceive what an additional charm might easily be given to many of our finest villages in the manner which we have suggested.

An instance of what can be done in this way may be seen at Williamstown, Mass. The principal street of this fine old village is a mile or more in length, and nearly three hundred feet broad. The road, in its course, meets three considerable hills not far apart, which give it a pleasant variety and even picturesqueness of appearance. The natural beauty of the street and of the village has long impressed those of appreciative taste. Several years ago, the late Professor Albert Hopkins, who was such a lover of nature, was prominent in an endeavor to bring the street and the grounds of the adjacent proprietors into a symmetrical and harmonious arrangement, and to secure a tasteful disposal of the whole. The wide street was made yet wider, in portions of it at least, by the removal of the fences in front of the college and its vicinity, and the college grounds themselves, embracing the two central elevations over which the road passes, were taken in hand and brought into proper shape and made very attractive. The various college societies, which own some of the finest buildings in the village, have also been prompt to bring their premises into a neat and tasteful condition.

Thus gradually has the village been gaining in appearance for several years. But within a short time a decided impulse has been given to the work of improvement here by Mr. Cyrus W. Field, who—with a noble generosity all the more noteworthy because he has no personal relationship with the place—has already expended more than five thousand dollars, a portion of it in the embellishment of the college buildings and grounds, but a larger share of it in converting into a lovely park that part of the street which formerly constituted the church green. This work is now so far completed as to show what the effect is to be, and to commend the enterprise of Mr. Field as an example to others who have the needful wealth for such undertakings. When the contemplated plans of improvement are carried out to their completion, Williamstown will sit more than ever as a queen of beauty among her surrounding hills, and, with her noble college, will become more attractive than ever for her unsurpassed beauty and her cultured society.

And now, in the interest of humanity, before dismissing the consideration of the subject before us, let us

suggest that our various town authorities ought to be
somewhat more mindful than they sometimes are that
their roads are occasionally traversed by persons from
a distance, who may be at a loss to know how directly
any particular road may be conducting them towards
their destination, or how far they may be from it at
any particular time. For the benefit of such, as well
as for the comfort of the horses which may be thirsty
by the way, there should be consideration enough to
see that guide-boards are maintained at the junctions
of all roads with others, together with mile-stones, or
some other means of designating distances; and then,
at suitable intervals, where some spring gushes from
the hill-side, or where water may be conveniently obtained, let there be drinking-troughs. A mossy old
log hollowed out, or a simple tub, is all that is needed, and is more inviting in the country even to a
horse, we must think, than any fanciful cast-iron affairs—dolphins or swans—such as we sometimes see.

Then, finally, let them sternly abate those nuisances
in the form of advertisements of patent medicines, dry-
goods, and groceries, and things innumerable which now
so often bedaub and disfigure the rocks and fences by
the roadside, as well as our bridges and many a lovely
and picturesque spot, shocking good taste by their staring effrontery, and even endangering life by affrighting
the horses which draw us on our errands of business or
pleasure.

But while considering the importance of good roads, we ought not to confine our attention to those which are designed for the use of vehicles; nor ought we to provide a better pathway for our cattle and horses than for ourselves. Yet this we often do. We pretend, at least, to make proper roads for the transportation of our property, and we make them with some reference, certainly, to the safety and comfort of the animals which are expected to traverse them. But how rarely in our villages is there any adequate provision for the convenient intercourse of those who have occasion to pass from one place to another on foot! One has commonly to choose between the dusty or muddy highway made for the cattle and the grass and stones and bushes which border it. Even in many of our closely settled villages, how difficult it is often for one to get to the nearest neighbor's house for a friendly call! If there has been a rain recently, the chance is that one cannot cross the street comfortably on account of the mud; and even in pleasant weather the grass, heavy with dew, practically forbids all going out until late in the morning, when the sun has dried up the excessive moisture. The result is, that our country people hardly know the pleasure, the luxury even, of a good daily walk. They really do not know how to walk. · If a call of business or pleasure is to be made at the distance of half a mile, instead of starting off vigorously on foot, the boy jumps upon his

horse's back and the girl asks her brother to get the
wagon ready for her.   Pedestrianism is a lost art in the
country.   The people, if they walk at all, go shambling
along like their cattle.   A country boy's walk is laugh-
able, and a country girl's is little better.   They may
sneer at city counter-jumpers and the like, but there are
thousands of men and women, merchants, clerks, and
Fifth-avenue ladies who daily take walks, and find
pleasure in them, which would utterly fatigue what are
deemed our hearty and robust country girls and women.
This comes in good part because in the city there are
smooth pavements on which to walk, while in the country there are hardly any paths over which the pedestri-
an can go at all times with comfort.   The lack of proper
footways in the country is one of the greatest hindrances
to that social intercourse which is so desirable and so
much needed to make village life more attractive and
satisfying.   There are few things which would do more
for the social life and true enjoyment of a village than
the making of good footpaths.   Until we can have these
we would encourage our country girls and women to
do as did the late Miss Catharine M. Sedgwick.   We
remember seeing her morning after morning, when she
was nearly, if not quite, seventy years of age, and at an
hour earlier than that at which most people take their
breakfast, the skirts of her dress shortened so as to
avoid the wet grass, and with stout shoes, starting off
for a walk with a vigor and a rapidity of pace that put
to shame the whole village in which she was for the

time a resident. How much this habit of taking daily exercise on foot had to do with the prolongation of her life, and how much her outdoor rambles had to do with the healthful tone which pervades all her numerous writings, we are not prepared to say. But we are confident that such a habit in our mothers and daughters, and in all our people, would be healthful in the extreme both to body and mind, and add greatly to the enjoyment of life.

STREET LIGHTS.

If roads and footpaths are desirable as facilitating intercourse between people, and so becoming the signs and instruments of civilization and social advancement, then it would seem that their usefulness requires that they should be so lighted during the customary hours of use that those passing over them, or desiring to do so, can find their way without difficulty. And at hardly any time do we more need the use of our roads, especially in the more densely populated villages, than in the evening. It is after the day's work is over that we have most leisure as well as the strongest desire for the interchange of social intercourse. It is then especially that we like to cross a neighbor's threshold and feel that we have common interests and concerns. There should be no unnecessary impediments to such intercourse. The darkness should not hinder this commingling of those who dwell in the same vicinity. In these days of cheap illuminators, the cost of a dozen kerosene

or naphtha lamps, properly screened from the wind by
lanterns, ought not to be felt as a burdensome tax upon
any village. Once adopted, such an aid to social intercourse and general well-being will soon be deemed something indispensable. It is one of the signs of progress
that so many of our villages are turning their attention
to this subject.

BRIDGES.

After what we have said of roads, little needs to be
added in regard to bridges. Designed for the purpose
of conveying persons and goods across streams—roadways over the water—the first requisite in their construction is strength; but attention has been limited too
exclusively to this. The result is that we have a great
many structures spanning our larger and smaller streams
that are not only unsightly in themselves, but which
mar the beauty of the landscape of which they often
form a prominent feature. · Why should not objects so
conspicuous as bridges almost always are be made pleasant features of our towns and villages instead of being
repulsive? Our utilitarianism has left in neglect what
might be an important source of beauty and pleasure in
our village life. If, instead of those huge wooden tun-
nels, often of a glaring red color, which so frequently
thrust their great bulk across our water-courses—their
stiff, level lines quite out of harmony with the curves of
the stream and of the land on either side—we could see
a graceful arch of stone, how much pleasanter would be
the sight! An addition of positive beauty would be

made to the landscape.	At the same time, such a struct-
ure would be more durable, and in the long run cheap-
er, than any other.	Or if we do not choose to build of
stone, we can have bridges of iron or wood which will
be objects of real beauty, while serving the purposes of
utility.	With hardly any additional cost, bridges may
be so made as to elicit the admiration of every one who
crosses them or beholds them from a distance.	Such
structures so placed, as they almost necessarily are, are
peculiarly adapted to become ornamental features of
the scenery of which they form a part.	One cannot
visit Europe without being made to feel that a bridge
is something more than a mere convenience for getting
across a stream.	There we find them classing among
the most beautiful works of architecture, the stone
moulded into gracefully curving lines which harmo-
nize with the curving lines of the rivers and their
banks.	Very likely they will be adorned with the
mosses of age, or decorated with mantling vines that
run luxuriantly over arch and wall, and link bridge and
water together.	Our youthfulness as a nation and our
limited resources have hitherto been our excuse for
great deficiency in matters of an æsthetic character.
But we are old enough now, and rich enough, to have
some appropriate fruits of age and ample wealth.	Our
bridges, among other things, ought to show this.	And
our smaller streams, not less than the larger, should be
spanned by structures of a tasteful character.	Even
the little runlets that cross our country roads so often,
11*

and over which we frequently throw such tasteless and
crazy structures—two roughly hewn logs perhaps, with
a few warped and rattling loose planks laid across them
—how easy it would be to make the numerous crossings
of them the occasions of positive pleasure by means of
graceful bridges, the cost of which would not be felt!
In many places a charming effect might be gained by
the construction of rustic bridges, which would be so
completely in harmony with all the scene around, as
especially in some wooded or rocky region, a little re-
mote, perhaps, from the more populous portions of the
town or village.   Any ordinary carpenter, almost any
one who has a little tasteful feeling, can build such a
bridge.   It is only necessary to take two or three logs,
not hewn or shaped by axe or saw, but with the bark
left upon them, for the supports of the bridge floor;
then let some of the larger branches of the trees which
have been cut, their bark also left upon them, be tak-
en and pinned together to form the necessary rails or
guards for the sides.   Smaller branches still may be
inwoven with these at pleasure, to give some effect
of ornament, and the work is done; and you have a
structure all-sufficient for the purposes of travel, while
it is in accord with the scenery around; and instead
of hiding the stream from the passer-by, as so many of
our bridges do, this invites him to pause and contem-
plate the beauty of the water and of the fields and
woods, which get an additional loveliness as they are
bathed by it or reflected in its liquid mirror.

CHAPTER XXI.

PRESERVATION OF WOODLANDS.

"A man was famous according as he had lifted up axes upon the thick trees."—Psa. lxxiv. 5.

"The destruction of the woods, then, was man's first geographical conquest, his first violation of the harmonies of inanimate nature."—G. P. MARSH: *Man and Nature.*

WHEN the settlement of our country by the whites began, it was so heavily timbered that in many places the first problem was, how to get rid of the trees, so as to have sufficient open space for the tillage needful for the support of the settler and his family. The forests were in the way. They were regarded as a nuisance almost, rather than anything of value. In their haste to clear up the soil, the settlers could not cut away the trees fast enough. So they girdled and left to fall by slow decay what they could not destroy with the axe and consume at once.

As the settlement of the country has advanced and various industries have arisen, as towns and cities have come into being, as manufactures have increased, there have come new demands upon our forests, and these demands have been supplied not only with readiness, but with recklessness, until there has come to be well-founded alarm lest our timber supply shall fail us. Our finest timber has been cut and consumed for fuel wherever a price has been offered for it that would leave any present profit after deducting the expense of chopping and carrying to market. It has been estimated that a single iron furnace in blast will consume from year to year all the wood that can be properly spared from a region extending three miles from it in every direction. In other words, it would require nearly an ordinary township of land, or a tract six miles square, to keep a furnace supplied with fuel. Our railroads also are enormous consumers of forests, both for the construction of their road-beds, for fences, and for fuel. They consume them for the latter purpose until scarcity carries up the price so far as to lead to the partial or complete use of coal. The fencing of our railroads alone requires lumber to the value of $6,000,000. Our 110,076 miles of telegraph lines have consumed 4,000,000 trees, and require 500,000 for their annual repair and increase. It was estimated several years ago that the railroads of Ohio consumed 700,000 cords of wood annually for fuel. These roads required also more than 10,000,000 ties for their construction, and these would need to be renewed, on the average, every six years. There were in the same state, at that time, sixteen miles of wooden railroad bridges and ten miles of trestle-work, the timber of which would have to be renewed almost as often as the railroad ties.

What is true of Ohio is true also of many other

states, some of which, on account of having a smaller
proportional area covered with forest, are less able to
meet the demands made upon them. Then one has
only to look at the lumber trade of our country to be
astonished at the havoc we are making with our trees.
For instance, a gentleman writing from Wisconsin says
that there were 10,000,000 acres of land in Wisconsin
and Michigan, north of the 44th degree of latitude,
which were originally covered with valuable timber.
Since the settlements have commenced in that part of
the country, at least half of this has been cut off and sold,
and 1,000,000 acres of hard-wood timber have also been
felled and burned upon the ground by the farmers while
clearing up their lands. All along the rivers flowing
out from this region, lumber-mills have been erected,
many of which are of such capacity that they are able
each to cut annually 100,000,000 feet of lumber. Not
less than 1,750,000,000 feet of lumber were taken from
this vicinity in a single year some time ago. The average yield of pine timber in this locality is estimated at
300,000 feet for forty acres. Reckoning it at 333,000
feet, it would require more than 200,000 acres annually
to furnish the lumber product of this district. Then,
if we add 100,000 acres for railroad ties, telegraph posts,
hewn timber, shingles, and firewood, as determined by
the known amount received from this district in the
Chicago market, and 30,000 acres for the amount cut
and burned on the ground in the process of clearing the
land, we have 330,000 acres stripped every year of their

growth of wood, or more than 1000 acres for every working-day of the year.

It may give some a more definite impression of the rapidity with which the consumption of our forests is going on when we say that the clearing of the above-mentioned number of acres is equal to the cutting of the timber on nearly 500 square miles, or more than one third the area of the State of Rhode Island.

It is difficult to make an accurate estimate of the amount of lumber produced in our entire country, or the total consequent consumption of our forests, because there is no report of the trees cut by farmers and others in a small way, and worked up in the lesser saw-mills which are to be found all over the country and upon all our smaller streams. We have reports only from the great mills in the so-called lumber regions of the country, and from certain chief centres of the lumber trade, such as Chicago and St. Louis in the West, and Albany, Boston, Saco, etc., in the East; and even in these places the statistics are incomplete. From such reports as we have, however, it appears that the work of felling our forest trees, and converting them into lumber for various uses, is one of the principal occupations of our people. Taking the great lumber region of the Northwest, we find the product for the year 1882 as follows:

Lumber......................	7,552,151,916 feet.
Shingles, etc., equal to..........	1,000,000,000 "
Total...................	8,552,151,916 "

To these figures may be added for other parts of the country—

Pennsylvania	1,773,844,000	feet.
New York	1,184,220,000	"
Maine	566,656,000	"
Georgia	451,788,000	"
Florida	247,627,000	"
Alabama	251,851,000	"

The total is thus carried up to 12,988,137,916 feet. These estimates, moreover, are for pine lumber alone, and leave out the hard-wood of various kinds, which is used so largely in the manufacture of tools and implements of many sorts, furniture, and various other articles of use and comfort.*

If now we add the product of the Pacific coast, from which there is an estimated annual export of more than 400,000,000 feet, we shall see that we have an annual product of lumber, mainly pine, exceeding 13,000,000,000 feet. It is reasonable to think that if we could have an account of the lumber made at the small mills all over the country, and the timber used for railroad building,

---

* There are in our country seventy or more occupations which use wood, in whole or in part, for their raw material, employing 1,000,000 hands. There are nearly 70,000 establishments manufacturing articles made entirely of wood, employing 393,387 persons, and using material worth $300,000,000 annually.

Even so seemingly insignificant a manufacture as that of friction matches involves, according to Mr. George P. Marsh, the use of not less than 230,000 feet of the best pine lumber, or the product of between 60 and 70 acres; while the production of shoe-pegs in our country consumes 1,000,000 dollars' worth of white birch.

for bridges, and fences, and for the thousand purposes of the arts, the figures would be at least double those which we have reached.

It has been estimated that as long ago as the year 1869 the consumption of wood for fuel by the railroads necessitated the cutting-off of 350,000 acres of woodland every year. In 1874 there were 72,623 miles of railroad in operation. The addition of double tracks and sidings will probably increase the mileage to 85,000. Supposing the life of a railroad tie to be seven years, 34,000,000 ties would be required annually, or what could be cut from 68,000 acres of woodland.

Some of these figures are so large that we cannot comprehend them as they stand. Let us try to bring them within our grasp. If we take the lumbermen's estimate that forty acres will ordinarily yield 333,000 feet of lumber, then it appears that in order to furnish the amount reported by the census of 1880, not fewer than 21,781,334 acres of woodland had to be swept clean by the axe, or an area nearly double that of the states of New Hampshire and Vermont. By another estimate this amount would load 90,000 vessels, each carrying 200,000 feet, the average cargo carried by the vessels employed in the lumber trade of our Great Lakes, or it would fill 2,584,479 railway cars with 7000 feet each, the ordinary car-load. This would make a train of cars 15,380 miles long, or two thirds the distance around the globe.

But great as is the consumption of our forests by the

axe of the lumberman, it is estimated by the most competent judges that as large an area of our woodlands is
annually consumed by forest fires. It was ascertained,
for instance, that in the census year 1880 not fewer
than 20,000 acres of forest were destroyed by fire in
the State of Massachusetts alone. All such destruction
is an utter and most deplorable waste without any in-
cidental compensation.

But we are beginning to discover that the destruction
of our woodlands means also something besides the ex-
haustion of a valuable article of commerce and of use
in the arts. It means a change in climate and in the
productiveness of the soil. It means a change in the
water supply of great regions, and consequently affects
health as well as the prosecution of many industries
which are dependent upon the water-power of streams.
The healthfulness of a region is dependent in no small
degree upon its being well wooded. Trees are large
absorbers of carbonic acid, a poison to human beings;
while they give off from their leaves large quantities of
oxygen, the life-sustaining element of the atmosphere.
They are also great equalizers of temperature and moisture. The presence of trees, therefore, especially in the
vicinity of populous towns and villages, is one of our
best assurances of a healthful atmosphere. If it were
not for the winds, which waft the better air of the
wooded regions to the cities and to those districts which
are comparatively destitute of forests, they would be
far less healthy than they now are.

Trees have another important office—that of shielding from sweeping winds, which, by their force, their piercing cold, or for any other reason, might be harmful to us or the crops we seek to produce on our lands. Even a single row of evergreens planted on the exposed sides of a house is sufficient to make a perceptible change in respect to the comfort of living. A belt of such trees consisting of only a few rows is equivalent in effect to a change of several degrees of latitude, and will enable one to grow many kinds of fruits and vegetables which could not otherwise be successfully cultivated. The same effect is produced by the vicinity of a piece of woodland covered with deciduous trees; for though these have not the dense foliage of the evergreens, and lose their leaves altogether during the colder seasons of the year, yet every one who is at home in the country knows that the most violent winds penetrate but a little way into the forests, even when stripped of their foliage, and that the woodchoppers are able to carry on their work in the coldest weather of winter with comparative comfort, because the interior of the woodland is still. It is the effect of air in motion, rather than its absolute temperature, which we most feel, and which is most felt by vegetable as well as animal organisms. Air itself is a poor—that is, slow—conductor of heat and cold. This is shown by the familiar effect of double windows on our houses. The confined stratum of air, enclosed by the windows, interposes an effectual barrier between the cold atmosphere without and the warm within, so that the one is but little affected by the other. But air in motion, and in proportion to the rapidity of its motion, imparts its own heat to bodies colder than itself, or absorbs the heat of those that are warmer. Hence we can bear, in a still day, the exposure to an atmosphere below zero in its temperature without much inconvenience, whereas we should shrink from a temperature twenty degrees higher if the air were in rapid motion. It is not so much the still cold nor the calm heat that produces discomfort, as it is the sweeping blast, whether of winter or summer. Locomotive engineers observe that in cold, windy weather they can keep up the steam in their engines more easily when passing through the shelter of woodlands than when in the open country; and on the prairies of the West it is sometimes a matter of great difficulty to maintain a good head of steam when encountering the violent winds of that region.

A committee of the French Government, of which the distinguished Arago was a member, in a report made in the year 1836, said that the cutting of a belt of forest on the coast of Normandy and Brittany would improve the climate of the interior by admitting the warm ocean winds, while the cutting of a similar belt on the German side would admit the glacial winds from the Alps and make the winters more severe. The clearing of the Apennines is thought to have materially changed the climate of the valley of the Po. The sirocco, formerly unknown, now prevails on the right bank of that stream.

The latest researches of naturalists seem to show also that, as in the animal system, so likewise in the vegetable, the vital processes are attended with the production of heat. Living trees have a temperature of 54° to 56° when the air near them is from 37° to 47°. Nor does the temperature of the trees vary in the same measure as that of the air. So long as the atmosphere is below 67°, the tree is always highest in temperature; when above this, the tree is lowest. Boussingault has also noticed the evolution of heat in flowers at particular times. It is likewise common in the winter to see ice which has formed around trees, melted for a certain distance on every side, so as to leave a clear space, or a space filled more or less with water, which can be accounted for only as the effect of the vital heat of the trees; and Mr. George P. Marsh, one of our most intelligent and careful observers in connection with this whole subject, suggests as a reason why the evergreens resist the cold better than deciduous trees the fact that they have a more persistent vitality, as shown by the retention of their leaves throughout the year.

By the mechanical obstruction, therefore, which trees in masses make to the sweep of injurious or uncomfortable winds, as well as by the vital heat which they emit, they tend to modify and equalize the temperature of the region where they are, and thereby to improve it for the uses of man.

But they exert also a positively healthful influence in another way. There is good reason to believe that trees not only contribute to the purification of the atmosphere, by absorbing, as they do, carbonic acid and exhaling oxygen, but that they deprive miasmatic air passing through them of its pestilential germs, and so render it healthful. Whether this effect is merely mechanical or is also chemical is not ascertained; but the fact is now very generally admitted. Even small screens of trees have often proved effective in this respect. In Italy poplar-trees have been planted in districts affected by malaria as a remedy, and narrow belts consisting of only three or four rows of trees have been thought to intercept a large portion of the malarious influences. Even rows of sunflowers have seemed to be very efficient to the same end. We are disposed to regard swamps as unfavorable to health. But the great swamps of Virginia and the Carolinas are proved to be healthy even to the whites, until the woods in and about them are cut away; and there have been cases where swamps from which the trees have been removed have become unfavorable to health, but which have become healthful again when the trees have been allowed to grow up once more.

It is well ascertained, also, that the presence or absence of trees in any region has an important connection with the rainfall of that region, thus modifying its climate as well as its agricultural capacity. A treeless country is a dry and comparatively barren country. We may not be able to say exactly why it should be so. How far it is to be attributed to electrical and how far to other causes we may not be able to determine. But the fact is indisputable. We have the observations of Humboldt, Herschel, Boussingault, and others, all attesting this. On an elevated plain near the city of Caraccas, South America, for instance, the chocolate plant flourished. In the endeavor to extend the profitable culture of this plant, the whole plain was stripped of the forests which abounded upon it. The result was that rains almost ceased to fall upon the plain, and the cultivation of the plant had to be abandoned. Since then the trees have been allowed to grow again, and the cultivation of chocolate has been successfully resumed. The island of St. Helena at one time had become almost barren, as the result of the removal of its forests. Latterly the trees have been restored, and the rainfall has nearly doubled and the productiveness of the island increased. Fifty years ago Mehemet Ali planted from forty to fifty millions of trees in Egypt, for the purpose of increasing the rain in that country, where sometimes none would fall for a twelvemonth. Now the annual average of rain there is thirty days.

The common opinion that the presence of trees in large masses increases the fall of rain seems to be substantiated by a large number of facts. But if the total amount of rain from year to year is not increased by trees, they very certainly promote a more uniform degree of moisture than prevails in the open areas, and cause the showers to fall more frequently, if not more copiously.

The presence of trees in large masses has a still more manifest connection with the subsequent distribution of the rains, and their ultimate and economical uses. When the forests are allowed to remain upon the slopes and hill-sides, the foliage, as it drops and decays from year to year, forms a porous, spongy soil, which is at the same time held in place by the roots of the trees. This soil absorbs the rain as it falls and retains it, so that it does not run off at once and in torrents, but oozes gradually away, moistening the fields and feeding the brooks and streams with a steady supply throughout the year. On the contrary, when the woods are cut off, the spongy soil soon becomes dry from exposure to the sun and wind; and when the tree-roots have decayed, there is nothing to hold it longer in place. The result is that the soil itself is soon washed from the hill-sides, to a considerable extent, making them barren; and the rains, having nothing to absorb them as formerly, go rushing down at once in torrents into the meadows and lowlands, covering them often with sand and débris, and producing also destructive inundations, attended not unfrequently with great loss of life. For the same reason, the water being no longer held by the spongy soil and distributed gradually, but flowing off at once, in the intervals between the rains the streams become low. So there is an alternation of floods and droughts in place of the steady flow which the forests formerly insured. Of course, the streams thus variable become less valuable for manufacturing and com-

mercial purposes. As a consequence, mill-owners are
obliged to place in their factories auxiliary steam-engines, to give them sufficient power in the seasons of
scarcity, or to construct artificial reservoirs, at great expense, in which to store up the superfluous water of one
season for the needs of another.

For the same reason, our streams are less valuable for
purposes of navigation than formerly. Forty years
ago, for instance, large barges, loaded with goods, went
up and down the Cuyahoga River, in Ohio, where now
a canoe can hardly pass. Steamboats which could once
ascend the Mississippi River as far as St. Louis at all
seasons of the year can now go no higher than Mem-
phis. The same may be said in substance of other
streams in all parts of the country.

The evil effects of the extensive and indiscriminate
destruction of our forests are already so apparent that
measures cannot be taken too soon to remedy them.
The following, from the *Virginia Enterprise*, Nevada,
shows the need of such measures even in the newest
portions of our country :

"It will be but a very short time before we shall be able to observe
the effect that stripping the pine forests from the sides and summit of
the Sierras will have on the climate of this state and California. In a
few years every accessible tree, even to such as are only of value as firewood, will be swept from the mountains. Even now this has been done
in some places. It is to be hoped that a new growth of pines or timber
trees of some kind may spring up on the ground that has been cleared,
but we do not hear that any such growth has yet started.

"Already one great change has occurred that is evident to the most
ordinary observer, which is the speedy melting-away of the snow on the

mountains. It now goes off at once, in a flood, with the first warm weather of spring; whereas formerly, being shaded and protected by the pines and evergreen trees, it melted slowly, and all summer sent down to the valleys on both the eastern and western slopes of the Sierras constant and copious streams of water. Instead of a good stage of water in our streams throughout summer, as in former times, there is a flood in the spring, and when this is passed by our rivers speedily run down, and being no longer fed from the mountains, evaporation leaves their beds almost dry when the hot weather of summer comes on."

The general interests of the country, its climate, its productiveness, demand that some restriction shall be placed upon the consumption of its forests. Either by legal enactment or by public opinion, the indiscriminate removal of our forests should be prevented. We have still an abundance of woodland in most of our states, if it is properly cared for, if its use and consumption are duly regulated.

In Europe the care and preservation of forests has long been a matter which has claimed attention and which has been regulated by law. The effects of the indiscriminate and wholesale cutting of the forests have been felt so disastrously that self-preservation has become almost dependent upon this cutting being restricted and upon the restoration of the forests where they have been removed. We know as yet comparatively little of such effects in our country, though they are manifest enough to put us on our guard and lead us to take measures to avoid the sad experience of the countries of the Old World. There these evil effects have been wrought for centuries, and any one who inquires into the facts in regard to this subject cannot

12

fail to be surprised at the record of losses and devasta-
tions occasioned by man's wanton interference with the
world in which he lives. Hon. Geo. P. Marsh, our late
Minister to Italy, and long in the government service
abroad, has given much attention to this matter. His
book entitled "Man and Nature; or, Physical Geography
as Modified by Human Action," is a treasury of facts
upon this subject and a recognized authority. Mr.
Marsh says, " There are parts of Asia Minor, of Northern Africa, of Greece, and even of Alpine Europe,
where causes set in action by man have brought the
face of the earth to a desolation as complete as that of
the moon, and yet they are known to have been once
covered with luxuriant woods, verdant pastures, and
fertile meadows; and a dense population formerly inhabited those now lonely districts. The fairest and
fruitfulest provinces of the Roman Empire, once en-
dowed with the greatest superiority of soil, climate,
and position, are completely exhausted of their fertility, or so diminished in their productiveness as, with
the exception of a few favored cases that have escaped
the general ruin, to be no longer capable of affording
sustenance to civilized man. If to this realm of desolation we add the now wasted and solitary soils of
Persia and the remoter East, that once fed their millions with milk and honey, we shall see that a territory
larger than all Europe, the abundance of which sus-
tained in bygone centuries a population scarcely inferior to that of the whole Christian world at the

present day, has been entirely withdrawn from human use, or, at best, is inhabited by tribes too few, poor, and uncultivated to contribute anything to the general, moral, or material interests of mankind.   The destructive changes occasioned by the agency of man upon the flanks of the Alps, the Apennines, the Pyrenees, and other mountain ranges of Central and Southern Europe, and the progress of physical deterioration, have become so rapid that in some localities a single generation has witnessed the beginning and the end of the melancholy revolution."   In France, for example, whole districts have been ruined for agricultural purposes by the masses of rocks and gravel which the mountain torrents, resulting from the cutting-away of the forests, have carried down into the plains below.   As a consequence the people have been obliged to migrate to other and less exposed regions.   The disastrous floods of the Po, a river about the size of our Connecticut, resulting from the removal of the forests on the Alps and Apennines, which are its sources, are a matter of frequent occurrence.   The European nations have therefore been compelled to give serious attention to the subject of forests in their relation to agriculture and the maintenance of population, as well as to health and salubrity of climate.   The necessity of preserving and restoring the woodlands has become imperative, and measures have been taken accordingly.   Forestry, or the science of restoring and maintaining a proper amount of forests, has now in Europe a recognized place as one of the most important concerns of the state. It has its schools in which learned professors give instruction in the art of growing and preserving large plantations of trees. Whole libraries of books have been published on the subject. In Germany, 1815 volumes on forestry were published prior to the year 1842, and an average of one hundred volumes are published annually in the German language. One of the Spanish Commissioners to our Centennial Exhibition, himself a forestral engineer, has prepared a list of treatises on forestry published in the Spanish language alone, which amount to more than eleven hundred in number. This shows the interest which this subject has abroad.

The state has a right to say that for the interests of public health, the highest productiveness of the soil, and the general interests of the people as a whole, a proper proportion between its forests and its cleared lands shall be preserved. Careful and long-extended investigation in Europe has shown that this proportion requires that from one fifth to one fourth of the land shall be kept in the condition of forest. In this country, owing to a difference of climate and other considerations, it is probable that not less than one fourth of the land should remain covered with trees. In some of our states, the eastern and southern especially, this proportion is preserved, though in portions of these, owing to unequal distribution, there is a deficiency of woodland. But in many other states, particularly those of the Upper Mississippi Valley, there is a great lack of forests.

Happily, the extreme scarcity of timber in those states has stimulated the settlers there in many cases to adopt measures to remedy this evil, and the planting of trees has been taken in hand so vigorously that there is already a manifest improvement, and the traveller is often surprised and pleased to see the belts of quick-growing trees surrounding the houses and portions of the farms on many of the Western prairies, and not unfrequently large groves and incipient forests which promise in a few years to bring great comfort and benefit to the people living there. Nebraska has her "Arbor Day," established by law, a rural holiday, observed on the 10th of April every year, on which the people are invited to give themselves to the planting of trees, to which they are also stimulated by the offer of premiums in the shape of a remission of taxes for a certain number of years, proportioned to the number of trees planted and preserved, and an offer by the State Agricultural Society of one hundred dollars to the Farmers' Society of the county which plants the largest number of trees on that day, and twenty-five dollars to the man who individually plants the most. It was estimated that more than a million trees were planted in 1876 on Arbor Day. In Missouri, Illinois, Iowa, California, New York, Massachusetts, Connecticut, and in other states, tree-planting has been encouraged by law or by agricultural societies. It would be a good and pleasant thing if we could have an "Arbor Day" in every state. It would be a good thing in many respects if, on a given day in the year, designated according to the climates of the different regions of our country, the people, old and young, and of all classes, were to be brought out for the purpose of planting trees both for use and ornament.

The time will probably soon come, also, if it has not come already, when it will be advisable to have, in connection perhaps with the Department of the Interior, a commissioner of forestry, who will do for us what officers of that name have done for European countries. Through such a commissioner, or by some other appropriate means, we need to have the importance of this subject set before our people in all its bearings. Care for our woodlands and forests is now one of our most pressing duties. We have land enough already cleared, even in rocky New England, to support three times our present population. There is no need of laying bare any more of the soil. If wood is wanted, whether for fuel or for the purposes of building and the arts, let the necessary trees be culled a few at a time from the forest, rather than sweep off the wood by the acre, as is now so often done. It would be well if our farmers, especially those living near cities and large towns, would make sure that a new tree is planted wherever an old one is cut down. In this way our supply of wood for all purposes would be maintained. Then we might hope also to regain one of our lost treasures— the blazing fire upon the hearth. It is enough to make one sad to go into so many of our country dwellings, in regions even where the forests are most abundant, and find the old fireplace that was once the very centre and soul of the house now shut up or destroyed in some way, and the family grouped and simmering around a dull, black stove, which vomits its sulphurous gases, perhaps, from every joint, poisoning the air of the dwelling—the very demon of unsociality and the pregnant mother of half the ills that flesh is heir to. And all for what? Because, it may be, the farmer can sell his wood and buy coal at a little saving of money at the outset—but with the risk of ill-health and large doctor's bills in the end—or because the good housekeeper thinks there will be some lessening of dust and sweeping of hearths and watching of fires if coal is used; and so the sacred fire on the altar of home is put out. Alas that it should be so! There were healthful influences to the soul as well as to the body coming from the old blazing fireplace. It was a moral power in the household, the loss of which money cannot make good.

We are confident, also, that the planting of trees where there is now a scarcity of them, and even in other places, would be one of the most profitable expenditures of labor in a pecuniary point of view, as well as on other accounts which we have mentioned. We have already abundant evidence that in those western states where timber is scarce, the efforts which have been made to secure the growth of trees have proved among the most profitable undertakings. An intelligent tree-planter in Illinois says that pine and larch trees attain a height of thirty to thirty-five feet, with a diameter of eight to twelve inches at the collar, in twelve years. One square yard to each would admit of 4840 trees on an acre. He proposes to plant in rows, every fourth tree pine, the remainder larches. He would cut out 2400 larches at the end of seven years, 1200 more at the end of fourteen years, 600 at the end of twenty-one years, and the remainder at the end of thirty years, leaving 300 pines twelve feet apart each way. He figures the yield as follows:

```
2400 trees fit for grape-stakes at 5 cents.........  $120
1200  "    fit for fence-posts (4000 at 25 cents)..  1000
 600  "    at $3.................................  1800
 300  "    at $20................................  6000
      Product in thirty years...................  $8920
```

Making allowance for any seeming extravagance in estimates here, enough would remain to show a good profit on the value of the land and the labor expended.

The whole subject, we repeat, deserves careful consideration. It especially deserves the attention of our agricultural societies and of the state and national governments. There are experiments to be tried which necessarily reach through a long course of years. Few individuals have patience for these. Few have the knowledge to make experiments most successful. There are encouraging evidences that increasing attention is given to this subject. Already there is a forestry association organized in Minnesota, and another in Ohio.

Many of our agricultural societies are also giving special consideration to the preservation or the establishment of forests. The Massachusetts Society for the Promotion of Agriculture has given its attention to the subject of tree-planting. It has offered prizes for the planting and cultivation of forest trees; and in connection with the offer has published a pamphlet, from the pen of its secretary, Professor C. S. Sargent, Director of the Botanic Garden and Arboretum of Harvard University, in which is condensed a great deal of information as to the value and qualities of different trees and the best method of planting them, as well as many facts in regard to the influence of forests upon the climate and productiveness of a country. The society offers $1000 for the best plantation of the European larch or the Scotch or the Corsican pine of not less than five acres; $600 for the next best, and $400 for the third best. It also offers $600 for the best plantation of American white ash of not less than five acres, and $400 for the next best. The awards are to be made ten years after the planting of the trees.

The society recommends very highly the European larch and the Scotch pine. These trees are now planted so extensively in Europe that they are propagated in immense quantities and furnished at low rates. Plants of the Scotch pine, one foot in height, can be imported and delivered in any part of Massachusetts for from fifty to sixty dollars the ten thousand. They can be procured also at about the same rate from Doug-

12*

las and Sons, of Waukegan, Ill., who have been engaged for many years in raising and planting forest trees. This pine is a rapid grower and very hardy, growing where the white pine will not flourish. Its lightness and stiffness render it superior to any other kind of timber for beams, girders, joists, rafters, and indeed for framing in general. It is largely used for railroad ties, and is the most durable of all pine woods. It will grow on poor soils and in exposed situations, and is especially valuable for the production of screens and wind-breaks about fields and buildings.

The European larch, a tree quite superior to the American larch, or hackmatack, as it is often called, is beginning to be imported and cultivated in this coun- try, and deserves attention. No tree, it is said, is capa- ble of producing so large an amount of such valuable timber in so short a time as this. It is one of the strongest and toughest of woods. Hardly any other bears so well exposure to the trying alternations of wet- ness and dryness. It is preferred in Europe to all other woods for railroad ties. For fencing material we have no wood so durable. It grows readily on poor soil, if only properly drained. Recently it has been a good deal planted, especially in the West; and we have some plantations of it in our country where the trees have reached the height of fifty feet, and proved that they can be easily grown in our climate and upon our soil. Twenty-five years or more ago, in the endeavor to es- tablish some profitable cultivation upon the sandy and stony waste-lands of Eastern Massachusetts, several plantations of considerable extent were made, and others have since been made through the encouragement given by those early experiments. In the year 1846, and during two or three following years, Mr. R. S. Fay planted on his estate near Lynn two hundred thousand imported trees, and as many more raised directly from the seed. Two hundred acres were thus covered. The sites were stony hill-sides, fully exposed to the winds and destitute of any good soil. A variety of trees were planted, but the European larch was principally used. No preparation of the ground was undertaken. The trees were inserted with the spade, and no after-care was given them except to protect them from fire and browsing animals. Twenty-nine years after the trees were planted many of them had reached a height of more than fifty feet with a diameter of twelve inches or more. Seven hundred cords of firewood, meantime, had been cut, besides all the fencing needed for the large estate. Firewood, fence-posts, and railroad ties to the value of thousands of dollars could now also be cut with advantage to the remaining trees. The experiment has been abundantly satisfactory to Mr. Fay. Apart from the value of the wood grown, he has by means of his planting converted his land—at the outset not worth five dollars an acre—into a plantation fit for the production of any crop whenever the forest is removed.

Similar experiments have been made on various portions of the sterile and exposed soil of Cape Cod, abundantly proving that the Scotch pine and the European larch especially may be successfully established on the poorest soils and in the most unfavorable situations to be found in our country. The results are conclusive in regard to the feasibility and profitableness of covering many of our rocky hill-sides and waste or worn-out lands with a growth of timber. It is estimated that eight million dollars might be added annually to the net agricultural product of Massachusetts alone by replanting only a small portion of its poorest lands with trees, for trees will grow where no other crop can be cultivated. Not only may we plant with the larch and the pine, but with other woods also more valuable than these for some purposes. It will be easy to cultivate in this way the butternut, the black walnut, and the ash—already so much used—not only for the manufacture of cabinet-work, but coming all the while into more extensive use for the interior finish of dwellings. To these may be added the hickories, the beech, the birches, the common wild-cherry, and the tulip or white-wood, all capable of being used for so many purposes. The ailanthus, also, once so fashionable as an ornamental tree, but now gone out of cultivation because of the unpleasant odor of its blossoms, is found to be one of the most valuable timber trees, being exceedingly durable, while it has a beauty of grain and texture which fit it eminently for use in cabinet-work and for the finish of houses.

Nor is there any danger that the supply of these and

other woods will outrun the demand for them and
make their cultivation less profitable in the future than
it is now. The development of the various arts among
us is constantly increasing the demand for the different
kinds of wood to be made into articles of utility and
convenience, as well as those which are merely tasteful
and ornamental. The natural increase of population
calls continually for an increased amount of wood for
the ordinary purposes of life—for fuel and for the uses
of building. And then there is a constantly increasing
demand for our lumber, soft and hard, for export to
other countries. Many of our woods are unknown in
the forests of Europe, and are much sought for as a desirable addition to those which grow there. The hickories are not natives there. The white ash is also unequalled for many purposes by any European tree, and
it is likely to be in great demand both at home and
abroad. There is a rapidly increasing export trade of
ash lumber to Europe, Australia, and the Pacific coast.
No other wood equals it in toughness and elasticity.
It is therefore specially valuable for the construction
of carriages, for the handles of shovels, hoes, spades,
rakes, and other hand implements. It is preferred to
all other woods for the manufacture of oars. It is also
coming into extensive use for furniture and the interior
finish of houses. As an ornamental tree for shade and
roadside planting, few trees excel the ash. There is
abundant reason, therefore, to think that the planting
and cultivation of this and many other of our trees will

for a long time to come prove to be one of our most profitable employments.

The Massachusetts Society for Promoting Agriculture, in offering prizes for the cultivation of trees on a large scale, gives also some general directions in regard to the planting of trees. These directions, coming from such a source, may of themselves stimulate some to engage in the work of tree-planting, and so we give them here. For larch and pine trees, it recommends that when the nature of the soil will permit, shallow furrows four feet apart should be run one way across the field to be planted (this is best done during the autumn previous to planting); then by planting in the furrows and inserting the plants four feet apart in the rows, the whole land will be covered with plants standing four feet apart each way. Planted at this distance, 2720 plants will be required to the acre. On hilly and rocky land, which is especially recommended for the cultivation of the European larch, and where it is impossible to run furrows, it will be only necessary to open with a spade holes large enough to admit the roots of the plants, care being taken to set them as near four feet apart each way as the nature of the ground will admit. In very exposed situations on the sea-coast, it is recommended to plant as many as 5000 trees to the acre, the plants being inserted more thickly on the outsides of the plantations in order that the young trees may furnish shelter to each other.

It is imperative to plant the larch as early in the season as the ground can be worked. No other tree begins to grow so early; and if the operation of transplanting it is delayed until the new shoots have pushed, it is generally followed by the destruction of the plant.

The Scotch and Corsican pines can be planted up to the 1st of May.

Land in condition to grow corn or an average hay-crop is suited to produce a profitable crop of white ash. Deep, moist land, rather than that which is light and gravelly, should be selected for this tree. The land should be ploughed, harrowed, and made as mellow as possible during the autumn previous, that the trees may be planted as soon as the ground can be worked in the spring.

As soon as the frost is out, mark out the field with furrows four feet apart, and insert the trees two feet apart in the rows. This will give 5445 plants to the acre, which, at the end of ten years, must be thinned one half. These thinnings are valuable for barrel-hoops, etc.

It is recommended to cultivate between the rows for two or three years, to keep down the weeds and prevent the soil from baking.

General Directions for Tree-planting.—Be careful not to expose the roots of trees to the wind and sun more than is necessary during the operation of transplanting. More failures in tree-planting arise from carelessness in this particular than from any other cause.

To prevent this, carry the trees to the field to be planted in bundles covered with mats; lay them down and cover the roots with *wet* loam, and only remove them from the bundles as they are actually required for planting.

In planting, the roots should be carefully spread out and the soil worked among them with the hand.

When the roots are covered, press the earth firmly about the plant with the foot.

Insert the plant to the depth at which it stood before being transplanted.

Select, if possible, for tree-planting, a cloudy or a rainy day. It is better to plant after the middle of the day than before it.

All young plantations *must be protected* from cattle and other browsing animals—the greatest enemies, next to man, to young trees and the spread of forest growth.

Note.—The experience of the last few years has reduced our estimate of the value of the Scotch Pine for planting in this country. It grows well for a few years, as almost all our plantings indicated; but after a growth of twenty or twenty-five years it shows signs of failure, and threatens to be with us a short-lived tree.

CHAPTER XXII.

SCHOOLS AND SCHOOL-HOUSES.

"Yet on her rocks, and on her sands,
    And wintry hills, the school-house stands;
    And what her rugged soil denies,
    The harvest of the mind supplies.

"The riches of the Commonwealth
    Are free, strong minds, and hearts of health;
    And more to her than gold or grain
    The cunning hand and cultured brain.

"For well she keeps her ancient stock,
    The stubborn strength of Pilgrim Rock;
    And still maintains, with milder laws
    And clearer light, the Good Old Cause!

"Nor heeds the sceptic's puny hand,
    While near her school the church-spire stands;
    Nor fears the blinded bigot's rule,
    While near her church-spire stands the school."

WHITTIER.

IF there are any outward symbols of village life, particularly in New England, they are the church and the school-house. From the beginning these have been the most conspicuous structures of our villages. Wherever our people have planted themselves, a building for the purposes of worship and a building for the purposes of education have been among the first things thought of and planned for. And as the tide of population has rolled westward, it has carried with it these tokens of New England life, these signs of its peculiar glory and power. Virtue and knowledge have been the corner-stones of our American life. It was a vital faith in a personal God, in distinction from all mere professions and ritualisms, or external shows of religion, which separated our fathers from their homes in the mother country and brought them to what was then a wilderness; and it was the conviction that knowledge is the basis of true virtue, as ignorance is the mother of superstition and formalism, which led them to cherish from the first the institutions of learning. And so the school-house ever went up by the side of the church, or "meeting-house," as it was called; and the minister and the school-master were the highest dignitaries of the community. Those structures deserve to be thought of with veneration and thankfulness by every Christian and every patriot, in view of the work which has been wrought in them and the great benefit which they have been to the country and the world. What influences have gone forth from those, as they seem to us, very humble and inartistic buildings! What characters have been nurtured in them! What safeguards have they been to the nation against the blandishments of a sensuous and corrupted civilization and the seductiveness of religious formalism! It was needful, doubtless, and altogether best, that our foundations should be laid deep and strong by those who, in their reaction from the corruptions which prevailed in the mother-country two centuries and a half ago, became cast in the stiff, stern mould of a puritanism which thought little of external graces, whether in habit or habitation, but made the inward spirit and life everything. We should not have grown to our present stature as a nation, we should not have held the high place we do among the nations, if our beginnings had been shaped by a less rigid spirit.

The old village church, a square, uncouth structure —a "meeting-house," rightly called, or place where the people might meet together—and having little in itself that was particularly suggestive of worship or religious use, was commonly perched upon the top of the highest hill, where it could be seen from afar, there to wrestle with all the winds and storms of heaven. Thither the people climbed, with almost equal difficulty, whether in winter or summer. But in those tempest-beaten struct-ures on the hill-tops they learned to battle also with the tempests raging in the soul, and, by the struggle, to grow strong; and they carried down into the work of daily life a new sense of the invisible and the spiritual which went with them in all their occupations, and made life noble, if it was somewhat stern in aspect.

The school-house was another "meeting-house," though for a different purpose. And yet the school was almost a church—the children's church; for the New Testament and the catechism were the chief, if not the only, reading-books of that day. The Sabbath-school had not yet come with its abundant religious in-

struction, and it was regarded as one of the well-under-
stood duties of the parish minister to be a regular visitor at the school - house and, as a superintendent of
schools by a divine right almost, there to exercise his
function at his will.

The school-houses were plain structures indeed. They
were planted here and there with no regard to beauty
in themselves or their surroundings. Equality of rights
demanded that they should be as nearly as possible equi-
distant from all who were to have the benefit of them.
If this carried them into some swamp or upon some
bleak hill-side, it mattered not. There was little thought
of comfort or pleasure in connection with school, either
on the part of parents or children. Duty and drill were
the two simple factors in the scheme of education. The
softer side of human nature was little touched. The
amenities of life were seldom considered. The feelings
and tastes were hardly recognized as having existence,
and, of course, were rarely appealed to. Surrounded by
natural objects full of beauty and interest, the world
ready to pour its treasures of knowledge into their
minds, the children, nevertheless, hardly knew the word
"nature." But the "three R's" taught in those rude
school - houses — taught, however imperfectly — have
wrought for us as a nation what is beyond estimate.
We may almost say they have made the nation.

All honor to them for what they have done. But
the village school-house and the village school of to-day
are not so far in advance of those of the early times as

they should be. Our dwelling-houses have begun to assume the look of taste and adaptation to family character. The old square structure, with its one huge chimney rising from the middle of its roof, its clapboarded sides painted red, or not painted at all, has given place not unfrequently to something more comely and convenient, and all its surroundings often show the marks of taste and thoughtful consideration. But our school-houses are too often but slight improvements upon those of primitive times. It hardly seems possible, when one thinks seriously of the subject of education, that the people of our villages should be content with the structures which so commonly meet the eye, and in which is wrought a work in comparison with which—if it is what it purports to be—all the work of farm and store and workshop is as nothing. It is a shame that we should permit the work of education to be carried on in such places as many of our school-houses are. The work of moulding the human mind, of drawing out its subtle powers and developing them to their full stature and wondrous beauty; the culture of the finer tastes and delicate sensibilities of our nature; the formation of character—this is the noblest work that can be done, can be thought of. What should be the place in which it is wrought? What its fittings-up and surroundings? If we are ready to fashion our factories and machine-shops with comeliness of proportion, and even to put upon them often not a little of adornment, if we are willing to expend freely upon these both money and taste, what should be the character of the buildings where the work of education is carried on? Should they not be very palaces of beauty? Should they not be the architectural gems of our villages, the very crystallizations of our utmost care and taste? Should they not be made attractive and adapted to their purpose by every appropriate comfort and convenience? A moment's thought would seem enough to answer these questions in the affirmative. And in our cities and larger towns the school-houses have begun to assume their rightful prominence and character. They take their places among the structures which have some architectural merit. They are arranged within with some sense of fitness and adaptation to the work to be done in them. Here and there also in our villages the same is true. But in too many of them the case is quite different. In how many places, even such as have some pre-eminence on the score of taste and enterprise, may you still find the "old red school-house" of half a century ago! It is a low, oblong box of a building, which in its plan had no reference to proportion, and very little to comfort. It was designed simply to furnish space enough for a certain number of persons, and its dimensions were fixed as would be those of a barn designed to contain so many cattle, only probably comfort and convenience would be likely to be considered more in the latter case than in the former. Rude seats and desks have insured constant uneasiness and offered irresistible temptations to the jack-knives of the boys.

Then, moreover, this architectural nondescript has been daubed with a hideous red pigment, out of harmony in color with every object near it, having the sole merit of cheapness—the cheapness which has been aimed at throughout. And now, to crown all, cheapness has decided that this most important structure in the whole town shall be placed on some vacant bit of ground left at the meeting of two or three cross-roads, or, if land has been purchased, it has probably been just enough to be covered by the building itself, leaving no room for playground but the public highway, and no opportunity to make the surroundings of the school-house in any way pleasant or attractive. If now we add that there is no place for the storing of fuel, but that through the long four or six months of winter the pupils are dependent upon the comfort which they can get from a pile of green or refuse wood, dumped upon the ground and exposed to storms of rain and snow, so that a large part of the school-hours are lost to study; and then if we say that there is an almost total absence of blackboards, maps, globes, dictionaries, and other apparatus, we shall have described in a general way the too prevalent village school-house.

And the teaching is often as far behind the real demands of the time as is the school-house. In the primitive and colonial days, the teachers of the schools were the best to be obtained. The position of school-teacher was honorable, and the best which the time afforded were placed in this office. Now, with the many other occupations which are open to the enterprising and the qualified, and the changed condition of society, teachers are often employed on the ground of cheapness or personal favoritism rather than that of competency for the work of instruction. School-teaching is often made a stepping-stone to something else, or is taken up as a convenient and easy way of earning a little money in the cold season of the year, when other kinds of employment are not abundant, or during the years that lie between youth and incipient manhood or womanhood. The teacher's work is seldom regarded on either side as a permanent employment. The people do not look for one who will stay among them for years and carry their children along in a steady and intelligent course of instruction. The teacher is not encouraged, therefore, to give his whole soul to the one work of teaching, and thereby make himself an accomplished instructor. And so, while there are some schools deserving the name, and some teachers who abundantly honor their calling, too many of both are far from being what they should be.

It is difficult to decide what to say, and what not to say, when treating a theme like this in a limited compass. When one thinks what education properly is—the drawing out, *e-duco*, what is in the young mind, rather than the pouring into it of anything from outside, or the recitation of any number of memorized lessons ; that it is the training and development of the nice perceptive powers and the cultivation of the finest feelings

and impulses of the soul; in short, the culture of the
whole man in its germinant state—one can hardly keep
his patience in view of the work as it is often carried on.
All honor to those teachers and superintendents of public instruction and others, some in almost every community, who are giving themselves with so much earnestness, and patience at the same time, to the noble endeavor to make our schools what they should be.   If
any deserve our gratitude and thanks, they do.   If any
are true benefactors of their country and their kind,
these are they.   In time to come many will think of
their work with gratitude, and will bless them for what
they have done to make their life happy and useful.
Already the fruit of their work is seen.

But much yet remains to be done for most of our
schools, both without and within.   The school-house
should be a model of taste and architectural beauty, so
that it may be itself an instrument for the culture of
taste in the children.   It should be surrounded with
well-arranged and well-kept grounds, and in this respect
compare favorably with the best private grounds of the
neighborhood.   There should be pleasant walks leading
up to the school-house and around it, and shady bowers,
and borders of beautiful flowers, and climbing vines, and
abundant trees, and room enough, besides, for an ample
playground in the rear.   Can any one say why the
whole village or district should not combine to make
the place where all their children assemble together to
spend a large part of their time, during the most im-

pressible period of their lives, more pleasant and beautiful than any single dwelling-place among them? Why should they not lavish upon it their thought and care and money, and adorn it within and without, so that the feet of the children, instead of loitering on the way to school, as is now so often the case, should linger rather as they go from it when the day is ended? With such surroundings of the place of education as we have suggested, how many lessons of the best kind, and touching the most important points of character and culture, might the teacher instil into young minds and hearts when walking with them amid such objects! Nay, how many such lessons would get into the hearts of the young without any aid of the teacher, infused into them by the silent teachings of the place itself! The influence would be altogether and unspeakably healthful, shaping the life and character permanently for good. Twenty years or more ago, the proprietors of some of the great factories at Lowell planted the grounds around their mills with shrubs and flowering plants, and trained vines upon the walls. The work-people of the factories were told that these were designed for their gratification, and the only restraint put upon the operatives in regard to them was a placard standing up amid the flowers on which were inscribed the words, "Let us grow." And we have it on the testimony of one of the managers that not a flower was plucked except by the one who had the care of the grounds. Shall we do less for our children than for the operatives in our mills?

13

And if children see that such things are designed for
their benefit, and thus are made to feel a personal interest in them, nothing is more certain than that they
will care for them and guard them from injury. How
easy, in this way, it would be to bring up our children
to cherish and care for all beautiful things, instead of
being, as they now too often are, their wanton destroy-
ers!

And then, why should there not be corresponding educational influences within the school-room also? Why
should not all be beautiful and tasteful there? Why
should not pleasant pictures be hung upon the walls as
well as the skeleton maps which now are often their only
adornment, if adornment they can be called? And
now, happily, we have respectable works of art within
the reach of the smallest village school. If we cannot
command the picture fresh from the painter's easel, we
have chromos and engravings and autotypes which may
safely be employed in their place, and which are afforded very cheaply. Suppose our school committees, or
some person, were to offer as a prize for best scholar-
ship or best deportment a fine picture, or one of Rogers's
admirable groups, only stipulating that the prize, instead
of being taken home by the successful competitor, to be
hidden away in some spare room, shut up for most of
the year, and so its influence lost, should remain in the
school-room as the property of the school, to be seen
daily, and to be a daily educating force as well as a
source of most refined pleasure. If such prizes were to

be given from year to year in our schools, how soon would the school-houses become galleries of beauty and taste! What refining influences would they exert upon our children! Then, if supplementing these means of culture, the teachers were, once a week perhaps, during the pleasanter seasons of the year, to shut up the books and the school-room, and take their pupils out into the woods and fields, and cultivate their perceptive powers and their sensibilities by bringing them thus face to face with nature, teaching them to observe and love the living things with which the Creator has stored the world, how much would be gained for the real purposes of education! Is it too much to hope that the day is at hand when we shall see some advancement made in this direction?

CHAPTER XXIII.

THE VILLAGE CHURCH.

"The Sabbath-day, the Sabbath-day,
  How softly shines the morn!
IIow gently from the heathery brae
  The fresh hill-breeze is borne!
Sweetly the village bell doth toll,
  And thus it seems to say,
Come rest thee, rest thee, weary soul,
  On God's dear Sabbath-day!"
                     BLACKIE.

IF there is any place which should be peculiarly dear
to the people, it would seem to be the village church.
It stands as the representative, and also the instrument,
of what is above all other things in value—the spiritual
welfare of the people. All secular and material interests are of little importance in comparison with this.
They are temporary; this is eternal. The place where
the soul and its interests are specially ministered to,
the place where the people meet to offer their worship
to God and to be instructed in respect to their relations
to him, it would seem that they would cherish with utmost regard, and bestow upon it their most scrupulous
care. It would seem that they would be ready and
eager to make the place of worship—the building which

they call "the house of God," and dedicate to him—in its structure and position, worthy of its high character and important uses. It might well be supposed that they would bring to it all that their wealth and care could do to make it what it should be, that all the resources of the builder's art would be brought into requisition, and all the adornments which the best taste and the warmest and most devout feeling could supply would be lavished upon it. It might be expected that the most beautiful and commanding spot would be selected for its site, so that the worshipper, as often as he might go up to the place or catch the sight of it from a distance, would be moved to exclaim with the Psalmist, "Beautiful for situation is Mount Zion."

One would naturally expect, also, that when the doors of such a place were thrown open at the appointed times of worship, it would be thronged by old and young, all classes and conditions, ready to pour forth their grateful offerings of prayer and praise to the Sustainer of their daily life and the Source of their hope of life eternal. It would seem that here they would gather with joy and gladness, and that all the services would be engaged in with manifest heartiness and delight.

In some instances these expectations are realized in a good measure; often, however, the case is far otherwise. The ordinary village church is distinguished from the mass of buildings around it chiefly by its larger dimensions and a certain conventional structure or appendage rising from its roof and commonly called a steeple. It is usually constructed of wood, and with its clap-board sides, pierced with two or three times as many windows as are at all needful, it has a thin, frail look, as though the whole thing was meant for only temporary use and was expected soon to pass away. It is built with little regard to proportion or any beauty of form, and is frequently a positively unsightly object. Then, to make the matter worse, it is very likely to be coated with glaring white paint, out of harmony, of course, with all objects near it, unless it be the neighboring houses, which probably have the same chalky, dazzling hue.

The building, thus flimsy and disproportioned, and staring in its ugliness, is perhaps erected on some bare and unprotected hill-top, that it " may be seen of men," or is set down at a junction of roads, or in some other equally unattractive place, like a huge boulder lodged there by chance. Not a tree, it may be, is planted near to shield from sun or storm, or help to give pleasantness to the spot. No well-kept walks or shaven sward indicates any thoughtful care for the surroundings of the house of God, nor does any adequate enclosure guard them from unwelcome intrusion, but the straying cattle quite likely make their pasture up to the very steps of the sanctuary.

So much for the outward aspect of the place. And now if one goes within, the appearance is equally unattractive. A square box of a room presents itself, with ranges of straight-backed and most uncomfortable pews,

having seats too narrow for adults to keep their places
upon them with any ease, and too high for half the occupants to touch the floor with their feet. The walls,
of course, are cold and cheerless with their white plastering, unless they have been fouled with smoke from
leaky stove-pipes, or disfigured by some paper fresco
or imitation of marble or granite, which is probably
peeled off in spots to make the sham perfectly apparent. The honest wood-work of pine, which, left to itself, would have taken on a richer tone of color from
year to year, has had the usual misfortune of falling
under the hands of the grainer, to be daubed over in
imitation of oak or some more valuable wood, and so,
but that the imitation is so poor that no one is deceived by it, the house of the God of truth is converted
into a glaring falsehood. Dingy carpets, or no carpets
at all, cover the floor. Two lines of black stove-pipe
extend from end to end of the room, a disfigurement at
the best, and dripping their dark creosote stains upon
walls and floors. The light pours in from the unshield-
ed and too numerous windows in such profusion as to
be oppressive, or streams in crosswise through the inter-
stices of the half-open shutters like a thousand Lillipu-
tian darts, no one of which, by itself, might be of serious effect, but in the combination producing a general
uneasiness and discomfort only the worse because so
few discern its real cause. And now if we add the fact
that there is so seldom any adequate provision for ventilation, and, therefore, during the larger portion of the

year, when the warmth does not induce the opening of the windows, the people are lulled into somnolence or something worse by the vitiated atmosphere breathed over and over, the average house of worship is seen to be as unattractive within as it is without.

If we turn, now, from the character of the place, and consider the character of what is done in it, what will be the conclusion? The place is called, of course, a house of *worship*. But how much of worship is there in the place, or is there really expected to be? What incentives or helps to worship do the attendants find? There is certainly little in the aspect or furnishing of the place to excite devotional feelings, little to suggest the thought of the Divine Presence, or that the place is designed for any use special and peculiar. The people assembled, they find a rostrum at one end of the building, at which the clergyman officiates in the offering of prayer, acting simply as the mouthpiece of the assembly, they being expected to make the prayer each one his own by a mental and hearty adoption of the uttered words. But, as a matter of fact, half the assembly at least will often be found paying no attention to this part of the service. Their heads are not even lowered in outward token of devotion; their eyes are in the ends of the earth, or studying the fashion of the dress in the next pew; their thoughts are upon their business or pleasure.

Praise is a part of divine worship. It is an eminently fit expression of soul for every human being. But, instead of being the united and accordant act of the whole assembly, this is usually left to a company as far removed as possible from the minister, perched up in a loft by themselves, behind the congregation, and allowed, for the most part, to perform what musical or nonmusical pranks and outrages they please in the name of worship. And so we have quartet choirs in our village churches, and solos and operatic airs, and attempts at musical effect which result only in musical failure, and too frequently dissipate devotional feeling and give us third-rate Sunday concerts in place of honest aids to worship. One of the worst things about it is also that good, sensible, and pious people are deceived into the belief that this sort of thing is worship or a part of worship, instead of being only a desecration of the place and name of worship.

Nearly all that is left, therefore, is the sermon, and whatever there is of worship must be found in the devout feeling involved in listening to the exposition of the divine word, or that which is aroused by its exhibition. The preaching of the word has been the distinguishing feature of our religious services from the beginning. Our forefathers made it so, in the natural reaction from the faults and defects of the establishment in England; and it has since held a disproportionate place, perhaps, as compared with other acts of worship. The people have gone to hear sermons rather than to pour out their hearts to God in devout confession, supplication, and thanksgiving. The

13*

intellect has been fed or gratified at the expense of the heart, and our religion has been made overmuch an intellectual matter. The people have come to the church to be entertained rather than to worship. They have been drawn thither by the intellectual attraction of the preacher rather than by their sense of duty to God or the impulses of devout feeling. This has been demoralizing both to minister and people. The former, feeling that he could keep his place only by his oratorical attractions, has often been led to convert his pulpit into a platform for ministerial mountebankism, and the people have too frequently encouraged this by rewarding it with the largest salaries and the most profuse reports in the daily newspapers. This evil is not confined to our city congregations. It has infected, more or less, many of the country churches. More and more they are seeking for the sensational style in their ministers. They want a metropolitan star in their pulpit, and sobriety, fidelity, and even piety are at a discount. "He don't fill the bill," is the business-like judgment of some country tradesman or little politician who has occasionally spent a Sunday in New York, when the minister does not convert his church into a lyceum or a theatre, and pander to the love of novelty and excitement. And if he "don't fill the bill," the minister must understand that, as they say at Washington, "his resignation will be acceptable," though he were a John or a Paul. Such is the demoralized condition of our churches at this day, so

loose our ideas and practice in regard to the relation
of ministers and people, that it is in the power of two
or three dissatisfied persons so to disturb the tranquilli-
ty of a parish as to effect the dismission of a minister
at any time. The relation of a pastor to his flock is
of the loosest character. A system of terrorism widely
prevails. A minister's peace and continued usefulness,
and the quiet and comfort of the parish, are at the
mercy of any meddlesome and opinionated tinker or
garrulous old woman, whether of one sex or the other.
The minority governs rather than the majority. The
result of all this is that the clergy of all denominations
have become itinerant, like the Methodists. Three
years is about the average length of pastorates, whether
in one denomination or another, and our parishes are
much of the time in an unsettled state. The relation
of the pastor to the parish has been reduced, in many
parishes, to one of an almost purely commercial character. The minister has become a hireling, and, whatever may be the religious considerations avowed or the
religious forms made use of, he is really engaged and
dismissed on grounds of the same moral quality as
those which govern the engagement of Bridget in the
kitchen or Patrick on the farm. If he can fill the pews
and thereby raise his own salary at the smallest cost
to the individual pew-holder, it is well; otherwise the
conclusion is inevitable that "his usefulness is at an
end."

And now, having drawn this picture of what is too

often seen, let us sketch a different one, which is sometimes realized, and might be more frequently than it is.
In the centre of the village, or on some choice spot of
ground near by and accessible to all—not upon a bleak
hill-top, but upon some sheltered slope, nor thrust out
upon the dust or noise of the highway, but withdrawn
from it upon its own enclosure with the modesty and
partial seclusion which befit the religious feeling —
stands the village church. With a proper sense of
the abiding need of the Gospel, and its sufficiency for
the wants of any community to the end of time, it
is built of enduring stone, which very likely was
found upon the spot or near by, and not of perish-
able wood. No attempt has been made to erect a Gre-
cian temple in miniature, or a Gothic cathedral in lath
and plaster, or a structure modelled after any of the
five orders of architecture. No burdensome outlay of
expense has been made in the nice hewing or carving
of the stone. It is laid up in the rough, as it came
from its native bed, except perhaps the jambs of doors
and windows, which are smoothly cut. But the work
is done with honest and conscientious fidelity. A
pleasing effect is sought, not from elaborate ornament
and useless appendages, but from a harmonious disposition of parts and a just proportion reigning throughout the structure. The building is not piled high in
the air, having a stilted and unstable look ; it is not in
the cubical dry-goods-box form, and so ranking with
the stores and work-shops around, and having an equal-

ly secular look. But the walls are low and the requisite elevation within is gained by a somewhat sharp pitch of the roof, which, while it secures protection from the beating storms, also forms a proper gradation of line for the modest steeple or spire, which appears naturally to spring from it. The whole structure thus seems to rise out of the ground and lift itself up, as spontaneously as the trees around it, towards the heavens. It is the fit symbol of religion, having its foundations upon the earth, man's dwelling-place, amid his sins and wants; its altar where he may reach it and cling to it while he prays; its spire ever pointing him towards the source of his hope and help, and the home of his redeemed, regenerated, and glorified life.

Along the rough walls, which offer a ready holding-place for their fingers, and over the slated roof which suggests no fear of decay on account of their presence, climb the graceful vines, which, in fitting harmony, symbolize the Great Head of the Church, the True Vine, and shed over this simple house of worship a beauty which no chisel of the most cunning workman could ever have given it. And there it stands amid the embowering trees, as lovely as themselves, an attractive object to all eyes.

Going within, all is found in harmony with the external appearance. No great expanse of cubical space above makes one feel lost in vacancy. No stretch of cold white wall and ceiling chills the feeling at the outset; but the low walls and roof give a homelike and household feeling at once. Subdued and pleasing tints of color everywhere meet the eye. The windows are modestly colored, and the light comes in, not in dazzling and distressing streams from unprotected openings, but diffused throughout the building with mellow and restful radiance. The pulpit or reading-desk is not perched high above the people, but is only a step removed from them, and the choir and organ have their appropriate place by the side of the pulpit. Minister and choir being thus near each other and among the people, the latter recognize the fact that they are leaders in the various acts of worship, and not performers come into church to play their part, whether in oratory or music. Hymns of devout feeling are sung, to the accompaniment of familiar tunes and the subdued and modest notes of the organ, and the hearts and voices of the whole congregation go out together in grateful praise, mindful of the words of the inspired Psalmist, "Let the people praise thee, O God; let *all* the people praise thee." When the invitation to pray is given, the heads of all present are bowed with becoming reverence and propriety; and no one could doubt that this is a praying assembly. The common sins are confessed, the common wants are uttered, the common pardon is sought, and the common adoration is expressed. The people not only listen to the reading of the Scriptures, but they read them together, old and young uniting their voices in repeating the words of life.

These acts of worship having been engaged in, not in

a hurried, perfunctory, and formal manner, but in full measure and with devout feeling, now comes the office of instruction. This gives occasion for the sermon, which is no display of intellectual gymnastics or strange conceits, but a sober and affectionate unfolding of the word of God, and an earnest effort to guide the people in the way of true living. There is no parade of learning, though it is full of the best fruits of learning. There is no lack of strength, but it is strength guided by gentleness and love. Over all and through all there is the blending of sincerity and earnestness, of sweet and affectionate interest in the flock, which the minister, true to the name of *pastor*, is seeking to lead in green pastures and beside the still waters of salvation. Old and young listen with attention and interest, as to one whom they regard as their guide and friend. The sermon ended, a blessing upon the word is asked, a hymn is sung, and with the benediction the congregation go home, not to admire or criticise the preacher, but to ponder his words and try to profit by them, and to feel that the gates of Zion are precious.

Such is the village church as we sometimes see it, as we might see it almost everywhere if our little sectarianisms were laid aside and religion had its proper place in our regard. Such a church is indeed the centre, and appropriate centre, of the place where it is found. It is the people's home. There they meet together as one family. It is the strongest bond of social life, the strongest bond and instrument of all that is best and most pre-

cious. The longer it stands, the more precious it becomes. As generation after generation worship within
its walls, it gathers new value from many associations.
It becomes dear to the children because parents and
grandparents have worshipped in it, or have been carried out to burial from it with Christian triumph and
in hope of a glorious resurrection. As a portion of
the villagers go out to dwell in other places from time
to time, with the precious memories of the old church
of their early days go precious influences also to hold
them to rectitude and virtue; and as often as they may
return to the place of their nativity, there is no spot,
save the parental dwelling, to which they turn with
such interest and affection as this. And so the village
church stands, the sign and monument of all that is
sweetest and dearest and best. Individuals and families and generations may pass away, but the old church
remains, growing more and more dear with the lapse of
time, as its walls gather a more mellow and a richer
tone of color from the storms and sunshine of each
passing year. The people take pleasure in the stones
thereof. It speaks to the eye continually of all that is
most beautiful and best, and from its altar and pulpit
within continually go forth the precious teachings of
life and immortality. It is the abiding source of elevating, purifying, and ennobling influences which give
to village and village life their highest charm.

CHAPTER XXIV.

THE VILLAGE LIBRARY.

" Consider what you have in the smallest chosen library. A company
of the wisest and wittiest men that could be picked out of all civil countries, in a thousand years, have set in best order the results of their learning and wisdom. The men themselves were hid and inaccessible, solitary, impatient of interruption, fenced by etiquette; but the thought which
they did not uncover to their bosom friend is here written out in trans-
parent words to us, the strangers of another age."—EMERSON.

FROM the first our people have been a reading people
—a people of books. The early settlers of New England had a firm conviction of the importance of the
knowledge and culture which come from books—from
communion with educated minds. It was the boast of
the early churches of New England that they had scholars for their ministers, men who were the masters of
the one book that stands above all others, and who were
also familiar with the best learning of the times. Many
of them were graduates of Oxford and Cambridge, and
it was not long after the settlement at Plymouth that
the foundations of a university were laid in a new Cambridge. The story of the founding of Yale College,
taking that name only at a later date in honor of one
of its principal benefactors, is also familiar: how a com-

pany of Connecticut clergymen came together, moved
by the true spirit of scholars, and, bringing their contributions from their own libraries, laid them down, declaring that they gave those books for the founding of a
college. We see with constantly increasing admiration
what that seed planted in the early times has brought
forth.

The fathers of our country had a wholesome fear of
ignorance, as the mother of superstition and crime.
From religious and moral considerations, therefore, they
favored schools and books, and the learning and culture
which come from them. In the early times, there was
a library in the parsonage, if nowhere else. But there
were also libraries elsewhere; and, considering the limited resources of the people at that time, and the difficulty of procuring books, they were quite numerous.
The books were apt to be largely of a theological
and philosophical character. They were of the solid
sort, with not much of light literature among them.
But many of our foremost men have been ready to
attribute their power and their success in life to the
knowledge and training which they gained through the
reading of those solid, if somewhat dry, volumes in the
ample old chimney-corner—perhaps by the light of a
pine-knot which took the place of a candle, the expense of which could not be afforded.

In these days, when we hear the clang of the print-
ing-press in every considerable town, and newspapers
are flying around us almost as abundantly as the au-

tumn leaves, it is difficult to realize such a state of things. But too many of the leaves that come from our innumerable presses are as ephemeral and unsubstantial as those of the trees. While we have books and magazines and newspapers which are worthy of any time and any society, a large part of those in circulation are so trashy that it is a waste of time to read them; while many are so immoral that their reading cannot be otherwise than pernicious. There is danger that both time and character will be wasted by these, for the young, in their ignorance and inexperience, are especially liable to be influenced by the weakest and worst kind of reading. They are peculiarly exposed to harm at a time of life when they are most impressible, and when injury received is likely to be permanent. Among the most desirable social and moral influences, therefore, especially in our villages, is that of a good public library, a well-selected collection of books constantly accessible. Hardly anything else can be named which will do so much for our children, which will so train them to proper habits of reading, secure a desirable choice of books, furnish them with valuable knowledge for all the purposes of life, cultivate the taste, and at the same time supply sources of most pleasant and healthful entertainment.

School libraries are very useful, and many of our states have made a wise and ample provision for them. Their establishment deserves to be encouraged in every school district of the land. But they are only the beginning or foundation of something better. Their very existence and the work which they do, instead of enabling us to dispense with a town or village library, make the greater occasion for it. The school library can hardly grow beyond certain narrow limits. When these are reached, if not before, there will be a manifest need of something larger and better. How shall that larger and better library be secured? In establishing a village library, it is essential to success that proper provision be made to insure its continued growth by the constant addition to its shelves of the most desirable books which are published from year to year. If such additions are not made, the library will soon become a dead thing, though it may have books which are among the treasures for all time. It will cease to be attractive, and soon its volumes will be shut away from sight or scattered one by one; and the library as such, and for the proper uses of a library, will become extinct. Many town and village libraries have thus disappeared— enough to discourage, oftentimes, the attempts to found new ones.

The secret of success in founding a library is to give it a good start. The aim, therefore, should be to secure as large a fund as possible before any purchase of books is made. A library, to insure that it will be properly taken care of and its growth secured, needs to be so large at the outset as to make upon the people on whom it is to depend for its support and growth the impression that it is worth caring for and deserving to have its growth assured. Many libraries have been started with the right feeling and with a sufficiently good selection of books, but the number of volumes has been so small as to be hardly noticed except by a few greedy lovers of books. The number of books being thus small, they have not seemed of sufficient importance to insure a place of keeping by themselves, or a librarian to take proper care of them. They have had to go a-begging for a place of deposit. This has been, perhaps, a corner of the post-office or of the village store, or they have been reluctantly taken in at some farmhouse. In either place they have been so hidden from sight as to make little impression on the public, and out of sight they are soon likely to be out of mind; the public soon cease to use them; no contributions are made for the purpose of adding to their number; the care becomes simply neglect—that is, they are left to take care of themselves. And so the experiment of founding a library ends in failure.

It would be much better, if those who feel the importance of a library in any of our villages cannot secure money enough to start upon a liberal and somewhat imposing scale at once, that they should fund the subscriptions for a few years, until they have accumulated sufficiently to make a purchase of books in such number as to insure success. The library had better be in the shape of money than books until there can be books enough to give the library assured life. It is hardly safe to start with fewer than a thousand volumes, and two thousand would be better.   The moment that such a library is thrown open to the people, it will make a strong impression upon them.   Most of the villagers have probably never seen a thousand volumes in one place before.   And now, to think that all these are for their use gives them the sense of something valuable as well as the sense of something new.   They feel that these books are worth protection.   They are moved to make additional contributions, if need be, in order to provide the requisite place for their safe-keeping.   They feel, too, that some one must be secured to act as librarian, to care for the books and promote their circulation. They will be willing to pay for this needed service. The library becomes at once a conspicuous thing in the village; it is the chief thing talked about.   Its books are soon found on the tables and shelves of all the village houses.   Young and old are interested, and find something to their taste.   A new source of entertainment has been brought into the town.   There is a new element of interest pervading the community.   The evening lamp and the evening fireside have a new charm.   Conversation is quickened with new topics of interest, and the whole village life has a new impulse imparted to it.   Even those least familar with books, except, perhaps, those which they have read at school, feel that in the library something noble and dignified has been added to their village possessions, and they point to it with pride.   Thus a new educating force is established in the community, supplementing and adding efficiency to all other educational appliances. The little village is brought into contact with all the best thinking of the world; and the humblest toiler on the roughest farm may be a daily companion of the wisest and most gifted of all ages. Such is the office of books; such the value of a good library to any community. Its advantages, direct and indirect, are incalculable, and they are within the reach of the smallest of our villages.

Perhaps a brief sketch of the origin of one of these village libraries, and the mode of managing it, may be a help to the founding of others. In a certain New England town, not many years ago, a few persons, lovers of books, and most of them possessors of respectable libraries, became desirous to establish a public library, that they might enlarge their own range of reading, and have their fellow-townsmen share with them the many benefits of books. While carefully considering the ways and means of starting this important enterprise—their own resources being small—a liberal-minded person offered to give one thousand dollars for the immediate purchase of books, and another thousand, the interest of which should be appropriated to the annual increase of the library, on condition that a thousand dollars should be given by others for it, and a suitable building should be provided for its safe-keeping. Stimulated by this unexpected aid, the citizens soon subscribed nearly twice the prescribed sum. Contributions were welcomed from the poorest, and in the smallest sums; for those who had the matter in hand

were aiming, from the outset, to get the whole community interested, and they felt that there was no surer
way to gain one's interest in the library than by getting
a money pledge to it.

Thus far all went well, and a committee was soon
diligently at work in preparing a list of the most desirable books for purchase. The only difficulty now in
the way was the providing of a suitable building for
the library. To secure the money requisite for its purchase or erection was not easy after making such liberal
subscriptions for books. But, almost before any pledges
had been made for this purpose, a lady gave a valuable
piece of land for a site, and another generous person
offered to erect the building at his own cost. The library was now assured, and there was left for consideration only the question of management. How should
it be made of widest use and greatest benefit to the village? How should be met the expense incident to management, the needful addition of books, and the replace-
ment of those which would be all the while wearing
out? The interest of the fund of a thousand dollars
would not be sufficient. Should a charge be made of a
small sum for each book taken? It was felt that even
the charge of a few cents might be enough to prevent those not accustomed to books, or who had not a
taste for them, from visiting the library and using its
books; and it was one of the prime motives for the
establishment of the library to reach and benefit just
this class of persons. It was resolved, therefore, by the

managers to appeal to the town to recognize the library as an institution for the general benefit, and to make an appropriation from its treasury for its partial support, on condition that the library should be free to all. The appeal was made, and after only a little debate a very liberal appropriation was secured.

In due time the library building was completed, and thrown open to the public with two thousand well-chosen volumes on its shelves, and a reading-room well supplied with magazines and papers. It was a marked and memorable day in the history of the village. The people felt at once that they had a treasure worth preserving. The library became the centre of interest to the community. Its books went by twos and threes to all the village homes, and by favor even over the borders into the adjacent towns.

It was hardly expected by any, at the outset, that the library would be opened to the public more than once in each week; but the same spirit which led the founders to establish the library with the design of making it useful to the largest extent made them resolve to have it open so constantly, if possible, that there should be no impediment on this score to its fullest and freest use. Accordingly, they determined that it should be opened on every afternoon of the week except Sunday and Monday. It has thus been open, with a lady acting as librarian, at a charge not too great for the funds provided by the town; and from the beginning it has been cherished by the people with increasing regard. Its

14

books have been widely read; its stores are constantly added to, and its reading-room is the village exchange, where young and old meet daily in the pleasantest and most social way. And so the library has become a bond of union and good feeling to the entire community, and is constantly elevating and improving the tone of society, and making the place where it is a better place in which to live.

Such a library may be the adornment and blessing of any of our villages. The secret of success lies, as we have said, in a good start, a vigorous and general effort at the outset, insuring such a number of books as will make the library an object of interest at once and something worth caring for.

And how many desirable things for the improvement of village life naturally group themselves around such an institution! how many things to make country life bright and happy! Such a library will appropriately give origin to reading circles in different portions of the town, where some book will be read aloud and its contents be familiarly discussed, thus forming pleasant neighborhood reunions. Debating societies will naturally spring up in connection with it. It will fall within the province of the managers of such an institution to establish courses of lectures from year to year, and to provide this kind of entertainment and instruction for the people. These may be varied by occasional concerts, of such a character as will displace the low minstrelsy of travelling troups and noisy vulgar buffoons,

who often find our villages rich harvest-places to them,
because nothing better is offered, and the natural yearn-
ing for amusement leads the people to such empty
performances. A village-library association may very
properly establish dramatic.entertainments of an unob-
jectionable character, and thus minister to one of the
strongest instincts of our nature, while affording one of
the highest pleasures which man can enjoy. It would
not be amiss, either, if, in connection with the library,
there were a room where games of skill—like chess—
might be engaged in, and pleasant conversation might
be carried on, with accompaniment of coffee, ices, and
fruits in their season—thus becoming a place of resort
which would attract many who otherwise might spend
their leisure time in places fraught, more or less, with
temptations to evil, or where their companions would
not be of a beneficial character.

The library-room, as was the fact in the case of the
library we have mentioned, might also serve as a museum, by gathering along with the books—in appropriate cases, to preserve them from injury—any curiosities,
heirlooms, or objects illustrating the history of the village; portraits of its eminent citizens; specimens of
minerals or birds and other animals abounding in the
place ; in short, anything of interest, whether to old or
young. Every village might thus have its museum.

In these and other ways, it is easily seen a village
library may be the source and centre of many most
desirable adjuncts of village life. We must not be

over-scrupulous about means and methods. A library
association in the country may do much that it would
shrink from doing in the city. It may fitly do all that
a village-improvement society would properly do; and
it can easily do much to remove the dulness which
characterizes many of our country places, and to enliven
and purify and elevate the tone of life.

CHAPTER XXV.

WORK AND PLAY.

"How often have I blest the coming day
When toil remitting lent its turn to play,
And all the village train, from labor free,
Led up their sports beneath the spreading tree;
While many a pastime circled in the shade,
The young contending as the old surveyed;
And many a gambol frolicked o'er the ground,
And sleights of art and feats of strength went round!
And still as each repeated pleasure tired,
Succeeding sports the mirthful band inspired;
The dancing pair that simply sought renown
By holding out to tire each other down;
The swain mistrustless of his smutted face,
While secret laughter tittered round the place:
The bashful virgin's sidelong looks of love,
The matron's glance that would those looks reprove—
These were thy charms, sweet village! sports like these,
With sweet succession, taught e'en toil to please."

GOLDSMITH.

"Let the world have their May-games, wakes, whitsunals; their danc-
ings and concerts; their puppet-shows, hobby-horses, tabors, bag-pipes,
balls, barley-breaks, and whatever sports and recreations please them best,
provided they be followed with discretion."—BURTON: *Anatomy of Melancholy.*

WE are the hardest-worked people in the world. By
all our antecedents, by all our history, the people of this
country seem to be started in life as under a doom of

work.   Work, with us, takes almost the place of a religion.   The alternative, and the only alternative, is complete idleness.   And so society is broadly divided into
two classes—those who are all the while toiling and
those who are idle.   You see everywhere men rushing and driving at full speed, ready to run down all
opposition and dash over every obstacle to their plans;
and, on the other hand, a class of idlers—men with
their hands in their pockets or pipes in their mouths,
perhaps both, sauntering about with no apparent object in view, merely living, animated, but as the snails
and sloths are animated.

Those old Puritans, weary of the frivolities of their
time and the neglect of all serious and important things,
came to think that everything in the nature of sport
and play was of the devil.   So they denounced it, and
for themselves lived lives of austere labor, and left it as
a legacy to their posterity.   Starting on this side of the
Atlantic a new society with this legacy, and having, in
addition, the difficulties attendant upon a new settlement
in a new world, separated by three thousand miles from
all other people, from the first we have been given up
to work as the one law of life, as no people before ever
were.   So ingrained is the feeling with us that life is
work, that when we do turn aside from our work, and
give ourselves to play, as nature impels us to at times,
our play is generally of a laborious sort—work again,
only under another name.   Our sports are not light and
graceful, but toilsome.   They are not free, but we seem

to be under some constraint in them all the while, and as though taking a respite from work under protest.

Now, this feeling is unnatural. We are, as to this, like insane persons, who think that all the rest of the world are lunatics and they alone are sane. Work is not the normal condition of life, but rather play. No one likes to work, no one chooses to work, except as he sees this to be the condition or means of a superior end which he seeks. One may, indeed, after long years of toil feel uneasy unless he is engaged in work of some kind. But this is a morbid state of the man. If he had given the play element of his nature proper scope all along the way of life, he would never have come into such a diseased condition.

If we would see the true state of the case, let us look at children and at all the animal tribes. The child's life is all play, and would continue so but for the necessity which comes to most, after a time, to engage in labor of some sort and to some extent in order to provide for the many needs of civilized life. Work comes to the child, as it does to the cattle, as a necessity. No boy likes to be put to his tasks at school. When he has grown to manhood, his love of knowledge may lead him to find play in an amount of study which was formerly only a drudgery and a task. And one difficulty with our schemes of education thus far has been that they have not brought the play element into exercise in connection with study as they might have done; that is, have not made the processes of education such as to interest the

mind and draw out its impulses and energies in a spon-
taneous devotion to knowledge. The Kindergarten system, on this account, seems the nearest approach we have
yet made to a proper educational method. We want
more of education through the senses, as distinguished
from that which is merely of the intellect. As says the
author of "Rab and his Friends," "the great thing with
knowledge and the young is to secure that it shall be
their own—that it be not merely external to their inner
and real self, but shall go *in succum et sanguinem;* and
therefore it is that the self-teaching that a baby and a
child give themselves remains with them forever—it is
of their essence; whereas what is given them *ab extra,*
especially if it be received mechanically, without relish
and without any energizing of the entire nature, remains pitifully useless and *wersh.* . . . Now exercise—
the joy of interest, of origination, of activity, of excitement—the play of the faculties—this is the true life of
a boy, not the accumulation of mere words." The natural sciences are full of interest to the young as well as
to the old, and the mind finds play as well as work in
the study of them. Therefore in our schools, especially
those in the country, there should be taught the elements of botany and of the art of agriculture. If less
attention were given to general geography and more to
the local geography of the scholar's own town or school
district, there would be a great gain upon the system
usually pursued. If our teachers had enough of proper
knowledge to be able to take their pupils out from time

to time into the fields and make them conversant first
with the geological and mineralogical character of the
country immediately around the school-house, and then
with the plants and trees, so that the children would
feel acquainted with them and be able to recognize them
at sight, and be interested in noting their various habits
of growth—this, as mere mental discipline, would be
worth more than to be able to tell all about the capes
of Norway or the islands of the Indian Ocean; while, as
the means of engaging the attention and training the
observing faculties and making study a pleasure, there
would be no room for comparison between the two sys-
tems. The study of nature fosters the play element in
us, or tends to convert our toil into pleasure, at least to
relieve its drudgery and irksomeness. The life of such
a man as Agassiz was, in one sense, a life of toil. But
how full, also, of happiness! In what a high, serene atmosphere he lived! When invited once to participate
in a scheme which promised large pecuniary results, his
memorable reply was that he had no time to devote to
money-making. The pursuit of knowledge for its own
sweet sake was his life, and in that pursuit his whole
life may be said to have been play.

The play element will have a larger place in the
scheme of country life in proportion as the general intelligence is increased. In proportion as our villagers
refuse to be mere mechanical drudges, to be rated like
steam-engines at so many horse-power each, or to plough
and plant and reap by the signs of the moon or the tra-
14*

ditions of their grandfathers, the toil necessary to the pursuit of agriculture will not only be lessened absolutely, but the play element will so enter into the most arduous processes as to greatly mitigate their severity. The celebrated John Opie, when asked by some one with what he mixed the colors on his palette, replied, "With brains, sir." So when the farmer mixes more of brains with his work, and does not leave it to be mainly a matter of muscle, the result will not only be larger in a pecuniary point of view, but the whole process by which the result is brought about will itself be more pleasurable. When our farmers take note of the chemistries involved at every stage of their work, when they are at home in the laws of vegetable growth, when they keep themselves informed of the different constitutions and habits of the plants they cultivate, when they have a cultured eye to watch the thousand curious processes of nature, they can hardly strike a hoe into the ground, or turn a furrow in the field, without finding something that shall so engage attention and touch the feelings as to relieve the drudgery of their work and transform toil into pleasure.

But, apart from the relief from the irksome pressure of labor afforded by a more intelligent method of labor, and which the more general diffusion of intelligence and culture will everywhere tend to secure, we ought to take care in other ways that we are not brought into bondage to sheer work, and so broken down by it. While we are to work, we ought not to overwork. The greed of gain will push men, and their whole families with them, into a round of slavish toil, under which, if they do not shorten their lives, they dwarf and brutalize them, and sink themselves below their proper nature. "The life is more than meat, and the body than raiment." But how apt we are to lose sight of this! Man was not designed to be forever in bondage to toil for the sake of food and clothing. This is the temporary necessity of what we call his *fall*. And he ought now to assert his freedom in whatever measure he can. In the midst of his labors, let him take time for what is highest and best in him. Let him take time for relaxation. The bow, to do its best, must be at times unstrung. Let him not allow his bodily toils to weigh down his manly energies and choke the spontaneity of life, or wear away the freshness of his sensibilities. God has from the first given man his Sabbaths as days of emancipation and types of what all his life is sometime to be—days that come week by week to set him free from toil and give him the sweet assurance that he was made for something else than the drudgery of work. But it is his privilege even now to have other days of rest and liberty. And when the demands of labor—needful labor even—press hardest, let him assert his birthright of freedom, and give his nature times of play. In the busy summer season, when the days are both so busy and so long, let there be care taken against overwork. There is danger at such times that many a boy will have the work of a man put upon him, and so, like a young colt, be broken down before his bones are yet knit into proper firmness. There is danger that work may be put upon or assumed by the man which is beyond the powers of the man; and the result of a week's overwork may be a hopeless break-down for life. There are a great many more of these early broken-down, crippled, stiff-jointed men on our farms than there ought to be.

Let there be a fair halt on the farm at mid-day; and if the sun be unusually hot, let the halt begin earlier and last the longer. Let there be time for the noon meal to be eaten leisurely and after the body has rested a while, as health demands; and let it be accompanied with the sauce of pleasant conversation, to make it something more than the hasty swallowing of a certain amount of provender by so many greedy animals. Then let the stomachs of men and animals alike have some time to do their work of digestion before going to work again. In the long run this course will be found to pay better, alike in money and comfort and health, than the driving, hurrying course which strews our villages with so many hulks of men worn out before their proper time.

But guarding against overwork is not enough. Something more is needed and ought to be secured. Once in a while whole days should be taken, if but one at a time, when the harness shall be taken entirely off from man as well as beast, and the time be given up not only to rest, but to play, often the best kind of rest. Let the boys have their games, in which also the men shall join

by looking on, if not themselves active participants. Or
let the worker go off upon some excursion to the mountains or the sea-shore; or, if that be not practicable, let
him go a-fishing, or break up the routine of life by
camping out, if for only a single day, by the side of
some familiar brook—spending the time, if nothing else
offers, in catching butterflies. It will do him good.
Only let him not be selfish in his play-spell. Let it be
a play-spell for the whole family, for all alike need it.
The mother and daughters have probably toiled as hard
as the father and sons, perhaps harder. And then how
good to keep up the family unity and affection by such
a commingling in pleasure and recreation! Re-creation
it will be. All will be born, as it were, into a new life.
It is a very good thing, also, for whole neighborhoods
to go together on these pleasure excursions. We have
known such, when perhaps a large tent, with the addition, it may be, of a few lesser ones, has been taken by
fifty or sixty of the same village, and pitched by the
sea-shore or on some pleasant spot and made their temporary house. And they have enjoyed this life all the
more because it has allowed them to keep themselves
free from the restraining conventionalities which are
apt to prevail at places of public resort. We have
known, also, companies of old and young, two or three
neighboring families, the strong and the feeble together,
to go up to some spot on the mountain-side, taking with
them blankets and a few simple culinary utensils, and
there living in a very simple way for a week or two—get-

ting away thus from the haunts of men, resting, changing the whole current of life, breathing the pure open
air highly charged with oxygen, and coming back again
after so little time with a new lease of life and memories of delightful scenes, and all the more ready for
work again, and for more effective work because of
this respite and play-spell.

There is little danger in our country that we shall
play too much. On the contrary, the games which have
within a few years been revived among us, or introduced for the first time, are to be taken as a promising
change in our national habit of life. These and other
games and sports are to be encouraged. They may be
abused, as every good thing may be and is abused. Let
us encourage them, while we guard, as we may, against
their misuse. Let us not make our games and sports
themselves a labor. There is danger in this direction.
It were a good thing and a great gain to us if we had
more of the French capacity of mingling work and
play, and so of making the most of life. If we would
only abate our extravagances of living and cultivate
simplicity of taste, half our work would be enough to
satisfy our wants, and there would be time enough for
enjoyments which now we hardly know. We toil in
order to have a time of rest and enjoyment, but we
wear ourselves out too often with our toil before the
time of rest and enjoyment comes.

Quite in the line of these suggestions as to the need
of more of the play element in our village life, we have

our agricultural fairs, now so common in the autumnal season. There is nothing in itself more fitting and pleasant than this coming-together of the dwellers in the country, the old and young, bringing with them specimens of their flocks and herds, the fruits of their fields and the products of the housewifely industry within-doors, and then comparing together their methods and experiments, and interchanging pleasant talk and discussion about matters of common interest. It is a most healthful custom, and ought to be encouraged. They might be made pleasanter and better than they are. More of method in their management and a determination to make them interesting to all classes, by making all classes participants in them, would lift them up to a higher position of importance and attractiveness than they now hold. They should not be regarded as occasions on which a few competitors meet for the purpose of securing the petty premiums which are offered, but as true festivals for the whole community. All should be invited to contribute something of their work to the attraction of the occasion, and all would find something in it to interest them. The exhibitions connected with these fairs, if any such should be allowed, should be something above fat men or women, or six-legged calves, or monstrous snakes. Nor should horse-races be made the chief attraction. Managed as they might be, these fairs would become true festivals, social and intellectual, and the people of any village be the happier and better for them.

CHAPTER XXVI.

OUR VILLAGE FESTIVAL.

"Once more the liberal year laughs out
    O'er richer stores than gems or gold;
Once more with harvest-song and shout
    Is Nature's bloodless triumph told.

"Our common mother rests and sings,
    Like Ruth, among her garnered sheaves;
Her lap is full of goodly things,
    Her brow is bright with autumn leaves.

"O favors every year made new!
    O gifts with rain and sunshine sent!
The bounty overruns our due,
    The fulness shames our discontent."

                        WHITTIER.

IT has been charged that the people of this country,
even more than our English relatives across the water,
do not favor festivals. A funeral, it is said, is more to
their taste, more accordant with their habitual feeling.
There is some foundation, perhaps, for such utterances.
We are not a festive race. We are certainly not given
to hilarity. The springs of our life are not on the surface, where they are easily or quickly affected. They
lie deep down. We are not emotional, or, if we are, our
emotions are rather of the slow and sombre sort. Com-

pared with many other peoples, we do not take readily to festivals or sports. Doubtless it would be better for us if we could vary the heavy tread of life, oftener than we do, with a quickened step. It would be well if we could temper our sobriety and staidness of feeling with more of what is exhilarating and mirthful—cheerful, to say the least. And if we could have something in the nature of festivals oftener than we do—occasions in which we should be brought together in larger or smaller numbers, and show each other the sunny side of life, give a let-up to plodding care and anxious thought, bring the heart out upon the surface and share a joyous mood together—it would be the better for us. Nothing good would suffer from such a course. The wheels of life would run all the more smoothly and pleasantly for it.

But, deficient as we may be in festivals and the festive spirit, we have one festival at least which is peculiar to us, and deserves to be cherished with the heartiest zeal and good-will. "Thanksgiving" is a festival in the truest sense and of the highest type. Peculiar to New England until recently, and born of the deep, devout religious feeling of our Pilgrim fathers, it has been for more than two centuries one of the characteristic features of New England life. But the tide of emigration, setting so strongly westward in these latter years, has carried this festival into the newer states, though in a somewhat modified spirit; and some recent experiences in our national history, combined with the sense of its inherent propriety and worth, have finally combined to spread it over the land and to make it a national rather than a local festival.

From the first this has been pre-eminently a *family* festival, and for this reason it asserts for itself a very high place in our regard; for the family is the root and central idea both of the State and the Church, of civil and religious, of social and moral life. It is the conservator of all that is good in society. The Anglo-Saxon people hold and cherish the family as hardly any other people do.* This was characteristic of them far back in their German home and on the borders of the North Sea. It was as *families* especially that the first settlers of New England came hither and named their new home after the old one. It was the remembrance of the family homes of old England that led them to do so. And so, likewise, the various settlements made here were settlements by families, and not by individual adventurers. They went out from the original settlements or colonies by families or households. The family was the unit of measurement and valuation in all such movements. They formed new churches when, and only when, they had a sufficient number of families. They established their schools on the same basis. The family or household was the ruling idea throughout. The individual was of little account except as connected with a family. Society was built upon the family, and it was maintained by the family spirit, or with this as

---

* Green's "History of the English People."

its chief strength and organific power. And so all that is best and dearest to-day we inherit from that family spirit which lay at the very foundation of our civil and religious institutions; and these institutions will be pre-served, and will be worth preserving, in proportion as the family life is maintained in its purity and proper spirit.

Our annual Thanksgiving festival has been the ap-propriate symbol of this family spirit from the begin-ning. When our forefathers, as the year came around and the harvest was gathered, were moved by their de-vout feeling to render thanks to the bountiful Giver of all good, they did it by households. They not only went up to the sanctuary to make public recognition of their obligations to God and to give him thanks, but they made it a time of rejoicing by families. It was pre-eminently a family day. Now, if at no other time during the year, the importance of the family was recog-nized; now, if at no other time, the children were im-pressed with the fact that the little grouping of old and young which was gathered under one roof and had its life around a common fireside was held to be something of special account. Now the father stood as a patriarch at the head of his little realm, and was joyfully recog-nized as such; now he looked down upon his house-hold with special delight, and as being a special treas-ure. The children who had gone out from home, in the natural arrangement of things, to make new homes for themselves, now, if at no other time in the year,

came back to the old homestead, and recognized the fact
that they and theirs belonged to an older and a higher
household. What preparations were made to go and
visit the old father and mother at "Thanksgiving time!"
What journeyings were undertaken for this purpose!
Fifty, sometimes a hundred, miles, and even more, were
traversed on the old roads, and in the old-time wagon,
that the expected family reunion might be enjoyed.
And what a hearty, blessed time it was! No expenditure, no painstaking for it, was so great but that it was
amply repaid. How the old people became young again,
as grandfather and grandmother saw the little host of
grandchildren filling up their house! and how rich, too,
they felt beyond all the measure of gold and silver!
Those were precious times. How they knit families
together and kept alive the family feeling!

And now, in this "day of roads," when the day's
journey is extended, from the fifty miles, at best, of the
olden time to five hundred and even more, the facilities
for such reunions are greatly increased, and widely as
the children may be scattered, they can come home to
the festival more abundantly and more easily than before. Over all the country, but especially in New England, how the lengthened trains labor for a day or two
previous to "Thanksgiving," with their precious freight
of sons and daughters hastening to the ancestral homes!
And then, when the festival is over, how the cars are
crowded again with the thousands and tens of thousands
who have gone to the family feast, and must now go

back to their business again! Blessed be the railroads that they make such a thing possible! They are not merely the conveniences of traffic and the highways of trade, but they are also the instruments of civilization and the highways of affection. As the trains dart back and forth over the continent, from city to hamlet, and from hamlet to city again, with their precious freightage, they are so many shuttles of the great loom in which is weaving the fabric of our national unity, stability, and virtue.

So let the day—Thanksgiving-day—be cherished and kept as a thing most precious. It is the festival of the heart and the festival of home. Let it take its place with Decoration-day and Independence-day, a day not to be forgotten or left in neglect. No cost of time or money or travel incident to its observance can be too great. Let it be made a pleasant, cheerful day to all. Let it be kept, first of all, as a *family* day. Let the scattered children hasten home, and let them be called thither, if need be, by a mandate from the gray-haired father and mother in the name and by the authority of home and all which that blessed word implies. Let the reunion be not a matter of convenience or individual inclination merely, but a thing of principle and duty. Let the children and the children's children come back, and together around the family fireside burnish anew the links in the chain of household affection and interest. Let it be a day of good cheer in every way. Let it be a feast-day in the common understanding of the term. Let the table be spread with the good things which a kind Heavenly Father has provided for his children. But let the occasion be also more than this—more than a day of eating and drinking or mere animal pleasure. Let it be a day of delight in one another for one another's sake. Let the story of the life of each during another year now gone be told, the varied experiences, the ups and downs, the successes and the disappointments; and let love be seen to be the heightener of all joys and the balm of every trouble. Let the ties of kindred and family affection be knit afresh; and, as separation comes again, let each go out stronger for all duties and trials, and with a new anchorage to all virtue.

But the festival will not have its proper crown, will not rise to its true and proper character, except as the religious element has its rightful place in it. Our fathers were careful on this day to go up to the house of God and give thanks to him for his bountiful gifts and his abundant mercies. They went up by households. They would have been absent from the place of public worship on Sunday as soon as on Thanksgiving-day. And why not? We have declined from their feeling in this regard—at least, from the manifestation of a like feeling. In many cases the thanksgiving seems to be forgotten in the feasting. But if ever people—if ever households as such, old and young together—should be moved to go up to the house of God with joyful and thankful hearts, this would seem to be the time. At this season of ingathering, when barns and

storehouses are filled with the fruits which his dews
and rains and sunshine have brought to perfection; at
this season, when households come together, and parents and children look into each other's eyes and are
reminded that God "hath set men in families," it
would seem that the least susceptible and the least devout would be ready to go up to the house of God, and
gratefully make mention of his loving-kindness. Now,
if at no other time, it would seem that the Christian
sanctuary would be filled with a throng of grateful wor-
shippers. That feast is only half blessed for which
thanks have not first been offered to Him whose bounty spread the table; and that family union lacks the
sweetest savor which has not offered its grateful praise
with others in the courts of Him who is the common
father of all, and who calls us his children. Let not the
careful Marthas allow themselves to be so cumbered with
much serving that they cannot sit for an hour at the
feet of Christ in the sanctuary, and learn of him a higher service than that which ministers to material wants.

And as, at the season of flowers, we are wont to carry them into the place of worship, so, at this season of
fruits, it is a comely custom in some places, and might
be in all, to carry into the house of God the various
products of the field and of the husbandman's industry;
and there, in the midst of them all, and with the sight
of them to quicken memory and feeling, to lift up the
voice in praise to Him who alone giveth the increase,
whoever may plant, whoever water. The vision of one

such occasion comes back to us now, after the lapse of many years. We see just in front of the pulpit, in the old village church, a large vase heaped to the full with bright-hued apples of various sorts, from the midst of which upspring stalks of grain nodding high their golden heads, while around its base lie heaps of corn and other products of the garden and the field. As the service goes on and the hymns of thanksgiving are sung, we see the eyes of the farmers riveted upon the symbols of their work and the tokens of the divine goodness; and the sight reacts upon their hearts and gives a stronger and more significant expression to their gratitude as the glistening tear-drops mingle with their praises.

Thanksgiving-day is pre-eminently the village festival. As it had its origin among a rural people, so it seems to belong especially and most appropriately to the open country. The old farm-house, the gentle slope of grass near it, the apple-trees not far off, the spring and the babbling brook so dear to childhood, and the woods, where the sound of dropping nuts in the dreamy October days was so welcome—somehow these seem to be the frame in which the Thanksgiving festival has its most appropriate setting. So let it be cherished as the village festival. It should have its place only next to Christmas — the great soul-festival of the world. Our village life would lose one of its most impressive scenes, and one of its peculiar charms, if it had not its *Thanksgiving-day.*